Perfect
Little Ladies

By Abby Drake

PERFECT LITTLE LADIES
GOOD LITTLE WIVES

Perfect Little Ladies

Abby Drake

AVON

An Imprint of HarperCollinsPublishers

PERFECT LITTLE LADIES. Copyright © 2009 by Abby Drake. All rights reserved. Printed in the United States of America. No part of this book may be used or reproduced in any manner whatsoever without written permission except in the case of brief quotations embodied in critical articles and reviews. For information, address HarperCollins Publishers, 10 East 53rd Street, New York, NY 10022.

HarperCollins books may be purchased for educational, business, or sales promotional use. For information, please write: Special Markets Department, HarperCollins Publishers, 10 East 53rd Street, New York, NY 10022.

FIRST AVON PAPERBACK EDITION PUBLISHED 2009.

Designed by Diahann Sturge

Library of Congress Cataloging-in-Publication Data
   Drake, Abby.
     Perfect little ladies / Abby Drake.—1st Avon paperback ed.
       p.   cm.
     ISBN 978-0-06-164836-6
     1. Women—Fiction. 2. Secrets—Fiction. I. Title.
   PS3604. R345P47   2009
   813'.6—dc22   2009012854

09 10 11 12 13   OV/RRD 10 9 8 7 6 5 4 3 2 1

Perfect
Little Ladies

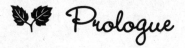 *Prologue*

Panties!

That was the word that caught Elinor's eye in the note that she held in her hand.

It was a colorful note, comprised of red and black and yellow and blue letters in different type sizes and styles, each letter, each word, pasted onto a single sheet of paper the old-fashioned way, not printed from a computer with thoughtless emotion.

It was a colorful note, a clever invitation perhaps, a ribald request for her presence at a ladies' luncheon, a charity auction, or maybe high tea. One or two of her friends, after all, were known to have slightly twisted senses of humor.

It was a colorful note, but . . .

After a moment, after a breath, she let her gaze travel the page.

Found: One pair Lavender Lace Panties!
Where: Dumpster, New York Lord Winslow Hotel!
Cost: $500,000 for their return!
Instructions to follow. Stay there and wait for my call.

Elinor supposed she'd had a worse day in her life, but right now she didn't know when.

 *One*

Alice and Poppy were drying their nails in the late August sun. They were poised on chaise lounges that were perched on the terrace of Elinor's country house north of Manhattan, far from the frenzy of Washington, D.C. The house had been a gift from Elinor's husband, Malcolm, right after the weight-loss drug Ranilin had won FDA approval and he'd received a sizable bonus for his efforts. Finally Elinor had been able to return home on weekends and be with her oldest and dearest friends, Alice and Poppy, whom she counted on for everything, including their opinions of the acrylics they were now testing for Elinor to wear to Jonas's engagement party, which was only a week away.

She did not count on advice from her sister, CJ, unless the

situation was dire. It did not matter that they were identical twins.

CJ (Catherine Janelle, named after their mother's mother) sat on the top step of the wide marble stairs that led from the terrace to the topiary garden and wondered why she'd been summoned along with the oldest and dearest. So far, they'd been there an hour; since then, Yolanda had been gluing and shaping while Elinor had been flitting, which Elinor didn't do well. Poppy was more the flitting type, but they were all nearing fifty, too old for that sort of thing.

"Seltzer?" Elinor (who'd been named for their father's mother, who'd only had one name because "one was sufficient") asked for the ninth or tenth time.

The o & d shook their heads. At their age, sipping meant peeing, which was not easy when one's nails were tacky.

"Elinor," Alice, the plucky one plucked, "will you please sit down? You're driving me mad with your wandering."

"Ditto," added Poppy, whose nickname had been coined from the color of her flame-red hair so long ago that CJ had forgotten what her name really was. Veronica. Victoria. Something like that.

Elinor sat but said nothing.

CJ sighed. She rose from the stairs and strolled toward her sister. "What's going on, E? You're nervous about something, but I doubt it's the party. You have far too much experience as hostess-with-the-most-est to be suffering simple frayed nerves."

Alice looked at Poppy, rolled her eyes, and wiggled her fingers. Poppy giggled and waggled her toes. Like Elinor, they'd been pampered girls who'd become pampered wives, so CJ forgave them their trespasses.

Elinor set the pitcher on the Italian flagstone and stared at the lime slices that dipped and bobbed as if they, too, were at sea.

"Well," she said. "Well."

Yolanda approached, shaking another bottle of enamel, that one creamy peach. Whichever shade was selected must blend with Elinor's mango Versace gown that said "Washington wife" with its straight, elegant lines, yet "playful" with its vivid tone. Elinor would look regal. She always did.

CJ would wear less obvious gray silk that she'd hand-painted with violet fringed tulips, like the ones Jonas had helped "Auntie CJ" plant at the cottage when he'd been a boy. The flowers were his favorites, he said every year, so it seemed only fitting. It would be their little secret, in a bittersweet way.

"Well, what?" Alice barked, because she could be as snappy as the old librarian who'd worked at McCready School for Girls when Elinor and CJ's father, Franklin Harding, had been headmaster, autocrat, person-in-charge.

"Well, give her a minute to think," Poppy excused, because she was as good at excusing as Elinor was at looking regal.

"Hold out your hand," Yolanda, the nail tech, demanded. "I don't have all day." She had, after all, a business to run, the top-notch hair and nails salon in New Falls, the next town over. Yolanda made house calls on special occasions.

Elinor shook her head. "Not now," she said soberly. "I'm being blackmailed."

Well, that made no sense, even to CJ, who was used to her twin sister's frequent cryptic-speak.

"E?" CJ asked. "What did you say?"

Alice and Poppy stopped wiggling and waggling. Yolanda screwed on the top and set down the bottle.

"I'm being blackmailed," Elinor repeated. "And I desperately need your help."

The Harding sisters were identical twins whose hair was what told them apart: Elinor's, always in a neat, ponytail-place, CJ's, short but askew, in need of combing. When they were kids they'd been cute, two little clones, too adorable for words. As adults, however, their identical-ness disturbed them both; neither wanted to be mistaken for the other, because it had taken them too long to just be themselves.

Still, a few years ago, when their ebony locks had started sparkling with silver, Elinor was appalled that CJ wanted to dye them. Washington, after all, wasn't New York, where only money mattered, or L.A., where looks were what reigned. In Washington, success was all about power and wisdom, and silver hair was oddly connected to that.

Or so Elinor said, anyway.

It hadn't mattered that CJ did not live in Washington but in the old family lakeside cottage in Mount Kasteel, named by Dutch settlers for the castle on the south side of town that overlooked the lake, the Hudson River, and part of Manhattan on a clear day.

In the end, CJ had not dyed her hair, and they'd remained looking alike.

CJ excused herself from the ladies, crossed the terrace, went through the French doors and into the house in search of vodka to add to the seltzer. It would take more than the flavor of a couple of limes to endure this latest Elinor complication.

Behind the bar in the main-floor billiard room she located a bottle of Skyy. She took out a small glass, filled it with an inch, then downed it quickly and neat.

"CJ," Elinor said. She stood in the doorway, her tall, lean, size 6 frame silhouetted against the afternoon backlight. "It's not nice to start drinking without me."

CJ poured another, downed that one, too. "I have a feeling I'm going to need it."

Elinor sighed, strode to the bar, and poured her own drink. It occurred to CJ that her sister was well suited to the Georgian house that might have been too big for a family of ten but was perfect for a larger-than-life woman despite the fact that her daughter was now out of grad school, her son was about to be married, and she and her husband also owned a sizable Washington town house. Elinor, of course, was the show-off, not Malcolm. He was too busy being a lobbyist-genius for DeBauer Pharmaceuticals, while Elinor was busy doing . . . well, it had been years since CJ had really known what her sister was doing.

"Does Malcolm know about the blackmail?"

Toying with her glass, which was Baccarat crystal (CJ had been there the day the delivery arrived from Neiman Marcus), Elinor said, "No. Malcolm isn't to know."

"Then why on earth have you chosen to alert Alice and Poppy and, for God's sake, Yolanda?"

"I told you," she said. "I need everyone's help."

It was not the first time Elinor had begged for assistance. But it was the first time she'd included an entourage.

"Why is someone blackmailing you, E? Is it about . . . ?"

"No," Elinor said, cutting CJ off. "If it were that, we would handle it ourselves."

CJ breathed again. Relief, she supposed. "Well then, you should call the police."

"I can't."

"A private investigator."

"I won't. There's too much at stake."

This house, CJ supposed. The town house in Washington. Elinor's perfect life with her perfect husband, and their reputation as Washington's go-to couple.

"Elinor, have you done something that deserves blackmail?" CJ didn't say "something *else*," because that wouldn't have been nice.

Elinor seized the Skyy and turned from her sister, her mirror image. "Come back to the terrace. I'll tell you my plan. Trust me, dear sister. It's better this way."

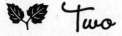 *Two*

"*Yolanda, I've asked you to join us because*
I respect you," Elinor began. "And because I believe you have
street smarts, which the rest of us sorely lack."

They assembled their chaises in a small circle, as if they
were campfire girls or wagon-train people.

Drinks were poured.

Silence fell.

And then Elinor related a tale of lavender lace and a Dumpster outside the New York Lord Winslow Hotel and a ransom
for a half million dollars.

Alice laughed. "Well, this is absurd. Do tell us that this is
absurd."

But Elinor said, "No, it isn't absurd. I suspect the panties
are my La Perlas. I bought them last year in Milan."

Poppy narrowed her eyes. "Haven't you always worn cream-
colored silk?"

CJ supposed Poppy knew that from too much togetherness in too many spas.

Yolanda simply listened, street smart as she was.

Closing her pewter-colored eyes, just as their father had done when he'd felt things were futile, Elinor said, "My lover prefers pastels to neutrals." Then her voice dropped. "Yes, ladies," she said, "I have a lover. I'm human, I've failed."

What had been silence became total dead air.

A lover? CJ thought. *Elinor has a lover?* CJ wasn't sure if she was more astonished by the sin or by the realization that she—and apparently the oldests and dearests—hadn't been told before now. This kind of secret was far too juicy to have been concealed from best friends.

Yolanda spoke first. "Is your lover the one who's blackmailing you?"

CJ wanted to ask who the lover was, how long Elinor had had him, and if he was young. There was so much of that in her sister's circle: the caterers, the masseurs, the page boys from the floor of the Senate.

"He wouldn't dare."

"Are you sure?" That came from Alice.

Poppy, in the meantime, had turned as pale as the marble statue of Venus that stood in the topiaries.

"Elinor," CJ said, "if you want our help, you'll have to tell us the details." She hoped that a jolt of reality would make Elinor reconsider spilling the rest of the beans.

"I can't tell you everything," Elinor said. "We'll just have to leave it at that."

"We can't 'leave it at that,'" CJ said. "Tell us who you are screwing, how often, and where."

Elinor laughed, though it wasn't a ha-ha kind of laugh.

"We're middle-aged women," she said. "We've probably all had at least one inappropriate relationship in our lives."

Alice grimaced.

Poppy twittered.

CJ made no comment; Yolanda didn't have to. They all knew the fury her marriage had caused in New Falls when she, the hairdresser, had run off with one of the Wall Street husbands, who'd later wound up dead, shot through the head.

"But do tell the truth," Elinor continued. "Don't you want to know why?"

CJ thought about Mac, her brother-in-law, about Janice and Jonas and the family her sister had built. She thought about the audience present: Alice, Poppy, Yolanda. Then she thought about her mother, who would be mortified that Elinor had chosen this grandiose terrace for airing her dirty laundry, La Perla though it was. "No," CJ replied. "It does not matter why."

"Well, that's too bad, because that's the easy part. The embarrassing truth is, Malcolm has been disinterested in me for a number of years, and, as I said, I am human. Believe it or not."

CJ sipped her vodka. The others did, too.

"If Mac's so disinterested," Alice finally said, "why not simply tell him about your affair?"

"He still is my husband."

No one knew that more than CJ. "Well," she said slowly, "in the unlikely event we can find the blackmailer, what do you intend to do next?"

"It depends on who it is." Elinor checked her watch, as if awaiting a call. "You'll have to go now. All of you. Malcolm will be home any minute, and the congressman and his wife are coming with their daughter." Their daughter was Lucinda, Jonas's intended.

"You won't be at the club tonight?" Poppy asked. "The club" meant the yacht club, where the elite of Mount Kasteel dressed up and gathered on Saturday nights in the summer if they weren't in Newport or the Hamptons.

"I don't think it's wise for me to be seen in public."

No one argued with that.

"In fact, it's also not wise for us to meet here. Let's say the cottage. Tomorrow morning, CJ?" Elinor still treated the cottage as if it belonged to the family, though CJ had bought it from their father's estate a dozen years earlier and had been paying the mortgage since then.

Still, CJ nodded. What else could she do?

Elinor stood up. "Eight o'clock. My guests are staying over, so eight will give me time to be back here for brunch. Between now and then each of you can ponder what we might do. By the way, I'm trusting all of you with my life. This is the most important confidence you'll ever be asked to keep."

Three women and a hairstylist asked to keep a confidence.

That time it was CJ who closed her eyes.

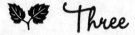 *Three*

Alice Sussman Bartlett was the only child of an esteemed Austrian baker and his Viennese-waltz-obsessed wife. Blonde, cobalt-eyed Alice had spent her early years in a cloud of flour and powdered wigs. It wasn't until she'd attended the renowned McCready School for Girls that she'd begun to see clearly, begun to learn that what mattered in life was neither hard work nor dancing but having a man who liked both. She would have preferred that Neal hadn't also been enamored by art deco abstracts that now lined the walls of their Federal-period, split-staircase, Mount Kasteel home, but what the heck, when he was around he was still decent in bed—apparently unlike Malcolm, who had hurled poor Elinor into the arms of a lover.

A lover.

Elinor.

!

Alice dropped onto the sofa in her living room and wondered why she felt so aghast. It wasn't as if she hadn't dallied outside the marital bounds. But that had been years ago, and with an old boyfriend, and she'd been slightly drunk, so it hadn't really counted. Leonard had been in town for his uncle's funeral, and Alice went out of respect. Well, okay, so she went because Neal was away on business and she was curious and so what?

Leonard had looked delicious, even in mourning. Standing by the sprays of lilies and gladiolas, he looked like the boy who'd stood nervously in the living room the night of the prom, who'd pinned a corsage of white gardenias too close to her young but full bosom, who'd later taught her the fine art of a blow job because Elinor once said a lady shouldn't go all the way. (Elinor had, even back then, been Alice's unwitting idol. How could she not have been? Elinor was so perfect!)

After Alice and Leonard bid the flowers and the folding chairs and his uncle adieu, they bought two bottles of wine, then went to the gymnasium parking lot at the McCready School, where they finally had a good fuck in the back of Alice's minivan between her daughters' softball gear and cheerleading pom-poms.

Leonard e-mailed her three times after that but had not threatened blackmail. They agreed it had simply been something they'd meant to do in the late seventies but had not had the courage. And that was the end of that.

The shrill ring of a phone shook Alice from her nostalgia. She waited for Neal to get it, then remembered he'd stayed in

Manhattan that weekend to work on a big presentation. He did that often—he was an advertising executive, after all, a veteran workaholic who sprang an erection whenever his BlackBerry buzzed.

Which was, of course, why Alice had been spending so much time lately schlepping her granddaughter around the country to auditions for *USA Sings*. Kiley Kate, at nine, had her great-grandmother's dancing talent—not for waltzes but for hip-hop. The traveling got Alice out of the house, out of Mount Kasteel, out where she could safely assuage the boredom that being Neal's wife sometimes wrought.

She had not, of course, admitted that to anyone, certainly not to Elinor, who had no tolerance for people who didn't play by the rules.

Or so Alice once thought.

She tried to wave off the surge of a hot flash as the telephone rang again.

"I've decided it can't possibly be true," Poppy blurted before Alice hardly had a chance at *"Hello."* "If she's been having an affair, wouldn't we have known?"

When they'd left Elinor's house, they'd walked to their vehicles, silence dragging behind them like an over-the-top bridal train. Apparently Poppy was ready to talk. "We know now," Alice said.

"Because she's being . . . oh! I can't even say it!" Her words were a rush of hyperventilation.

"No, and we shouldn't say it over the phone. Caution is called for." The hot flash abated; Alice returned to her senses. With Poppy, showing sense was essential.

"Oh, but who can it be? And why won't she tell us?"

"He must be a scoundrel. She must be embarrassed."

"But the engagement party is next Saturday. If this isn't over . . . well, good Lord, Alice, whatever will happen?"

The party was to be held at the Fairmont, an intimate, Washington-only affair. Alice and Poppy were dying to go, but the only outsider invited was CJ, and only because she was Jonas's aunt.

"We'll know more tomorrow. Will you be all right until then?" Poppy tended toward the delicate when it came to the traumas of life. It was why they turned a blind eye to her small indiscretions, like the way she helped herself to things that weren't hers. Compacts, silverware, nothing big, really. She was a good sort, with a childlike spirit, which was no doubt beneficial in enduring marriage to her husband, the parasite, Duane, who was there for her trust fund and, geez, talk about a philanderer. He'd once cornered Alice at a charity function and managed to brush his huge penis against her hip bone.

Yikes.

It had been awful and awesome at the same time, and she'd somehow been able to slip away without indicating she'd felt the big thing. The big, *hard* thing, the thought of which brought on its own kind of hot flash and still made her gasp when she let it.

But this wasn't about Poppy or Poppy's naughty husband; it was about Elinor, because while it was true that each of them had their own issues to deal with, blackmail was an unforeseen irony, like the way there was no logic to the fact that though Alice's estrogen was rapidly depleting, she thought about sex now more than ever. She especially thought about it when she was out of town, where men were so available and she was anonymous, and no one, not even Elinor, would know if Alice wasn't a lady and went all the way.

Not that she did.

Not that she would.

"Will you pick me up so I won't have to drive?" Poppy was asking when Alice came to.

"Of course."

"Do you remember the way to the cottage?"

Alice sighed. "We'll find it. Elinor says CJ has transformed the old place."

Which wasn't the worst news in the world. The last time they'd been there, after all, the gardener had been found in a bed of impatiens with pruning shears sticking out of his back.

She wondered if Poppy had ever regained her memory of that day, or if, as with much of her life, she'd found denial a more comfortable place.

Poppy hung up the phone and climbed the wide staircase to the master bedroom. She unzipped the long zipper of her white halter sundress, slipped it off, and stood naked. She would have looked into the full-length mirror if she'd thought she would have seen anything different. But Poppy was Poppy, still lean and little, still sporting high breasts and green eyes and a surprising, round little ass that Duane once had heralded as "The Best in the West." Duane was from Reno, where those words meant something. In New York they were tasteless, sort of like Duane, who now lay asleep, sprawled on their bed in the middle of the day, possibly drunk, or spent, or bored stiff.

Stiff? Ha ha, Poppy thought, that would be an understatement.

They'd been married seven years; he was her third husband—or was he the fourth? No, he was only the third. She kept forgetting that she hadn't married Roger. She'd meant to, but Momma had coerced her into going to Monte Carlo, and that's when Poppy met Duane, who was there for the gambling.

He was handsome and charming, more charming than Roger, and they'd fallen in love, and so there you had it.

Within weeks they were married in front of the long reflecting pool at the majestic pink and white Rothschild villa on Saint Jean Cap Ferrat.

Whirlwind, Momma had called it and not added her blessing.

Poppy supposed that if she'd been smart, she'd have waited until they'd returned to the States to tie the knot. Maybe then she would have learned that though Duane indeed came from a silver mining family as he claimed, his older brother had bankrupted the mines. Duane had been on the Riviera trying to win back his fortune, but he'd won Poppy and her trust fund instead, and he'd never gone back to Reno or his destitute brother.

Momma had said there wasn't much worse than old money now gone.

Still, it was too bad he couldn't have at least kept a bit of the silver. Momma thought trinkets were so very pretty.

Poppy went to her closet and slipped into a long satin robe. Once, she might have slid between the sheets where Duane lay, might have let him cuddle up to her round little ass.

But unlike Elinor, apparently, Poppy had grown weary of sex. Duane didn't work, and he didn't play golf: he claimed that "nature photography" was his passion, but Poppy knew it really was sex. Day, night, morning, afternoon. For pity's sake, she got tired. A few years ago, she'd faked female problems. She'd suggested that he call a "service"; she'd said that she'd understand.

They'd never discussed it again. Their lovemaking became thankfully sparse, and Duane often came home well after dark, long after the sun set on any pictures he might snap.

Moving into her bathroom, Poppy sat on the plush white stool at her vanity. She looked into the mirror at her pasty complexion that had grown even pastier since Elinor's announcement.

Blackmail wasn't a new concept to Poppy. Duane, after all, had been sort of blackmailing her all this time, had the ring on his finger and the funnel to her trust fund because of what he knew, or hinted that he knew. But Poppy wasn't stupid. Let others think she had a silly, blind eye. If all it took was a few thousand dollars to Duane every month, a few moments here and there of acting as if she didn't care how he spent his time, protecting her secret was worth it.

It was the least she could do for Momma after all she'd been through.

Poor Momma!

Well, Poppy wouldn't think about her right now.

She'd focus on the pleasantries of life and how at least Duane was still not bad to look at. There could be worse men to escort her to places like the yacht club, where they were going tonight, worse men to have in her wallet.

Men, she thought. *They could be such a bother.*

But as she pulled back her red hair and looked into the mirror, a sickening thought washed over Poppy:

What if Duane had grown tired of her and the pittance of his allowance?

What if he'd learned about Elinor's lover; what if Duane was the blackmailer?

Poppy stared at her reflection, blinked quickly three times, and decided she'd better not think about that right now, either.

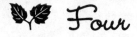 *Four*

"Mother," Jonas said, "you remember the congressman?"

"Of course, darling, don't be a goose." Elinor held out her hand to the Honorable Congressman William Perry (R-Ill.) (or Indiana, one of those oceanless states).

"Delighted to see you again, Mrs. Young," the congressman said. He had big hands, a big head full of big, white hair, and a deep, resonant voice. He looked rather uncomfortable in khakis and a polo shirt, as if he should have included a tie.

Still, he was perfectly civilized, and Elinor was determined to make this a nice evening, determined not to let anyone notice her occasional glance toward the phone, or otherwise reveal her fear that the *instructions to follow* would *follow* that evening in the presence of guests, *these* guests, of all people. The congressman and his wife, after all, were far-right right-wingers, who would not be enamored to know that their daughter's future mother-in-law had dropped her lavender lace panties in Midtown Manhattan, where they didn't belong.

Elinor attempted a relaxed, confident smile. "Please," she said, "call me Elinor."

The congressman grinned a polite grin. "Elinor," he said. "Your husband is showing Lucinda and my wife the topiaries. That's quite a garden you have."

"Thank you, we enjoy it."

"Your husband designed it?"

"Yes, with our daughter, Janice." Already her jaw was beginning to ache from her form-fitting smile.

The Honorable Congressman Perry turned to Jonas. "Betts and I haven't met Janice, have we?" Betts was the wife presently in the topiaries. She'd been one of Elinor's buttoned-up mentors when they'd first moved to Washington, one of the wives who'd invited Elinor to tea. She'd probably never even owned lavender panties, let alone had an affair.

"Janice is in Baltimore," Jonas said. "Johns Hopkins. She's a medical researcher."

"A medicine man, like her father, then." He made a slight noise that could have been a guffaw.

"Martini?" Elinor asked. The congressman nodded, and they wandered toward the living room, because that's where Elinor had set up the bar. He examined the Frederic Remington over the mantel and the Winslow Homer by the French doors, and he chatted with Jonas while she poured the drinks from the crystal pitcher that had been a gift from Joseph "Remy" Remillard back when he'd been a senator and Malcolm had overseen the care of his elderly father, who'd been diagnosed with Lou Gehrig's disease. Malcolm was always doing things like that—helping others not because he was a lobbyist but because he was just a good guy. If he crisscrossed any political boundaries or breached any conflicts of interest, no one seemed to notice or care.

Still, she poured from the pitcher, always with the hope someone would ask where it had come from because it was so lovely, and she could say, *"Oh, just a small gift from Remy,"* Remy, of course, who was now the vice president of these United States.

To date, no one had asked.

She set the triangular glasses atop a small tray and walked them over to the congressman and Jonas. Jonas was taller than his future father-in-law and much better looking, with a bright smile of youth, his mother's gray eyes, and thick ebony hair, which, though Elinor insisted he keep it trimmed short, really looked more attractive when it was a bit long.

The men snatched their drinks and Elinor snatched hers. She'd be smarter to have wine, but tonight she needed something stronger, something to prevent her from running, screaming, from the perfectly civilized room. Something to keep her face locked in its smile while she prayed that the phone didn't ring.

CJ fixed a salad for dinner and thought about Elinor and Malcolm, who were probably sipping Domaines Ott and nibbling bruschetta with the Perrys and Jonas. Elinor would be wearing a Vera Wang summer shift; CJ had changed into Crocs and her favorite, paint-splattered shirt. After dinner she'd go out to her studio and work on new fabric designs. It would be more pleasant than wondering how Elinor had ended up in this situation and how on earth it could be resolved. It would be more productive than thinking about Malcolm.

"Malcolm has been disinterested in me for a number of years," Elinor had said.

The very thought made CJ grow weak. She shook her head, then carried her salad to the small, round oak table that had "come with" the cottage, one of many things that had once furnished the lives of her parents and now furnished hers. Not much had ever originally "belonged" to CJ, except her ex-husband, and she'd tossed him like the salad before her.

She stabbed a grape tomato and three leaves of romaine. She wondered if having a lover had compromised Elinor's sanity. It had been a while since CJ had had a serious relationship, but she remembered too clearly how it could mess with your mind.

Still, Elinor had a history of emerging a winner.

Of the twins, Elinor had, after all, wound up with the husband, the family, the stable, full life filled with good works and wide interests and bright, eclectic people. She had money and connections and social power; she had houses and things that were hers.

Why had she needed a lover?

"Malcolm has been disinterested in me . . ."

CJ chewed the tomato, wishing she didn't feel just a teensy bit gratified that Elinor's home life was not as the world had been led to presume.

Smugness was a sin, she supposed, but what the hell. For years, CJ had wondered why Elinor had ended up with it all, when CJ had been the one who'd sacrificed everything, who'd had her art and her work but that really had been all.

The worst part was, it was her own fault.

It had started nearly three decades ago. CJ was in Paris,

studying at the Sorbonne. While she was away, Elinor married Malcolm, a research scientist fresh out of medical school. Within months, Elinor gave birth to a baby girl, Janice. Hours later, however, she developed a fast infection and was rushed into surgery. A hush-hush hysterectomy followed. Then deep depression.

"She needs your help," their father had said when he summoned CJ.

CJ went home without question. They might be different, but they were sisters.

So CJ had helped out with the baby, and with Elinor, who grieved for the other children she'd never have. She showed little interest in Janice, claiming it was too difficult to love an only child. Elinor was a twin, after all. As far as she knew, love came in twos. She told CJ and Malcolm that if only she could have one more baby, everything would be all right.

She was diagnosed with postpartum depression, though back then the condition was pretty much a mystery and there weren't many drugs that helped.

Then Elinor announced that she had a plan.

Elinor always had a plan. She was the alpha dog twin.

"We're identical," she said to CJ. "Our cheeks and our eyes and our smiles are the same. So is our DNA."

If CJ had Malcolm's baby, she reasoned, it would be no different than if the baby had been in Elinor's womb.

No one would know, so whom would it hurt?

Whom, indeed.

CJ stared at her salad now, her appetite suddenly gone. They'd been so young, and, of course, stupid. It had been long before technology was perfected, long before *surrogate* was a household word.

CJ and Malcolm would have to have sex.

"Once or twice ought to do it," Elinor had said.

It had taken eight times for CJ to get pregnant, but only once for CJ and Malcolm to fall in love. It had startled them both—horrified them, really. The only way they'd been able to rise above it had been to try and pretend it had never happened, *pretend* being the operative word.

Elinor and Malcolm had moved to D.C., and CJ moved with them. No one but their parents—not Alice, not Poppy—knew that the twins had switched roles for nine months.

Over the years the lie grew familiar, if not comfortable. Afraid there would always be sparks between Malcolm and her, CJ became adept at dodging family parties and holidays. It was stressful and painful and just plain depressing. But each time CJ looked at Jonas, each time she witnessed the product their love had wrought, she couldn't say she was sorry.

But now, if Malcolm was disinterested in Elinor—as shamefully gratifying as it felt—did it mean the worst thing CJ could imagine: that Malcolm had found someone else?

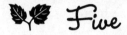 *Five*

Alice's daughter, Felicity, was twenty-five, too old to be snowboarding in Utah, where she lived off-season in a yurt. On the other hand, Alice's other daughter, Melissa, was twenty-seven, not old enough to be the mother of three, the oldest of whom was Kiley Kate. Like Elinor and Malcolm, Alice and Neal had married so young that the lives they now lived seemed too old for them.

Maybe that was why Elinor had sought distraction elsewhere: She'd been suffocating as a New-York-to-Washington wife.

Maybe that—not roller-coastering estrogen—was also why Alice had been looking this way and that, obsessing about the potential of out-of-town penises when she should have been focusing on her granddaughter's promising career.

She could ask Elinor if she agreed, but that would mean confessing her sins. Alice surely wasn't ready for that. Besides, it wasn't as if she'd had sex with the out-of-towners. (One night with Leonard had left her guilty enough.) Still, she did enjoy the little game she'd invented of flirting and teasing and knowing she still had what it took to turn a man's head.

Hers was a harmless game.

On the scale of infidelity, however, Alice supposed her behavior might be considered as culpable as Elinor's affair. Especially if Neal ever found out.

So, in lieu of confessing (at least not immediately), Alice decided to divert her attention by hopping into her big, white Cadillac SUV and driving to her daughter and son-in-law's to deliver a surprise for Kiley Kate: a sequin-splashed, to-die-for outfit for the upcoming *USA Sings* audition in Orlando. After all, Alice and Kiley Kate would leave on Thursday, whether Elinor's panties found their way home or not.

With a small sigh, Alice turned the Esplanade onto the back road that led to Melissa and David's house that Alice and Neal paid for because David was just getting started in a Wall Street career, and status began with property worth. It ended, of course, when . . . if . . . character imprudence was detected—at least in Mount Kasteel, where status often outranked common sense.

Was that what Alice had become? An imprudent character?

A slightly wicked smile crossed her lips. In light of Elinor's, well, indiscretion, it might be safe now—and kind of fun—to share her own silly truths with her friends.

"There was Donald in Dallas," she could begin.

"And Larry in Las Vegas.

"And Parker in San Jose.

"I found them online, arranged date after date, in cities and towns where auditions were held—the first rounds, the quarterfinals, the semifinals, too, not to mention the regional tryouts in between."

Elinor and Poppy would need a drink before Alice could continue. They would have wine, because this would be a long story.

"It began on a lark," Alice would explain, "something to pass the time while Kiley Kate was in chaperoned sessions or early-to-bed." There was, after all, little to do in a strange place for a few days. The other contestants and their families could hardly socialize; competition did not breed good friendships.

She would say she'd grown tired of being sequestered in hotel rooms, cranking up noisy air-conditioning units with each drippy new hot flash. She would say she'd needed to find a pastime more engaging.

She wasn't certain how much more she should tell. Should she mention that Chicago had been first? Danny. Alice had wondered what sort of grown man would call himself by a childhood nickname; she'd soon learned it was the sort who showed up for their date with a single red rose, who made up for below-average looks with kind, gentle words, who sent teardrop sapphire earrings ("To match your lovely eyes") the next day with a promise of dinner to be followed by "clothes-shredding sex." She'd sent back the earrings and said, "Thanks, but no thanks."

She could tell them that in Richmond there had been a Civil War reenactor, who had a tattoo of a Confederate flag on his chest and claimed that his dick was a musket.

Or that in St. Louis there had been a tall, thin man who'd

resembled the arch and was a descendant of Harland Bartho-
lomew, the great urban planner who'd designed the city.

She just didn't know how much to share with Elinor, her
once-perfect idol. Could she admit that this harmless game
had begun on a lark but had grown to salvage her day-to-
day sanity? That it massaged her dispirited life, which should
have been ideal, because, like Elinor, Alice Sussman Bartlett
had made sure she had gotten it all: home, husband, children,
health, wealth, and oh, yes, status, at least unless Mount
Kasteel learned the rest.

Had middle-aged mania spurred Elinor, too?

If Alice only knew who Elinor's lover was, it might help
her decide how much to share. Was he one of many, or was he
a real lover? Was he a man Elinor might leave Malcolm for?
No. Not hardly, any more than Alice would leave Neal for the
amusement she found on the road.

But yes, hers was a harmless game. It was simply something
to think about other than the infernal hot flashes that left her
feeling wrecked the better part of most every day.

Pulling into the driveway of her daughter's small but neat
Tudor, Alice nearly hit a flying football that dropped, then
bounced, onto the asphalt. She slammed on her brakes, grateful the ball wasn't a kid.

"Mother," called Melissa, Mom-of-the-year, as she trundled over the front lawn with seven-year old Steven and
five-year old David, Junior, trailing behind her. "We weren't
expecting you."

Alice turned off the ignition, grabbed the shopping bag,
and got out of the car. "Your father's in the city. I thought I'd
deliver Kiley Kate's new outfit for Orlando."

"She's inside," Melissa said, then pointed to the bag. "But

you can return that. She says she's not going to go to the try-outs. That she doesn't want to be a singer anymore."

"Of course you want to be a singer," Alice said once she was in the house and found Kiley Kate in her bedroom, playing with Coco, the calico kitten. Alice was ashamed to acknowledge to herself that her stomach had pitched like the football in the driveway when Melissa had said Kiley Kate was done with her career. She was ashamed that her out-of-town pastime had become so important. "Every kid in America wants to be on *USA Sings*. You're lucky enough to have a real chance."

That part was true: Kiley Kate was an energetic child with a power-packed voice, a thick head of blonde waves, and giant cobalt eyes, the same color as Alice's, the same color as Kiley Kate's Aunt Felicity's, who never enhanced them with a light schmear of shadow or swift stroke of liner. If *USA Sings* had a "best-looking" category, Kiley Kate surely would win. The judges, however, maintained that the decisions weren't based on looks but on talent, as if that's all it took to make it these days.

Alice sat on the bed and stroked her granddaughter's hair.

"Mommy says you and Grampy have spent a lot of money and I shouldn't disappoint you by dropping out."

Alice wished Kiley Kate hadn't reminded her it was *Grampy's* hard-earned, overachieved dollars that paid for her fun.

"Honey, if you want to drop out, you should. But first, make sure you know why. Is it because of Morgan Johnson? Or Taylor LeDuc?" Morgan and Taylor, rock and rap performers, had received recent attention from local judges. With the final-finals set for Philadelphia just weeks away, no doubt Kiley Kate did not want to fail.

"I can't win," she said. "I'll never win." She'd had a real chance for the free trip to Hollywood and a slot on the show before either Morgan or Taylor had arrived on the scene with high-priced coaches Alice suspected of being judge-related: brother-in-law, mother-in-law, whatever.

Alice picked up the kitten and held it close. She'd always hated letting things go. She supposed that was why she'd held onto Neal for so long.

As she rubbed Coco's fur, she thought about the theme-park magician named Bud. He was the latest man she'd found online, her Orlando game waiting to happen. She'd been looking forward to fun conversation, slice-of-life stories about stressed-out vacationing families, stories he'd no doubt reenact to show how entertaining he was, how clever, how charming, how able to conduct an irresistible prelude to foreplay.

Irresistible, no doubt, to him.

She supposed she'd known all along that she'd been taking chances. Someday Bud or Donald or Larry or Parker might not take no for an answer; someday Alice might not *want* to say no; someday it could be her panties, not Elinor's, found in a Dumpster, and a blackmail note could be delivered to her. Or to Neal.

"What's in the bag, Grammy?" Kiley Kate suddenly asked.

Alice nuzzled the kitten, then set it on the floor. "It was for Orlando. But maybe we shouldn't go after all." She stood up, picked up the bag. *Yes,* she thought, *maybe we shouldn't. Maybe it's time for the game to be over before I'm the one who ends up in a pickle.*

"Can I see, Grammy?" The sapphire eyes pleaded with Alice.

"No, honey. I'll return it. I'll buy you a pretty outfit for school."

"Please, Grammy? Can't I just peek?"

Well, maybe a peek wouldn't hurt. Alice pulled out pink and white sparkly shorts and a matching, dazzling fringed top. Despite her pronouncement, Kiley Kate gasped.

"Oh, Grammy, they're beautiful!" She quickly scrambled out of her clothes. "Help me try them on!"

Alice faltered only a second. Then she unzipped the zipper, slipped the top over Kiley Kate's beautiful waves, and said a quick prayer that Bud in Orlando would be benign like the others, that she'd merely been overreacting because of Elinor and the lavender lace.

 Six

Yolanda Valdes DeLano wouldn't have been where she was if her big brother hadn't joined the army and sent money home to the Bronx. The cash had been for beauty school, The Big Apple School of *Esthetology*—a word that had given Yolanda's mother a hoot.

"Well, aren't you something?" her mother had said.

Ten years later, Yolanda really *was* something, after she'd done a wash and set on a woman from New Falls, who'd been in town for a funeral. The woman had been cursed with coarse hair, and Yolanda had performed such a miracle that the woman found her a job in the classy-ass town that she'd said was "upstate"—if that's what the Hudson River Valley was called.

Upon her arrival, her new customers hadn't been able to tell if she was black or white or Hispanic, and they hadn't cared, as long as she did their hair and their nails. Then she met Vincent, and they fell in love, and the women looked at her differently, but not good. He tried to convince her to tell them that her father had come from Havana on a raft—a real, freaking *raft*. He said that if they knew the truth, they would take pity and love her like he did.

But she'd been embarrassed, and then she'd been pregnant, and then they'd gotten married, and the rest was ancient history, including the fact that Vincent, her husband, was now dead. But Yolanda had her little daughter, and she'd opened her own business, and she was doing well. She was finally receiving some respect from the wives of New Falls.

She still missed Vincent sometimes, but she didn't need a man. When she wanted a male's opinion, she had her big brother, Manny, which was why he now sat across from her at the kitchen table in the apartment upstairs from her shop, which she'd decorated herself.

"It's blackmail," she said. "Do you have any ideas?"

He laughed, sprinkling more Cheerios on the tray of Belita's high chair—Belita, the beautiful one. The little girl laughed, too, then stuck a tiny finger through the hole in the *o*.

"Your friend needs to call the police." It was easy for Manny to say; after the army, he'd joined the police force in Brooklyn and was now a detective, plainclothes.

"She can't. There are reasons."

He laughed again, as did Belita.

"Manuel, this is not funny. This woman is my friend."

"This woman is your customer."

"All right, she's my customer. But she's a good customer. And she's a good person."

"Who cheats on her husband." Manny was known as one of the few cops who still believed marriage was sacred, no cheating, no boozing, no gambling the money that had been hard-earned for the family. Too bad his wife hadn't agreed. He had full custody of his three kids (son, daughter, son), and was as good a dad as he was a cop. Except for the fact that he liked eyeing women, Manny could have been a priest from a time when the collar had meant something.

"Judge not, Manuel," Yolanda said. That shut him up; he hadn't always been so high and mighty back in the old neighborhood days.

He formed a *B* for "Belita" out of the Cheerios. "So what do you want me to do? I'm a cop. I can't get involved unless it's official. I shouldn't even know about it."

"You don't have to get involved. Just tell me what to do."

"So *you* can get involved."

"Consider it part of my business. They think I'm street smart."

"Because you're not one of them? Because you're Latino, so naturally you'd know about criminals? Like it's a birthright that comes with your skin? Why can't you just be like other women and meet a nice man and be a nice wife? How many times do I have to ask you to have dinner with Junior Diaz? He won't wait forever, you know." His voice had grown louder, and he'd shoved back his chair and was standing now. Belita's dark eyes followed his movement. Suddenly, they filled with tears.

Waaaaah. Waaaaah.

"Now look what you've done," Yolanda said. "You've scared my poor baby . . ."

She picked her up and hushed her, while Manny said, "Oh,

man, I'm sorry, Yo. Honest, I'm sorry. Do you want me to hold her?"

"No," Yolanda said, smoothing Belita's black hair. "I want you to forget about trying to fix me up and let me be myself. I want you to tell me what to do for my friend."

He poured more coffee. "Start at the hotel. Find out where your friend left her . . . her *things* . . . before they wound up in the Dumpster." Tough cop though he was, Manny got flustered when the talk was of a womanly nature. "Then you'll have to figure out who had access to them."

"So you'll help me help her?"

"Only if you don't tell anyone. Or I could get fired, Yo."

 ## Seven

CJ rose at dawn on Sunday morning, hitched her yellow Lab, Luna, onto a leash, then went for their predictable walk around the lake. Summer was nearly over; a few leaves on the birch trees had already turned yellow, though the thermometer was nearly sixty degrees and would no doubt reach eighty by noon.

Last night, she'd barely slept.

This business with Elinor was crazy, insane. Putting aside her feelings for Malcolm, it was hard to believe that Elinor was having an affair. If there had been an award in high school for "Least Likely to Screw Around on Your Husband," Elinor would have won, without question. In fact, rumor once had it that Elinor kept her legs and her spine so tight most of the time that it was surprising she'd landed a man at all, let alone Malcolm.

"Morning, CJ."

She hadn't heard the Williams boy—Ray's son—ride up on his bicycle, which was hitched to a cart that held stacks of Sunday *New York Times* for the lake neighbors.

"Good morning, Kevin."

Luna loped over in search of a scratch on her ears. Like his dad, whom CJ on-again-off-again dated, Kevin thought Luna was the second-best dog on the planet, rated only slightly behind his chocolate Lab named Jerome.

"Want your paper now?"

"Sure. We're almost home." She took the paper; Kevin waved and drove off, pumping down the dirt road that was not much more than a path. Luna lumbered after him for a bit, then charged into cattails that hugged the water's edge, stirring up the cicadas, the noisy, heat-lazy insects that had three legs, "like a wheelbarrow," her father had always said.

Though there were times CJ wistfully thought about living in Paris again, she'd never regretted making her home where she and Elinor had grown up during summers and school vacations when they hadn't been on the campus of McCready School. Their mother had been more relaxed, less formal here, their father less stern. He'd sat by the lake, smoked his pipe, and read Victorian classics to his girls: Dickens, Trollope, and CJ's favorite, George Eliot, a woman doing a man's job.

She supposed she'd become a George Eliot of her generation, needing to earn a man's wages to support herself. And Luna, of course.

If she'd had a husband like Malcolm, she wouldn't have

needed to sell hand-painted dresses and jackets and elegant shawls. But the only husband she'd had had been Cooper (his first name was Lionel, so even CJ called him by his last), who had gotten too close to the truth.

They'd been married five years and had lived in a SoHo loft. He wrote screenplays (a few actually sold!), she painted textiles, and it seemed like a good long-term fit. For a while CJ forgot about Malcolm, but then she got pregnant. She and Cooper were ecstatic for a few weeks . . . until she miscarried.

"It's just one of those things," the doctor at the downtown clinic had explained to Cooper. "She's had one healthy pregnancy, so chances are, she'll have another."

One healthy pregnancy?

CJ, of course, had not told Cooper about Elinor and Malcolm and Jonas and the rest.

She'd deemed it safer to divorce him than to tell him the truth and reveal the big family secret. Not many people understood the magic bond of the twin-psyche, the monozygotic connection.

So she'd broken Cooper's heart, and broken her own, and since then, she'd been alone, which, she told herself, wasn't so bad. When she missed the warmth of a man, she had Ray Williams to turn to. Ray was a neighbor, a friend, someone who'd fix her screen door and share a bottle of wine, which often led to a romantic occurrence. She'd been quite clear about not wanting to get involved. Besides, Ray had sole custody of Kevin and would not spend the night. Other than her ex-husband, CJ had never slept until dawn with a man, not even Malcolm, whose love had been limited to clandestine moments in surreptitious places until one day the guilt had been too much.

And now the ache swelled again in her chest, the one reborn yesterday at Elinor's, the "Malcolm ache" she'd once called it before she'd buried it—or thought that she'd buried it—so long ago. But there it was, rising up from the ashes, Malcolm the Phoenix.

Unless it was just loneliness, looking for a victim.

She shuddered, then quickly shook her head.

"Luna!" she called. "Come on, girl!" It was time to stop dawdling, as her mother would have called it, time to stop thinking waste-of-time thoughts, to get home and get ready for the guests who'd arrive soon to talk about blackmail.

She clutched the newspaper to her chest, waited for Luna to catch up, then marched briskly back toward the cottage.

At five minutes to eight on Sunday morning, Alice located the mailbox marked Twenty-three Lakeside Lane. She stopped the car, surveyed a tall stand of pine trees, soft bundles of ferns, and thick clusters of sun-colored daylilies. It was quiet and serene, like a watercolor, accented by the old gardener's shed off to one side and the former carriage house, which, Elinor once told her, now held CJ's studio. In the center of the frame was the familiar stone cottage. It seemed smaller now that CJ lived there alone.

"It's changed," Poppy said quietly from the seat beside her. "It no longer looks scary." Her words were reassuring, but her tone was rather lifeless.

"It's older," Alice replied. "So are we."

"Older and wiser."

"Well, older, anyway." Alice put the car into drive and slowly directed it down the gravel driveway. "You're okay, then?" she asked. "To be here?"

Poppy nodded. "I'm not going to faint, if that's what you mean."

"Well," Alice said, "that's good then." She wondered if Poppy had been in therapy and hadn't mentioned it, the way Elinor hadn't mentioned her affair. Life was more fun, she supposed, when they'd been young and naïve and had discussed life's minutiae at great, tedious length.

"Poppy," Elinor said as she greeted them at the back door. "I am so sorry. I completely forgot. I wouldn't have had us meet here—"

Poppy held up her hand. "It's all right, Elinor. I'm a grown woman now." She supposed none of them really believed that, but it seemed like the right thing to say. For once, she would try to be there for her friends—for Elinor this time—the way they'd always been there for her.

"Still, it was selfish of me . . ."

"Well, don't be silly." Poppy's head twittered a little, so she spun around. "Catherine Janelle!" she called out to CJ. "You have, indeed, done wonders with this place!"

Her eyes cruised the living room, with its plump, comfy furniture in natural, neutral shades that accented the copper-like veins of the nutmeg stone fireplace.

Poppy had no idea how she remembered the fireplace was of nutmeg stone. Memories of this place were usually so confusing.

She held one side of her cerulean skirt up by its hem and wondered if her heartbeat would ever slow down. She feared that if she let her mouth relax from its smile, her lips would start quivering as they had that day, and that this time they'd never stop.

With a light fingertip, she touched a bouquet of gerbera daisies that stood in a thin crystal vase. Then she pirouetted to a painting in vivid acrylics.

"Yours?" she asked CJ, and CJ said, "Yes."

"Fabulous!" Poppy twittered again, aware that everyone was watching her, as if they'd been suspended in her precarious air.

"Simply fabulous!" she repeated, her timbre a bit higher than she would have liked. She twirled back to CJ. "Now where is the kitchen? Do we have Bloody Marys? I believe I could use one or two."

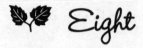 *Eight*

Yolanda was the only one who opted for coffee instead of a Bloody Mary. Then again, Yolanda hadn't been there when the gardener was murdered.

Alice meandered around the room, not wanting to witness Poppy's behavior, but not wanting to look out the window to the garden, where she surely would picture the yellow Police—Do Not Cross tape ribboned through the innocent pink and white blossoms.

She sat on the sofa and stared at the fireplace until a furnace flared up from her feet.

Finally, everyone had a beverage, everyone was seated, and everyone waited for Elinor to hold court.

"So," Elinor began, "do we have any ideas how we're going to find out who my blackmailer is?"

Alice cleared her throat. "What about the note? Did it come in the mail?"

"No. It was overnighted. A standard courier service. The sender was a phony name and address somewhere in Manhattan. I've already checked that out." A long fingernail traced the crease on her ivory cotton pants.

"What about the hotel?" Yolanda asked. "Were you at the Lord Winslow with your lover? Is that why your panties were there?"

Alice blanched.

Poppy blinked.

CJ seemed to take a deep breath.

Sometimes Yolanda was a little too outspoken for the ladies of Mount Kasteel.

"Yes," Elinor finally replied. "I met my lover there Thursday night," she continued. "We've often been careful to meet out of town."

Out of town? Alice gulped, even though this was not about her.

"We need to start there," Yolanda said. "Whoever it was might have been spying on you, maybe waiting to find evidence to hold up for ransom. Your panties were their mother lode."

They thought, they drank, they bit their lips and played with their hair. Actually, it was Poppy who played with her hair.

"Alice and Poppy," Yolanda continued, "the two of you should go to the hotel. You can tell the manager that you're Elinor's friends. Show them her picture. Say she left something behind and you've come to get it."

"Me?" Poppy asked. "Me?"

"Well, not me," the hairdresser-slash-nail-tech replied. "No one would believe I'm Elinor's friend."

They blanched and blinked and deep-breathed again.

"Why doesn't Elinor go herself?" Alice continued. "Or have CC go in her place?" She'd meant to say CJ, really she had, but "CC" had slipped out. It had been a tongue-in-cheek way she and Poppy had referred to CJ when they were kids, *CC* meaning "carbon copy," the besmirched, lesser twin who'd not been quite as grand or as snooty as Elinor. When they were fourteen, snooty had been good.

Yolanda stood up and walked to the fireplace. "If Elinor is being followed, the blackmailer might mistake CJ for her. If he thinks either one of them is snooping, who knows what he'll do." She looked at Elinor. "Did he say what his next step will be?"

"The note said to stay where I am, which I suppose means at the country house. I don't know if I'll hear more in a day or a week."

"In the meantime, maybe we can learn something."

"Oh," Poppy said, "I don't know if I can do this."

"Yes, you can," Alice said. "You're stronger than you used to be."

"I am? That's right. I am."

Yolanda ignored them. "You should bring a picture. Preferably one of the three of you: Elinor, Alice, and Poppy. That way, whoever you show the picture to will know that you're friends."

"What if the hotel people say, 'I remember her. But she left nothing behind'?" Alice asked.

"Ask if they're sure. Ask if someone else might have already picked something up."

"And if they say yes?"

"Ask what he looks like. Act as if it's fun, as if he must be another of Elinor's friends."

"What if it's not a he but a she?" That came from Poppy.

"I can't imagine a woman being this scary," CJ said.

No one mentioned Poppy's mother.

Then Elinor asked, "Do you think you can do this? Pretend you're my friend?"

Alice smiled. If nothing else, this game might be safer than the one she'd been playing. "We *are* your friends, Elinor. You'd do it for us." Wouldn't she?

"But what if the person we ask turns out to be the black-mailer?" Poppy asked.

Yolanda shrugged. "Look, I have no idea if this will work. But we can try."

"Please," Elinor said. "For the sake of my marriage."

More sighing and drinking and hair curling followed.

Then Yolanda said, "Do you have a recent picture? Of the three of you?"

Elinor opened her eyes and looked at her sister. "CJ?" she asked with a smile. "Surely you have a camera somewhere in the cottage. Would you be a dear and fetch it?"

Fetch it?

As if she was Luna?

Elinor was in fine form today.

Oh, Poppy, I'm so sorry. I completely forgot. And *please. For the sake of my marriage.*

Puuuhleeze, indeed, CJ thought. If Elinor weren't her twin, and if this wasn't CJ's house, and if CJ didn't know that all the bs was simply an indication that Elinor was totally terrified, she would have said, *"Good luck"* and left.

As for the others, well, Alice and Poppy should at least have known that when Elinor was involved, nothing turned out to be simple.

CJ went into the kitchen, leaned against the counter, and thought about Mac. Did she really know him anymore? She had turned off her feelings for the sake of the family, for the sake of her sister. Once, she'd actually thought that life could go on unaffected, that she could marry and have other children. Once, she'd thought she could accept that Jonas was not meant to be hers.

Maybe she'd been in need of as much help as Elinor.

Recalling a line about being able to pick your friends but not your relatives, CJ exhaled her frustration and opened the junk drawer. She bypassed a letter opener, a few old pens, a screwdriver, her cell phone charger. At last, she located the camera. Closing the drawer, her glance fell on the Sunday *Times* that sat on the counter where she had dropped it.

As she turned to leave, a front-page photo caught CJ's eye: A small group of men stood under the canopy at the front door of the New York Lord Winslow.

She halted.

That's odd, she thought. *Coincidental.*

Her eyes scanned the caption: the men had stayed at the hotel Thursday night after late meetings at the United Nations. Most prominent in the photo was Joseph Remillard, vice president of the United States.

Good grief, CJ thought. If Elinor had been at the hotel at the same time, she was lucky her lace panties hadn't been found by the vice president or the Secret Service or any of Mac's Washington cronies.

With a small laugh, CJ turned back toward the living room. Then her footsteps slowed. Her muscles went slack. A puddle of bile pooled in her throat.

Holy.

Shit.

No, she thought. *It can't be.*

Then CJ remembered that Elinor and Mac had had some sort of connection to the VP, which Elinor liked to flaunt with a martini pitcher.

Oh, CJ thought. *Oh, God.*

She went back to the newspaper. Stared at the photo. The New York Lord Winslow. Friday morning.

Her twin-psyche lurched into high gear.

"I can't tell you everything," Elinor had said. *"We'll just have to leave it at that."*

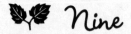 *Nine*

Elinor was the first to leave, which meant CJ didn't get the chance to ask her in private if she was sleeping with the vice president.

CJ had shuddered through the rest of the visit, during which Poppy had consumed three Bloody Marys while insisting that she had recovered from the incident with the gardener years ago and didn't even remember his name.

Did they?

Yolanda had been mute. CJ had shaken her head, and Alice had, too, though anyone who had been in the county when it had happened probably knew the name Sam Yates. Sixty-three-year-old World War II veteran. Caught peeping at fifteen-year-old girls. Yuck.

But rather than dredge up that ancient pile of manure, Alice had stood up and announced it was time to leave. CJ could have kissed her, because she had such an awful headache by then.

Besides, there had been nothing left to talk about. The others hadn't been willing to discuss Elinor in front of CJ, because no matter how strained the twin's relationship sometimes was, they no doubt knew that family ties were still stronger than theirs.

Finally left with dirty glasses, blessed silence, and Luna, who wanted to be fed, CJ scooped a bowl full of dry food, put out fresh water, grabbed the front section of the *Times*, and plunked herself at the table. She studied the picture as if it might hold a clue, a telltale remnant of Elinor, lipstick on his collar, panties peeking from his pocket.

When CJ saw no clue, she stared at the man. Joseph Remillard was on the short side, with football-player-wide shoulders and thinning hair. He had a slight paunch but a charming smile with a cleft in his chin that must have been good for a few female votes. Still, he was not as good looking as Malcolm.

"So what's the deal?" CJ asked the man in the photo. "Are you sleeping with my sister?"

It had been years since she'd seen Elinor naked, but CJ supposed she looked the way CJ did now—butt cheeks that weren't as taut as when they'd been teens, breasts not as perky, bellies still small but no longer appropriate for an itsy-bitsy bikini.

Not that they'd ever been allowed to wear one.

"No daughter of mine is going to pierce her ears (wear bell bottoms or miniskirts, smoke marijuana, get into a car with a boy)," their father had barked on more than one occasion. He'd claimed he had to be strict because his job was at stake, that if the Board of Trustees of the McCready School for Girls thought him incapable of rearing his own daughters correctly, he would not be headmaster for long.

So the trustees had been directly responsible for bringing up Elinor and CJ. Father had made certain his daughters' clothes and their friends and the food that they ate and the damn dolls they played with were all trustee-approved, at least in his eyes.

It was no wonder their mother had sipped cooking sherry when she knew their father wasn't looking.

Tossing down the newspaper, CJ wondered what her father would think of this latest Elinor charade. The odd part was this: Of the twins, Elinor was the one who was most like what he'd been—controlling, in control. Not at all like CJ-the-pushover, who'd spent her life trying to please others, though look where it had gotten her.

No, Elinor had never worried about pleasing anyone but herself. Unless, of course, that had all changed, and Elinor was now pleasing . . . him.

CJ's eyes fell back to the paper.

Yes, she thought. If Elinor were to have an affair, it would need to be with someone who had the ability to make her jaw drop along with her panties. It would need to be someone who was stronger than she was, more powerful, more capable of calling the shots. Elinor Harding Young would not lie down with just anyone. It had to be someone like Joseph Remillard.

The morning's Bloody Mary roiled in CJ's stomach. If the truth got out, it would humiliate Malcolm. It would no doubt be the end of Jonas's engagement. And Elinor would become fodder for the tabloids, a middle-aged mockery, a political joke, like that young intern and her tell-all blue dress.

Luna nuzzled CJ's hand, in search of an after-breakfast walk. "Sure thing," CJ said, scratching the Lab's head. "I could use some fresh air myself."

If Duane had needed a substantial influx of cash—say a half million dollars—would Poppy have noticed the signs? If it truly was possible that he was Elinor's blackmailer, could Poppy find out before any more damage was done?

Maybe it was the Bloody Marys, or the one-hour wait for the photo prints at the Mount Kasteel Pharmacy, but by the time Alice finally wheeled her big SUV up to the gate at Poppy's driveway, Poppy knew what she had to do.

"It's Duane," she suddenly blurted.

The vehicle stopped. "Duane?" Alice asked. "Your husband?"

"I think he's Elinor's blackmailer."

Alice drummed her thumbs on the thick leather steering wheel. "How would Duane know Elinor had a lover? *We* didn't even know, for God's sake."

When Poppy had bought this estate upon their return from Monte Carlo, newly married and giddy, she'd loved the high stone wall. She'd told Duane that the locked wrought-iron gates made her feel safe, as if the world couldn't get to her, no matter what. He'd laughed and said the gates made him feel like a big shot again, as he'd been in the heyday of silver. She should have known then that the marriage was doomed.

"For all we know, he could be her lover," Poppy added, then let Alice digest the possibility before saying, "As for the blackmail, well, I give him an allowance." It was something she'd never even admitted to her mother. "Maybe he's decided it's not enough."

Alice shrugged. "People have all kinds of arrangements, Poppy. It doesn't mean Duane's a criminal."

Folding her hands on the lap of her skirt, Poppy shivered from the air-conditioning. "Wouldn't it explain why we weren't invited to the engagement party?"

Alice stopped drumming. "You're talking in circles."

She shook her head. "No. I'm not. I am very hurt that we weren't invited. We've been Elinor's best friends since we were kids. Jonas is her son. Don't we deserve to go to a fancy Washington party?"

"First of all, we weren't invited because it's for the politicos. We live in New York and don't know any of them. Second, the party is being hosted by the parents of the bride. The *congressman*, Poppy. It's their party, not Elinor's."

"She could have insisted."

Alice shifted on the seat; the leather squeaked. "Sorry, kiddo, but I don't see how it fits."

"If Elinor is sleeping with Duane, or even if she just thinks he's blackmailing her, she wouldn't want us there. She couldn't invite you and Neal and not us."

The air-conditioning droned.

"But Poppy," Alice said, though her voice was quieter now, "if Elinor thinks Duane is involved, why would she ask for our help?"

"Because if we proved it was Duane, she'd know we wouldn't let it go public. Her reputation would be safe. Let's face it, Alice, Elinor might be using us." She supposed she should feel guilty for thinking such a thing, but it was safer to be angry with Elinor than with Duane, who'd know she would never ask for a divorce.

"No, Poppy, you're dreaming."

"Maybe so, but as soon as I get into the house, I'm going to find out."

Just then the gates yawned open. Duane's silver BMW convertible—Poppy's five-year anniversary present to him— nearly hit them head-on. He swerved and came to a stop on Alice's side. "Morning, ladies!" he cried, flashing his Duane-smile.

Alice put down the window.

"What are you lovely girls up to on this fine morning?"

"We've been at a charity breakfast," Poppy quickly shot back. "Are you going out?"

He patted a camera case on the seat beside him. "Pictures to take," he said, smiled again, then waved. "I'll be home later."

In a flash he was gone, leaving Poppy and Alice in silence, except for the air-conditioning that continued to drone.

Ten

Brunch had stretched into early afternoon, and there was little left to say to the esteemed congressman, his lovely wife, Betts, and the soon-to-be-daughter-in-law, Lucinda. So Elinor and Malcolm stood in the doorway and bade them a hearty good-bye-so-nice-that-you-came, and then Malcolm left, too, heading back to Washington, back to his work that paid for their comfortable life. Jonas had opted to stay in New York, muttering something about a job interview in Manhattan. Then he hauled the canoe from the yard where he'd left it the week before (someday he'd learn to put things away), strapped it onto the roof of the old Jeep that he kept in Mount Kasteel, and rushed off to hopefully catch a few trout on the lake. Elinor was pleased that her children were finally adults and she didn't need to know every detail of their comings or goings. Life was so much easier to navigate without dependents.

When she was certain she was alone, Elinor went into her bedroom, picked up her cell phone, and called CJ.

"I have to go to Grand Cayman to get the money," she said as soon as CJ answered the phone. Years ago Elinor had confided to CJ that she kept a secret tax-free account there in case of emergency. She'd explained that Malcolm didn't know. ("He's such a bore about doing anything that might question his character or his damn patriotism.") However, she hadn't admitted that the real reason behind the account was the fact that she was afraid Mac would leave her someday and she wanted to be financially prepared. She'd never dreamed financial preparation would involve underwear. She ran her hand through her hair now and tried to ignore the muscles in her throat that seemed to suddenly be constricting.

"It's nice you have it," CJ replied. "Not everyone can put their hands on a half million dollars. Cash."

Elinor bypassed the sarcasm. "It's a catch-twenty-two, Catherine. If we weren't worth a lot of money, I wouldn't be blackmailed."

CJ didn't admit that she had a point. "Are you sure you can do this without Malcolm finding out?"

"He's wrapped up in his work. Besides, between you and me, he might not even care. I don't know which would be more humiliating." She laughed, then walked to the window and stared down at her husband's prized topiaries. "I have to get the money, CJ. I have to be ready. In case we can't learn who's doing this. In case we can't stop him."

"But . . ."

Elinor shook her head, as if CJ could see her. "I need to do this before the engagement party, in case my friendly black-mailer decides to show up there . . ." She shut her eyes and stifled a scream.

"When will you leave?"

Elinor regained her composure. "Wednesday. And I need a favor."

Silence.

"Catherine?"

"I'm here, E."

Elinor hated when CJ went silent the way their mother so often had. Silence could be so judgmental. "Will you come to the house and stay here in case if the blackmailer calls?"

"Because our voices sound alike," CJ answered. It was, of course, part of being identical, in looks and voice, if not per-sonalities. "But Elinor, it's not as if you'll be trapped. You'll have your cell phone . . . can't you forward your house calls?"

"I don't know if the cell phone will work everywhere on the island." Elinor had learned from Father the importance of always having the answers.

"I won't need to go to your house. Leave your cell with me."

"I'm taking it with me."

"But you just said . . ."

"I can use it in the airports. I might be able to use it on the ground. I don't know which number this moron has. I need you to cover the house."

"Have the house calls forwarded to me."

Elinor tapped her foot. She had no patience for her sister right now. "What's the problem, CJ? Can't you just come over here? Pick a guest room. God knows we have several."

"What about Luna?"

"Bring her. Or leave her with that boy. It's not as if you never go away."

"And I always feel guilty about that. Poor Luna needs a family. Not just inattentive old me."

Then silence again.

"Please, CJ. No one has to know. Malcolm has gone to Washington. If he finds out you're here, tell him you're renovating the cottage or something. He never goes there, does he?"

"No. Of course not. But won't he wonder why you've left the country so close to the party?"

"Don't tell him I'm out of the country. Say I'm in Philly. That my dress needed last-minute alterations." She knew that her words sounded fabricated. She didn't remember whether or not she'd ever told Malcolm that her preferred seamstress now lived in Philadelphia, that she was the daughter of the woman who had been their mother's seamstress, the one Dianne Harding had depended on for every special event.

"Oh, E, I don't know . . . this involves so many lies."

"It's not just the phone call I'm worried about, CJ. I'm afraid the blackmailer will show up at my door. You could handle it. No one else could."

So CJ, of course, finally agreed. After all, she was the dependable one. Elinor knew that someday she should tell CJ that she was her anchor, that she was her strength. Someday, but not now. There simply was too much to do.

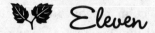 *Eleven*

Monday morning the temperature climbed toward the low nineties, and it was raining in Manhattan. Clusters of ghostly ectoplasms waltzed on the asphalt, a reminder that though it was almost September, the weather could still simmer like summer. Behind the wheel of her Esplanade (Neal only bought American), Alice had begun to sweat—or *perspire*, they'd been taught to call it at the Mc-Cready School for Girls, long before menopause had erupted and turned her into a near-nymphomaniac, as well as a perpetual swamp.

They'd come in on the Henry Hudson and taken a left up West Seventy-second, which brought them now to Central Park and Strawberry Fields, the area landscaped in memory of John Lennon. They were two and a half blocks from the Lord Winslow, the scene of Elinor's crime.

Alice wondered if Yoko had ever worn La Perlas.

In the seat beside her, Poppy twitched. She'd already told Alice that by the time Duane had come home last night, the Bloody Marys had worn off and she'd chickened out of asking what he knew about Elinor. Chickening out, of course, was more in keeping with Poppy.

"We'll be done before you know it," Alice tried to reassure her.

"I still think we're too early," Poppy said. "No one will believe we've come to town to shop. Not at ten o'clock in the morning."

She was right, of course. Wealthy women never shopped until after lunch, which had more to do with filling the hours between lunch wine and evening cocktails than with the digestive system.

They couldn't say they were in town to have their hair or nails done because on Mondays the best salons were always closed. Besides, that wouldn't have seemed right, what with Yolanda in the backseat.

"No one will care why you're in town," Yolanda said at that same moment, poking her head through the small opening between the cushy leather front seats. At the last minute, she'd decided to go with them, announcing that once at the Winslow, Alice and Poppy could get out and Yolanda could get behind the wheel and drive around the block until the mission was complete. It would save having to locate a garage or, worse, valet parking, which could be disastrous if a quick getaway was required.

"Do you have the picture?" Yolanda asked.

"You already asked her that," Alice said. Sometimes, for a hairstylist, Yolanda could be pushy.

"I have the picture," Poppy said and plucked the yellow envelope from her Miu Miu handbag, which was quite big and too heavy looking for her. She'd bought it on a whim one day when she and Alice had been in town for lunch and they'd seen Duane with a woman.

"Darling," he'd said when they'd approached his table at Gramercy Tavern, where they'd gone because Poppy had an appointment at her lawyer's in Union Square, which she'd said had something to do with her trust fund and her mother's private companions. "Do you know Mandy Gibbons? From the Gibbons-Gibbons firm?"

Well, of course Poppy hadn't known her, had never heard of Gibbons-Gibbons, which Duane probably made up on the spot.

"I'm trying to convince her to take part in next month's charity ball in New Falls."

Duane's choice of words had been nearly as ridiculous as the spandex worn by Mandy Gibbons that clung to every pore and was not exactly office attire even for someone who was twenty-five, give or take a few.

But Poppy had been her social self and said hello-how-nice-to-meet-you, then after lunch she'd dragged Alice into one shop then another, buying the Miu Miu and scores of other things she did not need and were neither appropriate for her wardrobe or suited to her taste.

Pulling up to the canopy at the Lord Winslow now, Alice pushed away the reminder of Duane's no doubt delicious penis. *God*, she thought, *I must need a shrink, or at least hormone replacement therapy.* "Okay," she said with a small sigh, "let's get this over with."

The doorman approached and opened the curbside door.

The reception desk was actually a counter, long and dark and gleaming, reminiscent of a hunt club or other good old boys' gathering place where brandy and cigars and perhaps a rendezvous or two were neither unexpected nor discouraged. Atop the desk sat an old-fashioned leather blotter, a classic fountain pen, and a dome-shaped silver call bell.

Alice decided to speak for them because Poppy's hand quivered as it touched the bell.

Ding-ding.

A young man came around a corner and took his place behind the counter. He was about the same age as Jonas, but he was thin and pretty.

"Hello. My name is Alice Richardson," she lied. Yolanda had recommended they not give their real last names. Using their first names, however, would help avoid slipups.

"How may I help you, Ms. Richardson?" His skin was shiny and dark, his accent lightly Caribbean.

She smiled her best smile, the one she saved for meeting the strangers in the other towns. "Larry?" she'd say. "How nice to meet you." Or, "Parker? Why, you're as enchanting as your e-mails." And the next one in Orlando, "Bud? Oh, my. You don't look like a theme-park magician."

Of course, there would be no Bud in Orlando if Kiley Kate backed out. Alice frowned and turned back to the business at hand.

"I am a friend of Elinor Harding," she said, as Poppy nudged the photograph toward her. "She was here last week. Thursday. Perhaps you remember her?" She showed the picture to the young man, whose nametag read Javier.

He smiled back, which was good. "I am sorry," he replied. "I see so many faces. We have so many guests." He didn't ask if there had been a problem.

"She stayed in room four-o-two," Alice said. "She overslept and packed in a hurry. She had a flight to catch." Alice made up that last part because she thought it added to the believability. It was not unlike the fabrications she'd become so adept at telling, such as, "I'm from Topeka," where she'd never been but liked the sound of. Middle America. Middle class. Middle everything. A few good talking points but not worth the bother after she left town. Before her first encounter, she'd researched Topeka online and learned about its Jayhawk "Air Refrigerated" Theatre and its wheat farms and tornadoes and the fact that Annette Bening hailed from there. (She'd later bragged that they'd been in the same high school class. What the heck, Alice had figured, once you'd told one fib, why not keep going?)

Javier looked at her blankly, his smile still in place.

Alice shifted on one foot and refrained from fanning her face with her hand. "Our friend left a few things behind. She asked if we'd collect them."

He glanced at Poppy, then back to Alice. "Perhaps you'd like the lost and found."

Alice pushed the photo toward him. "It would be easier if you remembered her."

He looked down at the picture, picked it up, and squinted. "I am sorry," he repeated. "We have so many guests."

"And we have so little time," Poppy suddenly spoke up and slid a bill across the counter. It might have been a ten or a twenty or a fifty, even. "Perhaps your manager can help us?"

Alice went on smiling because she didn't know what else to do.

"I am the manager," he said. "I'm called the night manager, though I work from midnight until noon. If you'd care to leave your friend's phone number, I will check with housekeeping and will be in touch."

They could hardly leave Elinor's phone number, so Alice related hers with two digits transposed. If he'd been a little older, and not so aloof, she might have turned on the charm. Instead, she picked up the picture, ignored the bill on the counter, then marched across the lobby without waiting for Poppy to catch up.

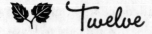 Twelve

"*Well, that was a waste of time,*" Alice said to Yolanda when they climbed into the Esplanade, traded places, turned the corner, and headed toward Amsterdam, then the West Side Highway. "The desk clerk—oh, excuse me, the *night manager*—wouldn't give us one iota of information. 'We have so many guests,'" she mimicked him. "And my friend here," she said, pointing to the back where Poppy had landed, "tried to buy him off. As if he were a maitre d' and the Lord Winslow was a trendy restaurant."

"Duane does it all the time," Poppy noted, which certainly explained it.

"Maybe it wasn't such a waste," Yolanda offered. "If the desk clerk is in on the blackmail, at least he knows something is happening. That Elinor is not going to take this lying down."

Lying down.

Ha.

"Well," Alice said, "I can't see what good will come of it. Personally, if I were Elinor, I'd tell my husband and keep the half million."

"But you're not Elinor," Poppy said. "And neither am I, and I'm not going to be the one to tell her what I think she should do. She's always been nice to Momma and me." Yolanda did not ask for details. "Besides," Poppy continued, "I have an idea. While we were standing at the reception desk, I noticed a security camera. Do you think the hotel has lots of cameras? Do you think one is aimed at the alley, near where the Dumpster is?"

Alice was about to comment on Poppy's brilliance when she heard a muffled *ding-ding*. Poppy, no doubt, had swiped the shiny silver bell from the reception desk at the hotel.

Staring out the windshield, Alice suspected this adventure was about to become an ordeal.

Elinor had no idea how—or if—she'd make it through the next hour, day, or week. She'd spent the morning e-mailing back and forth with Betts Perry, arranging and rearranging the seating chart for the engagement party (would the Republican from Idaho be welcomed by the Democrat from New Jersey?) and counting her blessings that Remy and the esteemed *second lady* would be seated on the opposite side of the room, away from the family, but with the House Speaker, who was rumored to speak very little in public.

It was even more tedious to help Betts make last-minute adjustments to the way-too-gourmet menu.

Grilled foie gras with Ceylon cinnamon and cider vinegar jus.

Ceasar of green asparagus.

Bhutanese red rice and caramelized Brussels sprouts.

Quail eggs, crab cakes, escabesche of diver scallops, fricassee of freaking wild mushrooms.

As if any of it mattered.

Elinor wondered what would happen if the blackmailer arrived at the Washington Fairmont demanding the ransom drop when the dessert cart arrived.

Raspberry chocolate pot du crème?

Profiteroles with Madagascar vanilla bean ice cream?

Half-million-dollar cheesecake, anyone?

She stared at the computer screen, grateful that Malcolm was back in Washington, preparing for what she deemed the "new year"—the post-Labor Day return to normalcy. It was a holdover from her upbringing, when all seasons had been defined by the McCready calendar: Classes Begin, Midterms, Finals, Christmas Break, which no doubt was now called "Holiday Break" in keeping with political correctness.

Life had order then. It had rules that were unspoken, such as when to wear white and when to not, and certain expectations, such as who would sit with whom at the engagement party for the offspring of a senior congressman and a longtime lobbyist. Such as what the food should be and if it really had to hail from a hundred different nations.

Elinor knew that, unlike her sister, she did much better when there were rules, when her days and nights, her weeks and months and years, had uniformity. Order. She did not do well feeling as if everything around her was collapsing. The way she felt now.

She propped her elbows on the keyboard tray and stared at the tiny dots on the screen. Not even CJ knew the pressures Elinor felt, had always felt. Not even CJ knew how hard it was always trying to be perfect, and always coming up second best in their father's eyes.

Oh, sure, Elinor was the one Father had turned to for advice. Elinor, after all, had learned to be like him: pragmatic, stern. He had taught her well.

But just once before he'd died she would have loved to have seen Father look at her the way he'd looked at CJ: his eyes warm with laughter, his outer shell a little softer.

"You're not as appealing as your sister," Father had told Elinor one afternoon at that god-awful lake house that CJ had insisted on keeping. "But you are clever, and you carry yourself well. Still, we'll need to find you the right man—a man with power and intelligence that will translate into privilege. A man like the fathers of your classmates." *A man with money*, Elinor, even at age thirteen, had understood he had meant.

When Elinor was in college, he'd found Malcolm for her.

Later, after Janice was born and Elinor had the hysterectomy, Father was alarmed. "A man needs a son," he said, apparently forgetting he was speaking to one of his only two children, both of whom were girls. She sensed he was more concerned that Malcolm would leave her if she only had one child. Having two children made leaving more difficult. Maybe that's why Father and Mother had stayed together all those years; maybe if Elinor and CJ had only been Elinor, or, better yet, had only been CJ, one child would not have been enough to keep the marriage glued.

Jonas had been Father's idea.

"Let's have them think the idea came from you, though," he had said. "It will be better that way."

So CJ and Malcolm thought the proposal was Elinor's concept, Elinor's coercion. Because it was what Father had wanted.

The mantra of her life was *Father Knows Best.*

Would he forgive me for not being as perfect as him, she wondered now *if he were still alive?*

Snapping off the computer, Elinor sat back in her chair and let the tears spill from her eyes.

CJ was out in her studio, pretending to be painting but thinking instead about what to pack, as if she was going on vacation and not merely to Elinor's. The batik sundress and matching shrug? The white swimsuit and hardly modest cover-up? Her favorite capris and crop top that made her feel sexy and young again? Certainly, a thick cardigan in case the air chilled at night.

She should be ashamed, she knew, for picking out the things she would like Malcolm to see her in.

She should be ashamed, but she was not. It was as if Elinor's infidelity had instilled a new twist on the rules.

What would their mother have advised?

"Do you love him?" Dianne Harding had asked CJ when CJ was heavy with a pregnant belly. Dianne had walked into the greenhouse at Elinor and Malcolm's new house in Washington and caught Malcolm and CJ in a kiss. Not just any kiss, but a breathless, tongue-touching, lip-melting kiss. Oh, and Malcolm's zipper was undone and CJ just happened to be holding his throbbing member in her hand, or at least that's the way Dianne Harding described it after Malcolm had zipped and CJ had turned red and they had pulled apart.

His throbbing member, CJ thought now with a hint of a smile. Her mother had sounded more like Poppy's, as if CJ and Mac had been in the middle of a romance novel and not a real-life family drama.

"Yes," CJ had answered. "I love him very much."

Dianne had paced the narrow rows of the aptly called "hothouse" that smelled of earth and dampness and of Malcolm and CJ and family betrayal.

"It must be your hormones," Dianne said. "When I was pregnant with you girls, I wanted to jump the mailman."

Their mother always had tried to be more contemporary than their father. ("The world is changing, Franklin. If CJ wants to study at the Sorbonne, perhaps that's where she belongs.") Still, this was the first CJ had heard that their mother had even known what hormones were. CJ had not, however, had the heart to tell her mother that her feelings for Malcolm—indeed, their feelings for each other—had begun that first night they had attempted to conceive, when they'd "been one" according to Elinor's plan and CJ's ovulating schedule.

Dianne had stopped and turned and looked back at the lovers, at Mac, who was as frozen as the small statue of Saint Francis of Assisi that he'd bought to watch over the shoots and roots and buds of the offspring in the greenhouse.

"I love her, too," he'd said before Dianne had a chance to ask.

She stood quietly for a moment, or maybe it was a year. Then she said, "Well, we can't have this, can we?"

She had not reminded them that Elinor was fragile, that she'd been through so much, that she *trusted* her husband and her sister with her life and, good heavens, with her child. She had not had to tell CJ that the headmaster would never allow it.

Instead, Dianne left CJ and Malcolm standing in the greenhouse.

Three weeks later, Jonas was born, and that was the end of that.

And now CJ thought about the black silk nightgown in her

lingerie drawer. She hadn't worn it since she'd walked out on her husband, Cooper, who had then moved to Denver, as if distance would help him forget. She stared at her paintbrush, trying to decide whether or not to pack the black silk, when the crunch of tires upon gravel interrupted her thoughts. Peering out the window, she saw the Esplanade and watched the three women clamber out.

 Thirteen

"I need a wig," Poppy announced when CJ met them in the driveway and they traipsed into the cottage. "Should I be a brunette or a blonde?"

They dropped, one at a time, onto CJ's furniture—even Yolanda, who now seemed quite at home.

"A blonde," Yolanda said. "You're too fair to be a brunette. No one will believe you."

"But will they believe she's lost her momma?" Alice asked.

Yolanda laughed and Poppy said, "They will! They will!" her cheeks flashing pink, the way they did when she was excited.

"Excuse me," CJ said, "what are you talking about?"

"Poppy wants to go back to the hotel tomorrow and pretend she's lost her momma," Alice said.

"Maybe I can access security," Poppy chattered. "Yolanda

says there must be a room where all the monitors are kept. If I can get in there, maybe I can see if there's a camera pointed at the Dumpster where Elinor's panties were found!"

CJ supposed a good shrink would diagnose Poppy as bipolar, with the emphasis on whichever pole was more manic. Between Poppy's erratic behavior, Elinor's need to control, and Alice spending her life mimicking Elinor, it was no wonder CJ had once gone off to Paris and left the others to their harebrained lives.

"She's hoping there's a tape of the blackmailer taking the panties out of the Dumpster," Yolanda said. "She thinks he'll turn and wave to the camera so we can see his face."

"I do not!" Poppy exclaimed. "Besides, none of you are coming up with alternative ideas!" Which made it sound as if she'd been speaking about alternative energy solutions or alternative medical miracles.

"If there is a tape, how the heck will we get it?" CJ asked. "And do they even make tapes anymore? Isn't everything digitally recorded?"

Poppy played with her hair. "I guess that's another thing we have to find out."

"And we need to hurry," CJ said. "On Wednesday, Elinor will be leaving the country for a couple of days. She's going to get ransom money."

No one asked where she was going or why she had to leave the country to get the cash. It was almost as if that part of the adventure was more information than they felt they should know.

Yolanda stood up. "Sorry to break up the party, ladies, but I have to get home. If you insist on doing this, Poppy, come by the shop. I'll fit you with a wig."

Yolanda left the cottage. The rest of them heard the roar

of the Jaguar that had belonged to Vincent, Yolanda's dead husband. Poppy looked at Alice and Alice looked at CJ and CJ said, "I think this is nuts," but Poppy said she thought it was nice to have something important to do.

Alice wasn't certain she agreed with Poppy's assessment that thinking they could find Elinor's blackmailer was important. Childish, maybe. Risky, perhaps. And maybe, as CJ said, nuts.

After leaving the cottage, Alice dropped off Poppy and headed home to focus on her own things to do. Within a few minutes she was in her garage, then her kitchen, where she nearly jumped a damn foot. Neal was sitting at the table with a bowl of minestrone and a petit baguette.

"Neal?"

Her first thought was that he'd been fired.

Or he'd heard about Elinor.

Or he'd learned of her out-of-town activities and had come home to confront her.

She rubbed her throat and dallied with the five-carat diamond necklace he'd presented to her on her fortieth birthday.

"Alice?" he replied with a note of sarcasm that he deferred to when he was trying to be funny.

She wondered if she'd turned off the computer in the media room, or if she'd left her e-mails displayed. She was still so unaccustomed to having something to hide.

Steam oozed up from her toes; she grabbed a place mat and fanned her face.

"Sit," Neal said. He gestured to the slim, postmodern Sacha Lakic chair that he'd insisted on buying because he'd said less was more.

She sat.

"We made the presentation this morning. It looks as if we've landed the account."

She couldn't remember if "the account" was the beauty products manufacturer or the national chain of health-food stores. After so many years, they all sounded the same. "That's great," she said. "Congratulations." Apparently the conversation would be about him, not unemployment or Elinor or Alice's indiscretions. She set down the place mat.

"They've invited management to dinner."

When the invitation was formal, it often meant wives were included—or, rather, domestic whatevers, since the management of Neal's firm now boasted one or two females and a homosexual man in order to attract clients who cared about that sort of thing.

"Well," she said, "it certainly seems as if you've landed it."

"They'll make the announcement at the dinner. I'm sure they think everyone will be thrilled to have an inside connection to the resorts and spas."

Resorts and spas. Neal must be referring to Tang Worldwide, named for an early Chinese dynasty famous for its delicate, hand-painted folding screens that brought inner peace and balance. Alice once remarked it sounded more like the orange powder mix they'd been encouraged to drink in school because the astronauts brought it with them to the moon.

She watched Neal's spoon scoop a piece of tomato and a red bean. "Will we get 'family' discounts? I'm sure the girls would love to go." How many cities and countries enjoyed a Tang Worldwide resort? Could it be a chance for Alice to go international with her new hobby? When Neal finished his minestrone, she'd have to go online. If he didn't get there first and figure out what she'd been doing.

"The dinner is Thursday," he said, as he stood up.

"Thursday?" she asked, her voice in a squeak. "But I won't be here Thursday. Kiley Kate has her competition in Orlando."

"I'm sure Melissa will go, under the circumstances."

Melissa was a sweet girl, though she'd gotten pregnant too young and robbed Alice of the fun of planning a big wedding. She was a good mother and a good wife, but she was terrified of flying. Neither Ativan nor Xanax seemed to penetrate her fear. "You know that's not possible, Neal."

"Well, David, then," he said as he carried the soup bowl to the sink because though he now could well afford domestic help, he'd been raised in a row house in Reading, Pennsylvania, where he'd shared a tiny bedroom with three brothers and a dog and cleaning up after yourself had been instilled. "For God's sake, Kiley Kate is their daughter, not yours."

Alice sighed. "David is not at a point in his career that he can take a few days off for something, well, unscheduled."

"Of course he can. I'll make the call."

Alice stood up. "No, Neal. That isn't fair. Helping Kiley Kate is one thing, interfering with David's job, quite another. It won't teach the children to be independent." Neither of them mentioned their *dependent* daughter, Felicity, whose Miss Porter's education had been a waste of time and hope, not to mention dollars. So, too, had been the girl's college years, which she'd turned into a career from Barnard to Boston College, from Swarthmore to Simon's Rock. She was such a bright girl, but sometimes brains just didn't count.

"Then ask the babysitter to go with Kiley. Good God, Alice, it's not as if I ask for much."

"It's hard to ask for anything when you're never home."

She supposed she shouldn't have said that. She supposed she

should be a dutiful, spoiled wife and say, "Okay, honey, whatever you want, honey, you're the one who wears the pants." Sometimes, however, the working-class roots of her father leaked through, and Alice spoke her mind.

"You seem to like the money I bring home." He turned around, leaned against the sink, and folded his arms. He was marking his turf, she supposed, the way a dog pees on his terrain. In Neal's case, the property was her.

She rose from the uncomfortable chair, tossed back her hair, and said, "They need to change the date. I won't disappoint my granddaughter. I'm sure they'll understand." With more attitude than she felt, Alice left the kitchen and headed for the computer room before Neal could beat her to it.

"She's going to dress up in disguise and say she's lost her momma. I'm going to fit her to a wig." Yolanda balanced Belita on one hip while she tossed laundry into the dryer. Her cell phone was tucked between her ear and neck. "She'll get into trouble, I'm afraid."

Manny let out a big whoosh of air. "And you want me to do what?"

"Go with her?"

He laughed. "You are insane."

"Tomorrow is Tuesday. It's your day off."

"Summer's over. The kids are back in school."

"Big deal. They're teenagers. They know how to get on and off the bus without you."

"I told you, Yo. I can't get involved."

"You live in Brooklyn. The Lord Winslow is in Manhattan. A thousand miles away."

"I have friends on the force there."

"Great. Maybe they'll help. You don't have to say what's going on. Just that some lady left behind unmentionables, and she'd like to find them before someone else does."

He laughed again. "These guys are pros. They'd see right through that."

Yolanda sighed. "Okay," she said. "I get it. It's just that Poppy is so delicate. I'm afraid she'll get caught and wreck everything."

"Her name is Poppy?" He didn't laugh again, but she could tell he wanted to.

She slammed the dryer door. "Manuel," she said, "forget it, okay? You think because you sent me to school and I live, as you say, 'uptown,' that my life is terrific. Well, I'm not one of those rich ladies who you think has nothing but air inside her head. I was born and raised in the Bronx, and I learned to care about other people, no matter what their name is or how much money they have in the bank. Maybe you've forgotten what that feels like because you're so important, Mr. Police Detective."

"Yo . . . ," he said, but she hung up before he could say more.

Fourteen

"*Momma? What are you doing in the orchid* garden? It's time for tea." Poppy never understood why Momma liked getting her hands dirty when there were day laborers for that.

"My red swans are magnificent this year. Come inhale their perfume—it's just like sandalwood and rose."

"I've smelled them, Momma. Now come in. Your tea is getting cold." Some years ago, they'd made the transition from Momma being the one to watch over Poppy to Poppy watching over Momma, though Poppy was never quite sure why that had happened or when. She supposed it was a mother-daughter thing that happened in most families, even the best.

Momma stepped out of rubber clogs and into purple flip-flops. She untied the sash of her wide-brimmed straw hat and hung it on a hook beside the potting table. Her bright white hair looked even brighter in the greenhouse light, like halogen illuminating a translucent face. Her bright blue eyes blinked and winked and smiled. "I must remember to have Lucky move a 'Jumbo Lace' into the house," she said. "I do enjoy its lilac fragrance in the powder room downstairs."

Lucky was Momma's longtime companion, paid to be at her beck and call, which was a full-time job. He made sure her orchids were as she wanted; he acted as her mouthpiece when anyone needed scolding; he escorted her to appointments and into Manhattan for lunch. Since the incident years ago, Momma had never been "quite right," a diagnosis that had grown more apparent with time. Still, Momma seemed content.

"I had Lila set out tea in the silver room," Poppy said, leading Momma by the arm, up two flagstone steps, through the covered walkway, and into the house that was too large for Momma, even with Lila, Lucky, Bern (driver and all-around handyman), Fiona (Bern's wife and Momma's personal secretary, though she hardly needed one anymore), and Cain and Abel, the two flat-headed Pekinese.

They settled in the Queen Anne chairs that had been handed down for generations, like the money from the railroads and the "skyscrapers" in Manhattan.

"Momma," Poppy said, "I need your advice." She poured the tea and passed the crumpets, then told her about Elinor and the lavender lace panties and the quest to find the blackmailer before Jonas's engagement party. Even with Momma's peculiar personality, Poppy still depended on her for wisdom when it counted. It wasn't as if she'd tell a solitary soul.

"I've always loved a good mystery," Momma said. She dotted strawberry jam on her crumpet, then took a tiny bite.

"I thought you might have a suggestion about my upcoming trip to the Lord Winslow," Poppy said. Though Momma had married only Papa ("There could never be another"), she'd had her share of lovers after a mugger shot Papa as he left the 1964 World's Fair, the theme of which had been Peace through Understanding. Momma maintained that most of life was irony, anyway. "I'm going to wear a wig," Poppy continued. "I've always wanted to be a blonde."

Momma took another bite, chewed a little, then closed her eyes as if it were naptime. After a thoughtful moment, she said, "I'm not sure blonde is a good idea. The less attention you call to yourself, the better. That way if questions come up later, you won't be memorable."

Momma was a genius, no matter what people said.

"Play down your looks," Momma continued. "Wear short heels, not stilettos. Leave your big purse here and take one of my small ones. And get rid of the coral nails."

Looking down at her nails, Poppy smiled. Then she delved into her Miu Miu with glee. "Oh, Momma, you are the best. And just for that, you get a prize." She pulled out the silver call bell and held it up for inspection.

Ding-ding, ding-ding.

Momma clapped her hands and jumped up from the Queen Anne. "From the Lord Winslow?" she asked and Poppy nodded and Momma snatched it from her and flip-flopped to the grand piano, where she added it to the "hotel collection" as she called it: the creamer from the Waldorf, the salt and peppers from the St. Regis, the water pitcher from the Plaza before the place had been gutted. Some were gifts from Poppy, others Momma had collected herself; all were shiny silver, like the stars. Next to growing orchids, Momma liked looking at "her" stars.

"I must go to Yolanda's now and try on a few wigs," Poppy said, then kissed her mother's paper cheek. "But first, I'll get a small purse from Lila. I love you, sweetest Momma."

But Momma, sweet or otherwise, was now distracted by her latest acquisition and didn't seem to notice that her only child was leaving the room.

"Momma says I shouldn't attract attention," Poppy said to Yolanda, when she arrived after a quick drive to New Falls. "So I'll be a brunette after all. Do you have something nondescript?"

Yolanda frowned. "You told your mother about Elinor?"

"Well, of course. Momma won't tell anyone. She's probably forgotten already." Poppy sat down at a big round mirror and stared at her reflection. She hadn't combed her hair since they'd left for Manhattan that morning. Maybe she could get Yolanda to do a comb-through while she was there. No sense looking like a banshee in case her husband was home when she got there. Duane was so particular about the way she looked.

Ooops! For a minute, she'd forgotten he might be a blackmailer. And sleeping with Elinor.

Yolanda brushed back Poppy's hair and sealed it in a do-rag, as if Poppy belonged in a gang. Then she snapped the dial of a yellow plastic radio that sat on the counter. "Baby monitor," she said. "My daughter is upstairs asleep. Would you keep an ear out for her while I go dig up the wigs?" Without waiting for an answer, she left the room.

Poppy stared at the walkie-talkie. She wondered what she

should do if sounds started coming out. She'd never really known if she'd wanted kids; if she was strong enough to endure pregnancy and childbirth, not to mention the crying and pooping and spitting up that followed, and the fact that you were totally responsible for their little lives. Yes, it was probably good that she'd never had kids. Momma said she might regret that decision in her old age, that kids were what kept you young. Alice and Elinor, however, always seemed older than Poppy.

"Hello?" a voice called out, not from the plastic device, but from behind her. She turned to see a handsome, latte-skinned man. He had wide, sturdy-looking shoulders, a crinkly face, and happy, dark eyes. His smile revealed perfect white teeth. "Is Yolanda here?"

She didn't move, not one little inch. Was he Yolanda's boyfriend? He was wearing nice pants, a short-sleeved shirt, a tie, and . . . a badge! Oh, no! He was a cop!

"Hello?" he said again, stepping into the shop and waving his hand.

"We're closed," Poppy replied. "It's Monday and we're closed."

He laughed. "I'm not here for a haircut." He loosened his tie, then rubbed his head. That's when she realized he was totally bald.

"Well, then, go away," Poppy said. "We haven't done anything wrong."

"Are you sure?" he asked. He kept walking toward her. She wished he wouldn't do that. The presence of policemen always made it difficult for her to breathe.

She tried to remember she'd come a long way. She sucked in her breath and slid off the chair. "Stop right where you are," she commanded, "or I'll call the police." Well, okay, so it sounded stupid. Maybe he was an imposter. These days, you couldn't be too careful.

"You must be Poppy," he said as he halted.

She tore the do-rag off her banshee hair and ran her fingers through the tangled mess.

"I'm Manny," he said, extending his hand for her to shake.

She shook. He looked older than Yolanda. Poppy had heard that Yolanda's dead husband had been older than her, too. It wasn't right for younger women to get the good ones and leave women like Poppy rummaging through the scraps.

Oh, wait! Why should she care? She was married to Duane!

Manny pressed his firm hand into hers. It occurred to her that she might gladly turn Duane over to Yolanda if she could have this one for herself.

"I'm Veronica," she said, but even as she said it, the name sounded foreign to her ears. She worked up a little smile. "Everyone calls me Poppy."

"I thought it must be you," he said, his eyes staying on her a moment, his hand pulling away too soon. He gestured toward the do-rag. "Are you trying on wigs?"

She watched him eye the knit cap that she held in her hand. She didn't know what to say.

He smiled again. "I think your hair is pretty just the way it is. The color's nice, you know?"

No, she didn't know. "It's a little red," she said, trying to finger-style it again without the use of comb, brush, or mirror.

"Well, look who's here," Yolanda said as she reappeared, carrying a plastic trash bag. "I see you've met Manuel."

"Yes," Poppy said. "I thought he'd come to arrest me." She

was trying to make a joke, but she realized it wasn't funny under the circumstances. She returned to her chair and tried to replace the do-rag by herself.

"He wouldn't dare," Yolanda said, then dumped the bag on Poppy's lap. "Take your pick. Twelve shades of brunette."

Poppy bit her lip and hesitantly reached inside the bag. She tried not to recoil from what felt like mounds of furry critters lying stealthily in wait.

"I like the red," Manny said again, and Poppy blushed.

"Men," Yolanda said. "Especially brothers. What do they know, anyway?"

Brothers? Manny wasn't Yolanda's boyfriend but her brother?

"Forget it," Yolanda said to Manny after Poppy left with three choices of wigs. "She's married."

"Forget it," Poppy said to herself when she climbed into her BMW and buckled up. "You're married. And you are not Elinor."

So they both forgot it.

Ha-ha.

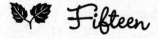 # Fifteen

If Elinor could only call him. She knew that if he would just hold her, if he would just touch her, everything would be all right.

But Tuesday morning, as she sat in the bedroom, with both her cell and her land lines close at hand, she knew there was no way she could call him.

Since the note had arrived, she'd lived with the reality that she'd have to figure this out without him, that she must endure the anguish and the waiting, not to mention the fact that she'd have to cough up the ransom, all while her nerves were unraveling like a cheap sweater.

She didn't know yet if she had been foolish to enlist her friends. She'd had little choice: She couldn't be proactive while sitting by the phone. And Elinor knew the importance of being proactive, of doing unto others before they could do unto you. It was the first lesson one learned in Washington.

Yes, it would be easier if she could call him.

But it had been an unspoken rule when their affair had begun, or rather, before it had begun, because it had, after all, been a scheduled event, like a Rose Garden press conference or a Camp David summit.

> *The Vice President of the United States of America requests your presence at a luncheon on February 6th at 12:30 p.m. to discuss your national health care recommendations. A car will be provided.*

She'd known from the start that it was a ruse. Elinor Harding Young had no more of an answer to the nation's health-care problems than anyone on the hill, in the country, or in the world, for that matter. The previous week she had, however, been standing in a long line that trickled from the ladies' room of the Jefferson Hotel after the mandarin gelato with mint wafer had been served, before the guest speaker from the Friends of the Homeless ascended the podium.

It had been a photo op, so the vice president was there; in fact, he was scheduled to introduce the speaker.

Elinor had known that. She hadn't known, however, that he would walk by just as she said to the woman in front of her, "If the vice president wants to introduce something really fixable, he should propose a law that every hotel in America have double the rest rooms for women as they do for men. It should be part of a national health care package. Think of the bladders he'd save."

"The vice president doesn't make laws," a sudden whisper

said in her ear. She knew the voice: Remy had been to their town house a few times when his father had been sick and Malcolm was helping. And, of course, he was a visible VP, famous for giving sound bites to CNN and the rest.

A slow blush had moved from her neck to her cheeks. She turned to apologize, but he had left, chuckling, no doubt, because he was known for his humor, along with his crooked half smile.

And then, a week later, she'd been swept to the Naval Observatory, the official residence of the nation's number-two official.

She'd never dreamed she'd go to his house without Malcolm, without the cover of business.

"To ladies' toilets," Remy had toasted with a glass of champagne when they'd been left alone in the family dining room. His wife was in Bangkok, their daughter at Radcliff. His blue eyes had twinkled, and Elinor was a goner. She'd always been attracted to power: proof that she and CJ weren't as identical as it appeared.

He'd set down his glass and folded his arms. "Bold women amuse me," he said. "It helps when they're beautiful."

He'd been lying, of course. She and CJ had never been beautiful. Cute, maybe. Pretty, perhaps. But beautiful? She digested the compliment along with the champagne.

"I'd like to see you," he said, "on a more intimate basis."

In case she hadn't understood what he meant (she had), he rose from the mahogany Taft-period chair, crossed to her side of the table, and asked her to get up.

Of course, she had.

He untied the silk bow of her blouse, then released the pearl buttons one at a time. And before Elinor knew it, his mouth was on hers, his fingers plucked her nipples, and her hands found their way to his zipper.

After their third rendezvous she stopped asking, "Why me?" and gave in to the pleasure in spite of the danger.

"I feel like a bungee jumper," she told him one hot afternoon after quick sex in the men's room at his office. *His office!*

"Risk is part of life," he replied with that crooked half smile.

They never talked about love or marriage or how many "risks" he had taken with whom. As long as words were unspoken, Elinor did not have to face them.

Until now.

She sat with her spine straight, perfectly proper, a testament to the McCready School. She stared at the phone. Did she dare make one little call?

She'd never called him before. Never intruded on his life, never asked for something as mundane as love.

But she was entitled to respect, wasn't she?

The way she'd been entitled to great sex?

Long ago, Elinor had decided that she had indeed been entitled, after all the years that she'd suffered, after all the torment she'd endured because of the actions of her husband and her own freaking sister—both of whom no doubt believed she hadn't guessed that long after Jonas had been conceived, born, and raised, they'd continued to do the same things with each other that Elinor now did with Remy.

Or had done with Remy.

Gripping her stomach, she leaned slightly forward.

Had done with Remy.

It was the first time Elinor considered that their affair would have to end now. Before the whole bloody world found out.

 *Sixteen*

At one o'clock in the afternoon, Poppy said good-bye to Alice and alighted from the Esplanade, which was parked at the front entrance of the Lord Winslow. Yolanda had stayed at her shop in New Falls, and CJ had made it clear that she, too, had to work. Not everyone had a husband or a trust fund, which, she'd made sure to add, "was just fine with her." Poppy hadn't taken offense.

Once inside the lobby, the brunette in low heels wandered from one end to the other, checking her watch at frequent intervals. One could never be sure who might be watching and what camera might be perched where. All Poppy could hope was that they'd timed it right and that Javier, the night manager, was off duty.

After a full fifteen minutes, she set her face in a scowl and meandered to the reception desk.

Ding-ding.

She smiled when she noticed that the call bell had been replaced. Then she glanced at the security camera.

Had the camera caught her in action yesterday?

Adjusting the short wig and turning her head, Poppy suddenly feared she'd be recognized. She considered departing just as a young woman appeared.

"May I help you?"

Poppy remembered the lines she'd practiced this morning in front of the mirror. "It's Momma," she said with a soft Southern drawl and a couple of prayers that the young woman couldn't see her heart racing. "I seem to have lost her."

"What room are you in?"

"Well, that's the worst of it. We're not staying here. I was supposed to meet Momma here in the lobby so we could enjoy your wonderful tearoom. But she's nowhere to be seen. And Momma's never late."

"Maybe she was held up in traffic."

"She lives just two blocks from here. She prefers to walk."

"What does she look like? Do you know what she's wearing?"

"She's small, about my height. And she has white hair. She said she'd be wearing her navy picture hat and a short-sleeve navy dress."

The young woman didn't ask what a "picture hat" was, as if she knew about all the fashion from the 1940s and '50s. "I'll call security."

Which, of course, was exactly what Poppy had hoped for.

In less than a minute, a gentleman in a gray Armani suit arrived.

"My goodness," she crooned, her drawl sliding out on a thin, syrupy stream, "your handsome attire is hardly befitting a security officer."

He assured her he was dressed for the comfort of the hotel guests. "We don't want anyone feeling as if big brother or sister is watching."

She took a quick, longing look at the new silver call bell—a pair would look lovely atop Momma's piano—then said, "But security is so important. At my daddy's cotton business down in Winston-Salem, they have cameras everywhere that see all the goings-on. Do you have cameras like that? Would they have seen Momma?" Her fingertips touched her throat as she spoke; Momma always said she'd have made a fine actress, she had such an ability to tune out the real world.

"Why don't you follow me, Miss . . ."

"Miss Bartlett." Poppy used Alice's last name because she couldn't be expected to make everything up right there on the polished-hardwood-floor spot.

They took the elevator to the basement, down a dark hall to a door marked Security. The man in the Armani waved a plastic card next to the door handle. Two green lights flashed and a beep beeped.

He pulled open the door to a tiny room that had no windows—just a console, two chairs, and about two dozen monitors lined up on the walls. When Poppy had come up with the plan, she hadn't considered that her claustrophobia would be a deterrent.

A man in black jeans and a black polo shirt sat at the console in one of the chairs.

"Hey, Jake," Poppy's escort said as he stepped into the room.

Poppy sucked in a reservoir of air, then followed him in. It smelled as if Jake had eaten Chinese takeout for lunch.

"A woman is missing," the Armani-man said, and Poppy restated Momma's made-up description.

Jake pressed a few buttons on the large console, which resembled a control panel on the Starship *Enterprise* from those silly old TV shows Duane liked to watch.

Struggling to scan the monitors without hyperventilating, Poppy wished she had a better idea of what a Dumpster looked like. Her only frame of reference was a green one in the back of the parking lot at Stop & Shop.

"My goodness," she said, "you have cameras everywhere."

The men didn't answer.

She fiddled with her wig.

"I can fast-forward through the last thirty minutes of the hotel lobby," Jake said.

Armani-man nodded.

Speeded-up images suddenly appeared on one screen; Jake slowed it down whenever anyone pushed through the glass and brass revolving door. Except for the fact that it was in black and white, the picture was eerily reminiscent of the video of Princess Diana and her boyfriend entering the Paris Ritz-Carlton on the last night of their lives.

Poppy's gaze flitted to the other monitors, searching for the Dumpster, the back door, the alley. But the other images looked like the X-rays that had been taken when Duane broke his foot on a ski slope in the Alps. She hadn't known what she was seeing then, either.

She tried taking in a breath now, but there was no air left in her lungs.

"Excuse me, gentlemen," she whimpered. "Perhaps I've been mistaken." She turned to the door just as there was a knock. Armani-man reached past Poppy, turned the handle, and pushed.

In the doorway stood the man with the badge. The same man, the same badge, she had witnessed at Yolanda's. It was Manny, the hairstylist's cute brother. "Detective Valdes from the twelfth over in Brooklyn. We're working on a case and I could use your assistance." He nodded at Poppy as if he'd never seen her. "Ma'am," he said coolly, "if you'll excuse us, this is official business."

Manny?

Manny!

Poppy skipped from the room into the dark hallway, her heart *all atwitter*, as Momma would describe it.

What was Manny doing there? Had he been following her? Though Momma believed life was irony, surely coincidence played a small part.

Suddenly, Poppy had to pee. Stress and excitement often did that to her. She glanced up and down the dark hall. She spotted a woman in a tan and white dress pushing a cart stacked with thick white towels.

Ah. A housekeeper.

"Please," Poppy asked, as she power-walked toward her, "is there a ladies' room nearby?"

The woman pointed to a door with a sign that read Staff Lounge. Wasting no time, Poppy skipped into a large, square room. A bank of gray lockers circled the inside perimeter. In the back corner was a doorway; beyond that stood several metal stalls. Poppy ducked into one, used the facilities, came out, then leaned against a well-worn enamel sink. Espionage was exhausting.

She closed her eyes and took a few Yoga breaths.

It was nice that Yolanda's brother had followed her. Was he playing Sir Lancelot to her Guinevere?

She wondered if that was what Elinor's lover did for Elinor— made her feel special when her husband no longer did.

Then Poppy remembered that Manny was not her lover. She didn't even, in fact, know his last name. What had he said? Sergeant *Valdes*? Maybe he'd made up his name the way she'd borrowed hers.

With a small sigh, Poppy opened her eyes. She turned on the faucet to wash her hands. That's when she saw a stack of laundry in the mirror's reflection—not towels like she'd seen on the cart, but tan and white uniforms like the one the house-keeper had worn.

Suddenly Poppy had another bright idea: what if the *housekeeper* had stolen Elinor's panties from the room? What if she'd wanted a special pair of La Perlas for herself? (Who wouldn't?)

What if the housekeeper had then learned that a rich lady from Mount Kasteel and Washington, D.C., had been in the room? Could she have realized she'd struck a lace gold mine?

Poppy's fingers flew to her throat once again, the little hollow at the base, where her pulse resumed its twittery race.

If any of this was true, could they prove it?

She supposed one of Elinor's friends could dress up as a housekeeper. Maybe then they could learn who'd cleaned room 402 after Elinor had been there. Maybe they could trace the La Perlas from there! Maybe Duane would be off the hook!

Oh! Poppy thought. *Oh!*

Before allowing herself to think anymore, she dashed to the pile of tan and white uniforms, yanked one out, and jammed it into the too-small purse Momma had suggested she bring.

Just then the door opened and the housekeeper walked in.

Poppy smiled, nodded with a slight jerk of her head, and straightened her wig. Then she tucked her purse under her arm and bolted from the staff lounge with her lips pressed tightly together, her chin held high, and her hands trembling from the rush.

"I've got it!" Poppy said to Alice when she scurried back into the SUV as if someone had been chasing her.

Alice pulled away from the awning and the curb. She decided not to mention the fact that Poppy's wig was off-kilter. "You know who's blackmailing Elinor?"

"Maybe!" She dug into her purse and pulled out what looked to be an unattractive dress. Polyester. *Drip-dry*, it used to be called.

Alice turned her attention back to the traffic. She wanted to tell Poppy it was time she stopped stealing things, but the subject would be unrelated to the current problem. "A dress," she said instead. "You've found a Wal-Mart dress. Hardly fair trade for Elinor's La Perlas."

"Unless the housekeeper did it."

Sometimes Poppy gave Alice a headache. She considered driving downtown to Grand Central and making Poppy take the train home rather than being subjected to any more Poppyness. But they'd been friends for so long, and Poppy had her share of issues, so the poor thing really couldn't help it. Alice dodged a rickshaw driver and two yellow cabs, and said, "Okay. Tell me what you're talking about."

So Poppy did.

"And you think a housekeeper would send a ransom note for half a million dollars?"

"Yes. If she learned that Elinor's rich."

"I disagree. I think a housekeeper might think about ten thousand dollars. A hundred thousand, max. I just don't think someone who barely makes a living wage would think in terms of half a million dollars. It's too much money, Poppy. It wouldn't be in her vocabulary."

From the corner of her eye, Alice saw Poppy pout.

"I don't think you can say that until we know who she is."

"And how will we find out?"

Poppy held up the dress again. "It's simple, silly Alice! One of us will dress up like a housekeeper. We will sneak into the Lord Winslow, up to room four-o-two. We will find the housekeeper who cleaned the room last Friday morning. And we will start asking questions!" Her cheeks were pinker than usual.

"You keep saying 'we.' But it looks as if you only have one dress."

"My mother told me to carry the small purse."

Alice did not ask her to elaborate.

"You can do it, can't you?" Poppy asked. "Tomorrow you can wear the dress and the wig and I can drive the getaway car. I think we'll figure this out, Alice. We'll help Elinor. It's sort of starting to be fun, don't you think?"

So their adventure had gone from being important to being fun. Alice cranked up the air. "Polyester is too warm for summer."

"It's only for a few minutes. You'll survive."

Somewhere in the Lord Winslow Hotel Poppy seemed

to have found chutzpah. "What about the security camera?" Alice asked. "Did you see if one's aimed at the Dumpster?"

Poppy scowled. "Oh. Oh, rats. I forgot about Yolanda's brother. I left him in the basement."

Alice turned onto the Henry Hudson Parkway, knowing she was going to have to ask Poppy to explain, but wondering if there was a way she could avoid it.

 *Seventeen*

CJ sat in her studio reviewing the China silk samples she'd ordered over the Internet and had been delivered earlier that day. Just because Elinor was being blackmailed did not mean that CJ could put her life on hold. The autumn crafts shows would soon be underway, and she needed to reinforce the inventory that would be depleted. Shawls and scarves were especially popular this year, which was great. They were so easy to paint.

The studio door opened and Jonas walked in. "I'd like to buy something for my bride," he said. "Do you have something in white?" He crossed the room to the drafting table where CJ sat and gave her a kiss on the cheek.

While she always relished a quick kiss from Jonas, she noted that this one was rather abrupt. She hoped her sense was not one of foreboding. "How about a white shawl with a pair of white swans?" she asked. "White on white? I think it would be lovely."

Jonas pulled up a chair and sat at the end of the table. "Perfect. I'm sure you'll make it great." He sounded cheerful, but he studied the floor.

"You didn't go to Washington with your dad and the others."

"I have an interview in Manhattan tomorrow. I'll take the train down from there."

It was odd that Elinor hadn't told CJ that Jonas was still at home, that he had a job interview in New York. She sometimes wondered if Elinor intentionally left her out of the details of Jonas's life to remind everyone who his mother was and who, clearly, was not.

"Where's the interview?" Unlike Janice, who'd known she'd wanted to be a biomedical researcher since before she'd known the word existed, Jonas was still floundering. If he had his way, he'd be a Broadway producer. But now he'd gone and fallen in love, so he needed a real job, a real future.

"The Elway," he said. "Do you believe it? They're looking for a theater manager." His eyes finally met hers and showed a hint of excitement. But a small shadow also lingered there.

"Oh, honey, that's terrific." She'd learned years ago to let Jonas talk, to trust that he'd tell her what he wanted when he was ready. In the meantime, CJ was thrilled for him. Jonas had studied theater arts and stagecraft in college. No one had ever declared that his creative penchant must have come from her, though she savored the obvious link, savored the fact that when she'd been married, Cooper had loved being his uncle.

"So I won't have to enter the management program at

Macy's," he said. "If I get the job, of course." Retail was his backup, the plan that came with health insurance and two weeks' vacation each year.

"What does Lucinda think about this?"

"Are you kidding? She's always wanted to act on the stage. She's been going on casting calls all over the city. We've decided our mothers can worry their heads off; we're going to go after our dreams."

Yes, Jonas and CJ were definitely linked. How that must annoy Elinor.

"In the meantime," he continued, "I'm worried about her."

Ah. There was the shadow. "Lucinda?"

"No. My mother."

CJ brushed a fleck of silk from her lap. So Jonas was concerned about how Elinor would react after all. Or perhaps he was worried about her involvement with the engagement party. "There's no need to worry about your mother," CJ said, interrupting her thoughts. "She has a way of making everything turn out all right."

But Jonas shook his head. "This time, I don't know how she can. She's being blackmailed. And she's really scared."

Well, that called for tea.

They went to the kitchen. CJ steeped a pot of ginseng, and they retreated to the sofas, where Luna curled up at Jonas's feet. He petted the dog gently, asked how she was doing. The scene tugged at CJ's heart: no one knew she'd adopted Luna because Elinor wouldn't allow Jonas to have a dog.

"Too messy."

"Too much work."

"No point," Elinor had said when Jonas had left for boarding school at age twelve.

So when CJ had moved to the cottage, Luna had joined her. The Lab offered a beloved canine connection whenever Jonas had a chance to stop by.

"What's going on, CJ? What has my mother done?"

"I'm not really sure. Tell me what you know."

"I think she's having an affair. Is she?"

CJ averted her eyes. "Perhaps you'd better ask her."

"Are you kidding? Me? Ask the buttoned-up Elinor Harding Young—the woman who used her maiden name before anyone else did, who wouldn't discuss Janice's abortion because she found it 'unpleasant,' who suggested I 'mind my own business' when I asked why she and Dad sleep in separate bedrooms—you want me to ask that woman if she's having an affair?"

Mac and Elinor slept in separate bedrooms? If CJ had been Poppy, she might have gasped.

She hauled her thoughts back to Jonas, to the subject-of-the-moment, to the fact that he was still so little-boy cute when he was befuddled. His freckles grew more pronounced; his dimples—his *dents*, he'd once called them—seemed to sink more adorably into his cheeks.

CJ's creativity; Malcolm's dimples.

She cleared her throat. "Jonas," she said, "I know it's not easy. But if your mother is having an affair, she probably wants to keep it to herself."

"But she's being blackmailed!"

Along with Jonas's creativity came sensitivity, a need to protect the people he loved. Another thing CJ had passed down to him. "Are you sure?" she asked slowly. Maybe he'd simply overheard E on the phone.... Maybe ...

"I saw the damn note! It was in her pocketbook. It's not like I go in there, but I was looking for the garage keys. And there it was, with letters that looked like they'd been cut out of a magazine. It said something about lavender lace panties and a half million dollars." He chugged his tea as if it were a beer.

If she'd spent her adult life in Washington as Elinor had, CJ might have known how to respond more adroitly, might have been more adept at verbal ping-pong.

"Do you know about this?" Jonas asked before she had conjured a response.

Well, she couldn't lie, of course, not when asked a direct question. "I know you need to trust that everything really will turn out okay."

He squared his jaw and folded his hands. "And my dad doesn't know?"

"Not that I'm aware of."

"Well, she's really done it now, hasn't she? Just in time for my engagement party." He no doubt was remembering when Elinor had missed the first high school play he had stage-managed, or when she'd mistakenly scheduled the ladies' cruise to Bermuda the same weekend as his Broadway debut. For someone who had wanted another child so badly, Elinor often forgot Jonas existed when her agenda was deemed more important.

He stood up. "So I guess she doesn't want input from me."

CJ stood, too. "She'll figure it out, Jonas." She gently touched his sleeve, as if it were his heart and she could mend it.

"And I shouldn't tell Janice."

"No."

"Or my father."

"No."

"And you want me to stay out of it."

"Yes."

"For my father's sake?"

"And your mother's. It will be for the best."

"I love them both, but I'm not sure I can do that." He kissed her cheek again and let himself out, and CJ started to ache.

"I'd like to speak with the vice president," Elinor said, when she'd finally screwed up her nerve, located his number from Malcolm's long list of contacts, and steadied her hand long enough to punch in the numbers.

It was late afternoon—she'd thought about this all day. She'd paced the house and the grounds of the Mount Kasteel estate and landed in the living room, next to the sideboard that held the crystal pitcher that had come from Remy way back when.

She'd had one phone call from Alice, telling her they hadn't learned anything concrete at the Lord Winslow, but there was a lead they would follow up on tomorrow.

Elinor didn't ask for specifics: she was too preoccupied thinking about Remy.

He needed to know what was going on. She convinced herself that if word leaked out, it would affect his life, too. His wife's life, his daughter's. The life of the whole damn nation.

Well, maybe not the *whole* nation. The blue states would love it; the red states would be livid.

"This is Mrs. Young. Elinor Young. The vice president has spoken with me about my recommendations for national health care matters."

"I'm sorry, the vice president is occupied. If you'd care to leave your number . . ."

Remy, of course, never returned phone calls; he had "people" to do that for him. He often joked that the last time he'd dialed a phone was when there had been actual dials, not buttons. He didn't have a private cell phone, either. He said they weren't very "private," at least not for a VP.

Which was, of course, why—after nearly seven months into their affair—he always made contact through an obscure, handwritten invitation or a mysterious call: *"The toilets will arrive tomorrow at one o'clock. Your driver will pick you up and bring you to the delivery area."*

The driver, of course, was Remy's driver. The delivery area was never disclosed. Elinor had learned to simply stand on the sidewalk in front of her town house and wait for the long black limo and the driver who only tipped his hat and never even said hello or good-bye.

Even their New York connections had been cloak-and-dagger, spy-novel stuff, coinciding with Remy's twice-monthly meetings at the United Nations. She would check into the suite (the same one every time) and spend all afternoon, evening, and sometimes into the night wondering when—if—he would show up for their hour of bliss, give or take.

She shuddered a little. Was her cell number now displayed on the caller ID screen at Remy's admin's desk? But this was the first time she'd called. Surely it would be safe.

"It's rather urgent," Elinor said. "There's been a change in directives that will affect our next meeting." She was both amused and impressed by her ciphered message.

There was a pause, then the admin said, "One moment, please."

She felt a flutter of anticipation, the kind she'd felt the first time he'd undone her pearl buttons and fucked her in his dining room.

Would he take her call? Would he dismiss senators or congressmen or whoever was in his office "occupying" him?

A lump of trepidation found its way into her throat. What if he was with another woman?

She laughed. Remy barely had time for her. He'd never have time for a harem.

Still, Elinor clutched the phone more tightly than necessary.

"Elinor?" She heard Remy's voice, just as another voice came from the doorway of the music room.

"Mom?" It was Jonas.

Elinor smiled at her son and quickly flipped the phone shut. "Hello, dear," she said, standing and dropping the phone into her purse. "I was confirming floral arrangements for the party. The details can be such a bore."

"Mom," he said, "we need to talk."

"I swear Betts asked me to handle the flowers because she thinks I have your dad's talent for that kind of thing."

"Mom . . ."

And then her phone rang in her purse. Remy, of course, would be calling back. She slung her purse over her shoulder. "Not now, honey," she said, striding across the room toward the terrace, hoping she'd get outside before the damn phone stopped ringing.

"Is this Elinor Young?" It was a male's voice, but not Remy's.

"Yes," she replied. Perspiration had formed on her upper lip; she tried to steady her voice. It must be Remy's driver on the other end of the line.

"Do you have the cash?"

The late-day sun radiated off the water lily pond that served as a centerpiece for the topiaries. Elinor was blinded, paralyzed. Finally, she blinked. "What?"

"The cash. The half million. Do you have it?"

Her throat felt as if Mac was standing on it, wearing the big boots that he wore when he planted trees in the garden. "I will," she said. "By Friday."

"Good," he said, then hung up without leaving instructions.

Elinor shut off the phone, dropped onto a chaise, and stared helplessly, hopelessly at the trees.

"Mom?" came Jonas's voice again. "Please, Mom. We really do need to talk."

 ## Eighteen

"*It's a bloody size sixteen,*" *Alice wailed into* the phone at Poppy. Neal wasn't home again, so Alice had poured a generous glass of wine and decided to rehearse the role that Poppy had convinced her to play tomorrow. It would be more fun than making dinner for one. But despite the slight menopausal spread of her hips, the dress hung on her frame like a discount-store window drape. "I know I'm bigger than the rest of you, but I'm a ten, Poppy. Not a sixteen."

Poppy sighed. "I bet Yolanda can help. She's domestic, isn't she?"

"Just because she cleans her own house and cooks her own meals I don't think that automatically means she knows how to sew."

"I bet she does," Poppy repeated. "Let's bring it over to her place."

"I'll pick you up in thirty minutes." Alice didn't ask if Duane was home. Long ago, the women had stopped asking about each other's husbands. They'd learned life was less dramatic that way, Elinor's current situation serving as a clear case in point.

Poppy changed from the demure summer suit she'd worn to the Lord Winslow into chocolate-colored jeans, high-heeled sandals, and a clingy turquoise top. If she had to go to Yolanda's, she might as well look as good as she could.

"Well," said Duane, "don't you look like a hottie."

Poppy responded with a tiny smile, because she knew how well the jeans hugged her round little ass.

"Come here," Duane said. "I want to have my way with you." He had that twinkle in his eye that she hadn't seen for a while, not since he'd started taking pictures after dark. Was it because he, indeed, was Elinor's lover and/or blackmailer and the danger totally turned him on?

"I'd love to, but Alice is picking me up. We're on a mission for poor Elinor. There's an engagement party in Washington this weekend and she's frantic right now." He didn't seem to wince when she mentioned Elinor's name.

"There's an engagement party and we're not invited?"

"It's only for Washington people, Duane. You know how they are." Well, of course he didn't, but that didn't matter.

He patted the sofa cushion next to him. "Five minutes," he said, then added, "please?"

Saying no might get her in trouble. Poppy checked her watch. She supposed five minutes would satisfy his unexpected need. Besides, if he really was involved in this muddle, Poppy didn't want him to think they were onto him and give him time to come up with a lie.

And, she supposed, a little sex wouldn't hurt Poppy, either, in case Manny showed up at Yolanda's. There was something about Manny's eyes, his smile, and his shiny gold badge . . .

When Poppy was a girl, Momma had told her it was always wise to masturbate before a date. She hadn't, of course, used that word. But she'd given Poppy a pretty little pink dildo, and told her to use it in her "special place" so she wouldn't be tempted to give in to her she-devil and let the boy do things she'd regret.

Duane wasn't a pink dildo, and Manny wasn't a teenager, but if Poppy had learned anything in life, it was that Momma usually was right.

All things considered, she should unzip her jeans, go to her husband, and let him have his way so Yolanda's brother would not.

But Poppy was Poppy, and if there was one thing she was no good at, it was pretending to love when she was no longer sure she did. She'd learned that with husbands number one and number two.

"Sorry," she said with an apologetic smile. "But we're already late."

"You're being blackmailed," Jonas said. "Don't lie, I saw the note."

Elinor blinked again. "What?" Her thoughts reeled. She couldn't gather a response.

"I read the note. About the panties."

Well, she could have died right there on the chaise; in fact, dying would have been preferable to having this discussion with her grown-up son.

Instead of dying, Elinor laughed. Would Jonas dare challenge her if she laughed?

"You saw the note?" *Ha ha.* "Do you mean the note with the words cut out of a magazine?" *Ha ha* some more, this time enhanced by a fine shake of her head.

"Mother, this isn't funny. I saw the note in your purse. I went in there to get the keys to the garage so I could put away the canoe. And there it was, big as life."

"And you thought I was being blackmailed? That I'd lost my panties in a Dumpster in Manhattan?" *Ha ha* again. "Really, Jonas, that's rather crude." She wanted to stand up. She wanted to make a sweeping, grand departure from the terrace, as if everything was fine, as if he was such a jokester and his accusation was absurd. But despite the laughter, Elinor had become numb, so she stayed planted right there on the chaise.

"Aunt CJ said as much."

Elinor closed her eyes, wishing she'd stop feeling as if her airway was being cut off. "It's a *joke*, Jonas. If you must know, Alice and Poppy played a trick on me. We were shopping in the city and I picked out a lovely pair of La Perlas for Lucinda's lingerie shower. I'm sure one of her friends will be planning one. Anyway, Alice and Poppy accused me of buying them for myself, if you must know."

She paused a brief second, hating that the lies came so easily, that being deceived had become Jonas's birthright. "For some ridiculous reason, the girls thought it would be a hoot to send me a blackmail note." She had no idea if the story made sense.

"The panties are for Lucinda?"

Elinor nodded. "Two hundred and ten dollars. A very nice style."

"May . . . may I see them?"

Her senses shot back into her limbs. She bolted up from the chaise. "Jonas!" she said with a hearty laugh. "Are you challenging me?"

He moved next to her. He was taller than Elinor, as tall as Malcolm. "No, Mom. But . . ."

She waved her hand. "But, nothing. For one thing, even if I wanted to, I couldn't show them to you. They're in Washington. At the town house." She knew she should have felt guilty, but she was too . . . oh, God, she was too freaking exhausted.

"I can't imagine what CJ is thinking or why, but she's mistaken. Now please, honey," she said, softening her voice and straightening the collar of his Hugo Boss linen shirt, "let's forget this nonsense and have an early dinner. Shall we go out for Italian?"

 **Nineteen**

"*The morons chose to pay the fine rather than* follow the bylaws," Ray Williams said as he sipped CJ's best Bordeaux. She'd asked him to dinner because she'd wanted some balance: as environmental manager of the lake association and architect of the Mount Kasteel Town Hall, Ray had turned the term *down-to-earth* into a science. He offered a refreshing change from Elinor's world, and maybe later CJ would get to have sex. It was never as tantalizing as it had been with Malcolm, or as satisfying as it had been with Cooper, but it would be sex, and it would be nice—a safe, familiar distraction.

"That's awful," she said, toying with the rim of her glass. Ray was referring to the Santoris, the new lakefront residents who'd built a five-million-dollar getaway, then decided the tall pines blocked their view of the water. They'd lopped off the branches halfway to the tops, then left the tops intact. The results resembled the tail of a French poodle, and Ray was justifiably upset.

"They claim the bylaws stipulate the trees can't be cut down. They say they didn't cut them down, that they only trimmed them in the middle." He had two matching furrows in his forehead, which might have been a result of having been married too long to Naomi, a woman who was more interested in archeology than in her husband and son. Naomi lived in Egypt these days: the last Kevin had heard from his mother she'd been with a group who'd found another king's tomb, which Ray had proclaimed was just what the world needed.

"Ray," CJ said abruptly. "I'm going away for a couple of days. Do you think Kevin would like to dog-sit?"

Ray winced. "Hey. I wasn't finished talking about the Santoris." He smiled.

"Sorry," she said. "I'm preoccupied tonight."

"You're going away. Somewhere fun?"

He wouldn't ask for details, because details did not define their relationship. It was good, of course, because CJ could hardly tell him she was going to her sister's to sit by the phone and wait for a blackmailer to call.

"No," she said. "Family business." She didn't say she'd only be across town, that she'd decided not to subject Elinor's gleaming hardwood floors to an eighty-pound, yellow Lab. Besides, Luna loved spending time with Kevin. They had equal parts of high energy.

"Upsetting business?"

CJ shook her had. "Jonas's engagement party is Saturday night. Elinor is becoming a madwoman."

Ray laughed. He knew Elinor, of course. They had been lake kids together—Elinor, CJ, Ray, and a half dozen others. Summer kids whose parents converged there each June and stayed until school reopened in September. Ray once told CJ that the year Elinor and CJ were twelve and he was thirteen, Elinor asked him to show her his penis because she'd never seen one and she said it was "time" that she did. Naturally, it was erect because he was an adolescent and they'd been swimming and Elinor was wearing a bathing suit that was not a bikini but showed her young curves.

She'd inspected his penis without touching it. Then she slid down her straps, showed him her breasts, and asked what he thought.

He'd said they looked like the anthills in the town picnic grove with tight little raisins stuck on the tops. He asked if her sister's looked just like hers.

Elinor had yanked up her top and told him to drop dead.

Ray had told CJ the story not long after she'd left Cooper and moved into the cottage, back when laughter had been essential and so hard to come by, back when they shared their first bottle of wine and she admitted to Ray that she was such a failure compared to her sister.

So he had made her laugh, because he was a good friend.

CJ supposed Elinor's action was indicative of the pragmatic, bold streak she would later fully develop. It hadn't occurred to her that Elinor might have simply been curious about sex. As for CJ, she'd never been so, well, sensually inclined.

Had she?

"Ray," CJ asked now, "did you and Elinor ever have sex?" The question popped out unexpectedly.

Ray nearly sprayed a mouthful of Bordeaux onto the couch.

"What?" he laughed, wiping his mouth. "What a question!" He stood up, meandered to the sound system, and became suddenly interested in the CDs on the rack.

It was odd that he hadn't said no. It was more odd that CJ suddenly felt uncomfortable.

"Never mind," she said. "I was just thinking of the story you told me about when we were kids, when Elinor showed you her breasts. I don't know why I asked that. How ludicrous of me."

He was a tall, thin man, who looked even thinner when he stood sideways, as he stood now, perusing the CDs as if they were rare works of art. "It was over a while ago."

CJ winced. "What?"

He shrugged. "The thing with Elinor. The affair, whatever you call it. It was over a while ago, CJ. It has nothing to do with you and me."

Alice set her glass of wine in the refrigerator. No sense traversing the back roads to New Falls with alcohol on her breath. The police had become so unfriendly about that.

She closed the refrigerator door and decided to change out of the polyester before driving to Yolanda's. Even worse than sniffing for alcohol, the cops might be inclined to wonder why a woman who resembled a housekeeper was driving an Esplanade.

As she moved through the kitchen, Neal suddenly appeared in her path.

"Oh," she said. "It's you." She might have added *"again,"* but she thought that might have sounded unfriendly.

"Imagine that," he said. "Your husband is home two nights in a row." He wasn't a bad guy. He was soft-spoken with her, though he wasn't that way in the boardroom, which was why they could afford to live in Mount Kasteel and half-support their grown children. His once dirty-blonde hair had washed into gray, but now most of that had washed away, too.

Still, she could have done worse. Neal was rock solid: a good husband, a good dad, a good provider. He still had gentle hazel eyes and clear skin without age lines, and he still wore only white shirts with pinstripes—blue, black, deep green, or maroon—and still wore his tie tac with the Sigma Pi logo, though he was no longer active in his college fraternity alumni association because he didn't have time.

All in all, Neal was a lot like Alice's father, who'd been gone for a dozen years, but whose gentle memory still brought her to quick tears.

"Nice dress," Neal commented. "But it's a little big, don't you think?"

Alice brushed back thoughts of her father and rolled her eyes. "I'm doing Poppy a favor. Don't ask what it is." She hoped she sounded carefree. "I'm going to change, then go out. Sorry. I won't be gone long."

He nodded, but he followed her up the stairs and into the bedroom. She hoped he wouldn't prod her for details.

"They can't reschedule the dinner," he said as Alice went into her dressing room. "For Thursday night. Can you please find another solution for Kiley Kate?"

"What about Emmie? She'd love to go to the dinner with you." Emmie was Neal's older sister, a New Age priestess who now was a certified Ayurveda consultant and spent a lot of time standing on her head. Neither Alice nor Neal would suggest that Emmie take Alice's place in Orlando, because she wasn't a responsible candidate for a chaperone. Too much marijuana in her twenties; too much meditation in her thirties. Alice had never pointed out that their daughter, Felicity, was a great deal like Emmie. Alice, after all, secretly envied their independence and their feral natures and the fact that neither had ever played follow the leader the way she had with Elinor, the way Melissa did with her husband.

He laughed. "Tang Industries might specialize in resort spas, but the only health thing that concerns them is the state of their bottom line."

"They're capitalists."

"Emmie's not."

"No kidding." She stepped out of the housekeeper's dress, unashamed to expose her middle-aged, slightly tattered body in front of her husband. She'd never been embarrassed, insecure, or ashamed of anything in front of Neal. More than once, she'd wondered why. Did it mean she wasn't ga-ga, head-over-heels in love with him? That she'd never felt the need to be perfect for him?

She'd married him, mostly, because Elinor had married Malcolm. She'd had Melissa because Elinor had Janice; Felicity, after Elinor had Jonas. One child would have been sufficient for Alice, but, as always, Elinor had set the pace for her life.

"If Elinor jumped off a bridge, would you?" her mother had asked on more than one occasion.

Well, of course the answer was *yes, probably*, though Alice never admitted it.

Pulling on a long, plum-colored, cotton skirt and matching tee, Alice slipped into ballet slippers of the same shade. "I'm sorry, Neal, but it's presumptuous of them to expect everyone to be available at the drop of a hat."

If he pushed her a little she might have acquiesced, might have decided to beg Melissa to go to Orlando in her place. But Neal apparently was done pushing, because he only said, "Never mind, then," and departed the room, leaving Alice to wonder if she took him for granted, and if she'd regret it one day.

Twenty

Elinor must have thought it was pretty funny when CJ had told her she was seeing Ray.

Pulling into the driveway of Elinor and Malcolm's "country house," CJ seethed. She'd never blamed Elinor for the tragedy of her life, for the emptiness she'd endured since Jonas had been conceived, for Cooper's lost love, which she'd relinquished to honor Elinor, Malcolm, Jonas.

She'd never blamed Elinor, and yet, and yet...

She ached. She ached.

She'd told Ray she had a headache and asked him to leave. How could she ever have sex with him again? How could she enjoy his closeness and his warmth knowing Elinor had—once again—been there first?

And when had it been, anyway?

Last week? Last month? Last year?

Had it been before Elinor had picked up with the vice president, if that was with whom she'd picked up?

It was almost eight o'clock now. CJ had sped to the house in anger, steeled to confront her sister, ready to blast her for all of her sins, primed to announce she was done coming in second. Maybe she'd say she was not going to house-sit, that it was time Elinor learned to clean up her own messes.

CJ flicked off the ignition and slammed the car door behind her. She marched up the front stairs and rang the bell.

Once.

Twice.

She waited a moment, then tried to peer into the library, but the drapes had been drawn.

She rang again. No response.

Perhaps Elinor and Jonas had gone out for dinner. Mother and son.

She ached again.

Wrapping her shawl tightly around her, CJ sat down on the stairs. She'd wait there for hours, if she had to.

But it was only twenty minutes later that Elinor's Mercedes pulled in.

"Everything's okay," Jonas announced as he plodded across the gravel to the stairs where CJ sat. "Mom isn't being blackmailed. It was all a joke." He laughed because he was a happy, trusting boy.

CJ stood up and moved her eyes to Elinor, who jangled her keys as she approached. "You're a day early," she said. "Did your decorators arrive ahead of schedule?"

If Jonas had been Malcolm, CJ might have spit out the truth. She might have told Elinor to stop lying and face up to what she had done. But Jonas was not Malcolm, so CJ said, "No." She would always protect Jonas, as if she'd been the prostitute whose child King Solomon had offered to cut in half to learn its true mother, to see which woman would renounce her baby rather than have him come to harm. "Something has come up," CJ continued. "We need to speak. Jonas, will you excuse us?"

"Sure," he said, though his smile faded. He no doubt saw the same shadow in CJ's eyes that had lingered in his hours earlier.

He took the keys from Elinor, said good night to CJ, and went into the house.

CJ swallowed her guilt.

"It's dark," Elinor noted. "What on earth is so urgent?"

"I'm here for the truth, Elinor. Why didn't you tell me about you and Ray? How many secrets do you have?"

CJ expected her sister to laugh. She expected her to say something glib, like, *"I never thought he was as good in bed as Malcolm, how 'bout you?"*

CJ expected almost anything out of Elinor. She did not expect her sister to sit down on the stairs, drop her face in her hands, and say, "My life is completely fucked up."

CJ sat quietly while Elinor cried. After a moment she put her arm around her sister's shoulders and tried—in vain—to pretend that she wasn't crying, too. Like it or not, she hurt when Elinor did, the mirror of their DNA.

"I've never been good at being faithful to Malcolm. It's not that I don't love him, you know."

CJ remained quiet, then finally asked, "It's him, isn't it? Your lover is the vice president."

Elinor hesitated before responding. "Please, CJ, please don't tell a soul." She didn't ask how CJ had figured it out. After all, she knew the twins' connection as well as CJ did.

"What if they find out? Alice? Poppy? Yolanda?"

"They won't. The blackmailer certainly isn't Remy."

"What if it's someone connected to the White House? Someone who might want to stop him before the next election?" Remy had been vice president for more than seven years. Most people presumed he'd be the party's choice for top dog next year.

"He won't run for president. He hates his job. He hates Washington."

CJ felt as if she'd been told something she shouldn't know, a top-secret-secret worth—what? Their dignity? Their lives? The future of America?

Good grief.

They sat in silence. Then Elinor said, "He called me today."

"Did you tell him about the blackmail?"

"No. Not Remy. The blackmailer called."

CJ sucked in the night air. "It's a man?"

"Yes."

"What did he say?"

"He asked if I had the money. I said I would have it by Friday night."

"And?"

"And he hung up."

In the distance, the night birds began their ballet as they settled into the pines. CJ wrapped her shawl around Elinor. "So now we know it isn't a hoax."

Elinor gave a short laugh. "It never occurred to me it was a hoax. A part of me knew from the start that nothing in Washington stays a secret forever."

The truth about Jonas had not yet been discovered, but CJ did not want to bring that up now. "Maybe we'll find the blackmailer. Maybe Alice and Poppy and Yolanda and I . . ."

Elinor stood up and wrapped CJ's shawl tightly around her the way CJ had. "And then what? What was I thinking? That we'll scare him off? That we'll bring him to justice? You were right . . . I shouldn't have dragged anyone else into this. We should have tried to resolve it, just you and me."

It was hard for Elinor to admit when she'd been wrong, so CJ didn't make things worse by saying it was too late for regrets. She stood up next to her sister, shoulder to shoulder, eye to eye. "We could tell the others to stop. We could say you found out it was a hoax. Or that you were just playing a game."

"It's too late for that."

"They don't know about Remy."

Elinor shrugged again. "If I tell them to stop, my bet is they won't. Poppy and Alice are too curious. Alice called to say they didn't learn anything concrete at the Lord Winslow today, but that they have another idea they're going to go after tomorrow. She didn't elaborate."

"Good grief," CJ said. "Let's face it, E, this is the most excitement they've had since—"

"Since the incident with the gardener."

They laughed a little, at the way their mother had always referred to that horrid day as *"The Incident with the Gardener,"* as if it had been the title of an Agatha Christie novel.

Then CJ said, "Come on, E, let's go inside. Whatever happens will happen, but we'll face it together."

She did not mention Ray Williams again. The topic seemed insignificant, in light of the rest.

Alice was in Yolanda's bathroom, putting on the housekeeper's dress, when Manny strolled into the kitchen. Poppy wondered what he would look like in a newly pressed uniform sporting a holster and a gun. The image was disturbing in a good sort of way.

"I see your friends managed to return without getting arrested," he announced.

"I thought you weren't going to get involved," Yolanda said. Belita said, "Da-Da," because she must have thought Manny was her Da-Da, not her uncle.

He went to the counter and poured a cup of coffee. "The Lord Winslow has more security than Fort Knox."

Poppy cleared her throat, because he hadn't looked at her as yet. "They didn't find 'Momma.'"

"They were humoring you," he said, stirring cream in his coffee, making eye contact with a carton of half-and-half and not her. "The minute you approached the manager, they had you pegged as a whacko."

Poppy recoiled.

"Manuel!" Yolanda scolded. "Watch your tongue."

"Sorry, but that's how they saw her. They assumed it was a phony routine, but if it wasn't, they figured she was looney."

Was that what he thought, too? That she was crazy? She pouted. Momma always said pouting was childish, but Poppy couldn't help it.

Manny dumped in sugar and stirred some more. "These people are trained to spot impersonators. And fake accents are a dead giveaway."

She'd thought her Winston-Salem imitation had been right on target. She'd never been there, of course, but a girl at McCready had been from that area, and Poppy thought she'd sounded just like her. *Shoot.* Her lower lip protruded a bit more.

He took a sip of coffee. Then his back stiffened and he looked into his mug. "You need to stay away from the hotel," he said. "All of you."

His tone was stern, the way Mr. Harding, Elinor and CJ's father, had been when they'd been girls back in school. Unlike Mr. Harding, Poppy's father had been quiet, agreeable, a sweet, gentle man. Her best memory of him came from the photo on the front porch swing, Poppy sitting beside him, his arm cradling her, keeping her safe and warm. His fortune had come from the backbone of his father and his father's father, from their railroads and skyscrapers. But the men who'd made the money had died before Poppy was born, so she'd never known either of them. If she'd grown up around stern men, like Mr. Harding, she might have been accustomed to stiff backs and cold stares. Instead, they made her twitch.

"But," she said. "Elinor—"

He held up a hand. "Forget it," he said. "I don't know what's going on, but you need to stay the hell out of it."

She winced again, as if she were a child in the headmaster's office.

"Look," Manny said, now leveling his dark eyes on hers. "The truth is, the Lord Winslow does not have a Dumpster."

Poppy curled a few strands of hair. "Of course it does. That's where the blackmailer found Elinor's panties!"

He blushed. He turned his eyes away again. "There is no Dumpster. Each floor has trash chutes. The trash is automatically compacted, then trucked out of the lower level."

Poppy was about to protest again when Alice emerged wearing the tan polyester.

"What's going on?" she asked.

"There isn't a Dumpster at the Lord Winslow," Yolanda explained. "The blackmailer lied."

"You have to back off," Manny continued. "For all of your sakes. Don't do anything else, unless your friend gets a phone call about the ransom drop."

"And if she does?" Poppy whispered, wishing he'd look at her again.

"Call the police." He tossed her a business card, drained his mug, and left Yolanda's without glancing back.

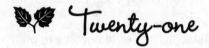 *Twenty-one*

It was after ten by the time Alice pulled up to the gates at Poppy's estate. They hadn't spoken all the way back from New Falls.

"Well?" Alice asked. "What do you think? Should we abort our mission tomorrow? Tell Elinor we've changed our minds?"

Poppy fiddled with Manny's business card, which she'd tucked in her pocket. "I don't know what to do. I hate abandoning Elinor, but Yolanda's brother is probably right. If the blackmailer lied about the Dumpster, he's probably dangerous."

"Of course he's dangerous. He's demanding a half million dollars, remember?"

Poppy relaxed her hand. "So what should we do?"

Alice shrugged. "Well, I have a polyester dress that now fits.

I really don't think any harm will come to us tomorrow. Then I'm off to Orlando and Elinor will be off to Washington for the party. I don't think we have much to lose. Besides, if we just do this one last thing, Elinor will know we didn't desert her. We don't have to tell Yolanda's brother. Or Yolanda, either, for that matter."

"But if anything happens to me, what would become of poor Momma?"

"Please. Your mother has more caretakers than the Biltmore Estate."

At least she hadn't called caretakers gardeners. That would have been so unkind. "Oh, Alice," Poppy said. "I just don't know."

"I'll be the one at risk," Alice said. "You'll be safe in the get-away car." The big headlights swept the front of the garage. A white Lexus was parked on the side. "Did you get a new car?" Alice asked.

Poppy's brow fell into a frown. She quickly recovered to avoid little lines. "Not that I know of."

"Well," Alice said, "you have company then."

"I wonder who it could be." She could have suggested that Duane had a guest, but she supposed Alice knew he had no friends. No male friends, at least.

"Maybe the car belongs to one of the maids."

"If it is, I'm paying her too much."

Alice stopped the vehicle, and Poppy got out, saying, "Guess I'll have to go in and find out who's here." She bobbed her hair and put on a tight smile. "I'll give you a call in the morning."

"All right," Alice replied. "But call me early. If I'm going to be a housekeeper at the Lord Winslow, I won't want to be late for my first day of work."

* * *

Poppy let herself into the garage through the side door. She held her breath until Alice was out of sight, then she listened. Had Duane noticed the vehicle pull into the driveway? Or was he too busy entertaining the owner of the white Lexus?

Was it a woman?

A few years ago he'd hinted that a ménage à trois might be fun. Poppy had been horrified. She'd locked herself in the bedroom for two whole days until he'd convinced her he'd only been joking. He'd never mentioned it since.

Still, today he'd been horny. And Poppy hadn't performed her wifely job.

She'd been too ashamed to tell Alice.

Leaning against the side of Duane's sports car, Poppy tried to figure out what to do next. She didn't want to barge in. If he was with a woman, she'd be too embarrassed for words.

It was bad enough she suspected he was a blackmailer, or at the least, sleeping with one of her best friends.

Oh! she moaned softly. *What have I done?* Why had she married him in the first place?

Why?

Why?

She thought about Manny, Yolanda's brother. Oh, sure, he looked really hot. And he seemed really nice. *But for God's sake, Poppy,* she cried to herself, *he is one of them!*

A two-timing,
money-hungry,
conniving
man!

Momma had been right not to trust any after Daddy was gone.

For the first time in forever, Poppy did not want to be inside her wrought-iron gates. She no longer felt safe.

Thankfully, Momma lived just a mile down the road. It had been years since Poppy had walked quite so far, and she'd never done such a thing in the dark, but she couldn't very well take one of the cars and risk alerting Duane that she had been home.

So Poppy let herself out and started walking in her high-heeled sandals, down the winding country road, toward Momma's.

In the morning, she would call Alice and say yes, she would go to the Lord Winslow. There was no reason to trust Manny or believe anything he had to say. He was a man, after all. And the girlfriends must stick together.

If Momma had been more . . . well . . . alert, Poppy might have considered talking to her about Duane the way she'd talked to her about Elinor. But since Momma had gone through all that she'd gone through, her wisdom came in occasional bursts—and lately, there had been few of those.

Because Poppy knew they frequently changed the alarm system code (Momma consistently feared someone would steal her orchids and trinkets), she went to the guesthouse where Lucky resided. It wasn't really a house but a three-room bungalow, tucked around back. Like the main house, it was made of stone—large gray boulders glued with cement that looked more like it belonged in Hansel and Gretel than in Mount Kasteel.

Poppy knocked on the wooden door. She slipped off her sandals and rubbed her poor little toes. She was grateful she'd made the full mile in one relative piece, without interruption from nocturnal critters or low-flying bats.

No lights came on inside the bungalow. Poppy knocked again. She'd already decided to say she'd locked herself out of the gates to her estate, that Duane was out of town, that she hadn't wanted to awaken the alarm service folks. She'd already decided to say she needed to stay at Momma's tonight, that she would deal with the locked gates tomorrow.

Lucky would be too professional to ask why whoever had dropped her off at the gates to Momma's estate hadn't waited to see that she'd entered safely.

She knocked again. She waited.

After another minute, Poppy said, "Damn."

She crossed the lawn, marched toward the garage, and climbed the stairs that led to Fiona and Bern's apartment. This time, her knock was more insistent.

Lights were lit; slippers shuffled across the hardwood floor. The door opened. Moments later, Bern was escorting Poppy toward the main house.

"Your momma's been having her spells again," Bern said. "When that happens, she likes it if Lucky stays in the house."

"But Lila's room is right down the hall."

"She's not much good in these situations."

Poppy realized then that Momma's life was a little drama, with people and roles and, no doubt, performances, too. "Why wasn't I told that her spells have come back?"

"Your momma didn't want to worry you. She says you have enough problems these days."

Bern unlocked the kitchen door and decoded the alarm. Poppy had a fleeting fear that they'd find Lucky under the covers with Momma, naked and hugging her old-moneyed bones.

What would Poppy say?

What would Lucky say?

Should she fire him on the spot, or would Momma protest?

Lucky was a dozen or more years younger than Momma. He had a low forehead and a pronounced facial tic, but he was dependable, and Momma liked that. She also liked the fact that he did everything for her, that he responded to her every whim. His demeanor always seemed professional enough, but Poppy suspected that not much stopped Momma when she was having a spell and needed brandy and warmth.

Poppy tagged along behind Bern as they made their way up the sweeping, curved staircase. She wondered if they should leave Momma alone . . . then she thought about Doris Duke and all the money her "companion" had made off with after her death . . . not to mention the rumors that he had somehow helped accelerate her demise.

Oh! Poppy thought. *Oh!*

But when they reached Momma's bedroom, they found Lucky parked on the settee outside the door. His head drooped as he dozed; his shirt was fully buttoned and his pants, fully zipped.

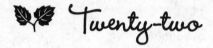 Twenty-two

The next morning, Poppy called Alice and asked if she'd please pick her up at Momma's and please not ask why she was wearing the same clothes she'd had on last night.

So Alice did and she didn't.

"Neal commented on the dress when I left," Alice said after Poppy was settled inside the Esplanade. "He asked since when had I taken to wearing polyester. I asked since when had he earned the right to question my fashion sense, Mr. White Shirt with Pinstripes." She'd hoped a little light humor might help erase the maudlin look on Poppy's face. It did not. She turned the AC vent toward her. "Good Lord, I was right. Polyester is hot."

Poppy didn't reply.

Alice drove down the driveway, past the chauffeur, who was washing the Lincoln stretch limo as if Poppy's mother had somewhere important to go.

"It's Duane," Poppy said suddenly, because she'd never been good at keeping secrets.

"I wasn't going to ask."

"The visitor last night was a woman."

"Who?"

"I have no idea. I didn't go in."

Alice steered the car along the shady country road toward the highway that led to the city. She wondered if their friends were as bothered by Poppy as she had become, or if it was another menopausal annoyance, like the occasional black hairs that sprung from nowhere in particular and instantly took root on her chin. "If you didn't go in, how do you know it was a woman? Did you peek in the windows of your own house?"

If Poppy was offended, she didn't show it. "I just know, Alice. Whether or not he's been sleeping with Elinor, Duane has been cheating on me for years. Do you think I am stupid?"

The question, of course, was an interesting one. Alice might have played along if it hadn't been for the fact that Poppy had crossed the boundary of their unspoken rule: she'd said something really bad about her husband, something not playful or malingering, like the fact he wore pinstripes. She'd said something really, really bad by acknowledging that marriage was not immune to unpleasantness even when housed in over-privileged rooms. CJ was the only one of them who remained unaffected. Then again, CJ never discussed her ex-husband, who had seemed like a pretty nice guy on the surface.

As did Neal, the bore.

And Malcolm, the disinterested.

Duane? Well, he'd never seemed what Alice could call nice. And now, good Lord, Poppy was considering his potential for perpetual adultery on top of the blackmail.

Alice could not disagree, which was such a pity when one considered that sweet stiffness to Duane's penis.

"Well?" Poppy asked. "Do you? Do you think I'm stupid?"

Alice fanned herself again and readjusted herself on the leather, wishing the tingles would abate. "Of course you're not stupid. Do you think Duane's . . . *visitor* . . . has something to do with Elinor's blackmail?" She glanced over at Poppy, whose eyes seemed rimmed with the same color red as her hair, as if she'd been crying all night.

"Idon'tknowIdon'tknowIdon'tknow." Poppy spewed out her thoughts as if they'd been one word, not three. Or nine.

Without looking either way, Alice pulled onto the shoulder and made a U-turn.

"What are you doing?" Poppy asked.

"We're going to Elinor's. We're going to ask if she thinks Duane is blackmailing her. I'm tired of pussyfooting around." She wasn't even sure if that's what they'd been doing, but she liked the way that it sounded.

Elinor loved her daughter. She'd often been pleased that Janice took after her, that she was self-sufficient and did not need a mother hovering about the way Elinor's mother had, the way her father had. The way *everyone* had, with silent expectations for the older twin, the less appealing one.

Like Elinor, Janice was clever, if not as attractive as Jonas. At twenty-eight, she hadn't yet found a man, perhaps because Malcolm hadn't corralled one, the way Father had corralled Malcolm for Elinor. Janice did have a career, which was off to a resounding start. Once in a while, however, she was prone to emotion-packed flare-ups that usually began with a surprise visit, like now, when she suddenly appeared in Elinor's bedroom, of all places, as Elinor was tossing a few things into her Chanel lambskin tote.

"Mother?"

"Janice?"

"What are you doing?"

"Shouldn't I ask you the same?"

"Why are you packing?"

"Why aren't you working?"

"I asked you first."

Good Lord. Elinor felt as if she was ten again, playing a game with CJ.

She sighed. "I'm packing for Washington. Your brother's engagement party is this weekend, in case you've forgotten."

"Of course I haven't forgotten. I'm staying at the Fairmont. Are you and Daddy?"

"I don't know yet. We might be at the town house." If circumstances were different, Elinor would have liked to stay at the hotel in the thick of the engagement party action, surrounded by any out-of-towners that might have been invited, pretending to play hostess, making everything look good. Now, she would prefer to hibernate if she could.

"Well, I don't intend to miss out on their scones in the morning," Janice continued. "I hear they're the best."

Janice resembled Malcolm, except she'd been cheated out of the dimples. Her hair was the same tawny color as his, though it was thick and unkempt, and would do a Rastafarian proud. Her eyes were the same shade of blue as Mac's, her cheekbones the same—high, well-defined. But Janice's jawline was set firmer than Malcolm's, more like her mother's, a cast of concrete that rarely relaxed into a genuine smile. Unlike her mother, Janice was awkward at small talk. Thankfully, she was smart and driven to research, and did not need to embrace the world's people.

Elinor sighed. "Janice, why are you here?"

"They think I've altered my results." She tried knifing a hand through her massive locks.

Elinor, of course, had no time for this. "Who thinks you altered what results?"

"My supervisor. She thinks I altered the results of my research."

"Did you?"

"Did I? *Did I?*"

"Now, Janice, you know I don't understand your work. Where is your father?"

"I thought he was here."

"He was here for the weekend with the congressman and Betts. He's gone back to work. Did you look at the town house?"

"I told you. I thought he was here." She stood in the doorway, hands in the pockets of her khakis. As Janice had never taken great pains with her hair, her wardrobe was equally mismatched to her genetics: DNA, mitochondria, whatever.

"What are you wearing to the party?" Elinor asked, because talking about style was easier for her than talking about Janice's job. She closed the tote with nonchalance, hoping Janice hadn't noticed that Elinor had packed a lightweight gauze sundress that was hardly Washington-wear.

"I might get fired."

"Before the party?" Well, of course, that was the wrong thing to say, which was no doubt why Janice spun on her Birkenstocks and stomped away.

Elinor's shoulders went rigid. She checked her watch. She needed to leave for the airport in twenty minutes. And where was CJ? She'd promised to be there by the time Elinor left. And now, what about Janice? Would she believe their lie about Elinor's seamstress and CJ's decorators?

And what if the blackmailer showed up right now?

The doorbell rang. It was loud. Insistent.

It must be CJ.

Unless . . .

Unless . . .

Elinor's mouth went dry. Her blood pressure skyrocketed, her chest compressed. She stood, perfectly coiffed, perfectly groomed, like the topiaries in Malcolm's garden. And, just like the trees, she was welded to the ground, unable to move, unable to speak.

Would a blackmailer ring the doorbell? Wouldn't he act with more theatrics, like breaking in through the French doors?

The bell rang again. Elinor felt frozen in an Alfred Hitchcock moment.

Then, the murmur of voices.

Male?

Female?

Friend?

Foe?

Was it Alfred himself, reincarnated?

"*Mottthhher,*" Janice bellowed up from downstairs, her syllables protracted with sarcasm. "You have company."

* * *

Elinor could run. She could flee down the back stairs and out to the garden. She could run through the woods and call CJ on her cell and order her to pick her up at the far end of the lake. They had explored every winding pathway of the land when they'd been kids. They'd even carved a few of their own. Surely Elinor wouldn't get lost.

That's what she would do. She'd run.

Any minute now.

As soon as she could get her feet or her legs or some part of her to move.

Then she remembered that her cell phone was in her purse on the breakfront in the dining room.

She clutched the Chanel as if it were a life preserver and she was going under. Then a voice called to her from the doorway.

"Elinor? Are you all right?"

It was Alice. And Poppy. What on earth did Alice have on?

The women stepped into the room. Elinor closed her eyes. "Janice said .. I thought ..."

Alice sighed. "Janice is gone. Did you two have a fight?"

Elinor let go of the Chanel and sank onto the bed. "We always fight. She wants me to be just like her father."

Alice and Poppy nodded as if they understood, which Poppy really couldn't, but Alice probably did because she had two children, too: one nearly normal, the other, regrettably odd.

"But tell me some good news." Elinor's gaze fell on Alice. "Like that isn't polyester you're wearing."

"Elinor," Poppy stepped in and said, quite breathlessly, "do you think my Duane is your blackmailer?"

Elinor's head started to hurt, the shards of a migraine poking at her eyes. "Duane? Your husband? Why? I barely know the man." This wasn't the time or the place to reveal to Poppy that Duane had once . . *Oh, never mind,* Elinor thought. That had been meaningless, and blackmail was not. "As much as I'd love to stay and chat," Elinor continued, forcing herself to stand up again and push through her pain, "I have a plane to catch."

"I'll drive you to the airport," Alice said. "We can talk on the way."

Elinor had planned to drive herself to JFK, but this was a better idea. If Janice still lingered on the premises, she'd think that Alice and Poppy were taking her to the club for Bloody Marys, or to a hair appointment, perhaps, at Yolanda's.

Besides, it was so hard to drive when one had a migraine and the sun was so fucking bright.

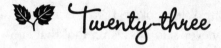 *Twenty-three*

Kevin was late getting to CJ's. She wondered if Ray had forgotten to pass the message on to his son, but she hadn't wanted to call the house. She hadn't yet decided what to do or not do about Ray; she hadn't yet decided why she was so bothered when all she had wanted was casual sex.

Finally the boy limped into the yard, pushing his bike. He had two bloody shins, and his bike had a flat tire.

"I hit a rut," he told CJ.

She spent the next twenty minutes picking gravel from his knees, cleaning his wounds, and bandaging them, while Luna watched with great interest.

Finally, CJ was done. As she sped toward Elinor's, her sister called.

"Where are you?"

"Sorry. Minor emergency. I'm on my way now."

"Well, hurry. I'm en route to the airport, thanks to Alice and Poppy. Be careful when you get to the house. Janice might be around."

CJ didn't have a chance to ask why.

"Pick me up Friday at four o'clock, okay? JFK?"

CJ said yes because she never said no. Damn fool that she was.

Once at the house, CJ parked in the garage and closed the door. No sense announcing to the blackmailer that someone was home if, as Elinor feared, he decided to show up.

Speaking of visitors, there was no sign of her niece.

CJ walked around back and let herself in with the key Elinor kept under the downspout by the kitchen window. It always amused CJ that Elinor had copied that childhood tradition, as if her palatial abode was no different from the small, headmaster's Tudor on the grounds of McCready's or the cottage at Lake Kasteel.

She carried her bag through the back hall, past the felt-landscaped billiard room, the softly buttered morning room, the stainless-steeled kitchen.

All was as it should be: elegant, sparkling, perfect. There were no people, of course. The day staff only appeared Tuesdays, Thursdays, and Saturday mornings. After all, it wasn't as if the family was there every day.

CJ trundled up the backstairs in search of a guest room. She'd brought a mystery she'd been meaning to read, along with a biography of a Supreme Court justice for balance. As long as she was going to be sequestered, she might as well relax and enjoy it. If there was something CJ was used to, it was being alone.

In the end, she'd chucked the sexy attire and packed non-descript cotton capris, knit camisoles, and a couple of big shirts. She'd thrown in a fleece nightshirt and fuzzy socks. It sometimes was freezing in Elinor's house, as if they had first dibs on the air-conditioning in Westchester County.

At the top of the stairs she set down her bag and examined her choices: to the right was a large room in taupe tones. A thick down comforter frosted the sprawling, king-size bed; a sitting area featured a posh, silk-covered chaise; a rich walnut writing desk sat in an alcove.

"Too big," CJ said as if she were Goldilocks who'd gone for a walk in the forest.

To the left was a smaller room done in pale greens. The bed was only a queen size, and in place of the chaise were a single wing chair and a footstool. There was no desk.

"Too small," she said with a smile.

She ambled down the hall past the room Janice used. It was loaded with books but no personal items: She hardly was there anymore.

At Jonas's room, CJ paused in the doorway. His presence was everywhere. From the poster-sized photograph of Times Square at night, to the caricatures of theater stars that had been signed and framed as if this were Sardi's; from the orange life vest that he'd stashed in the corner, to the shelf with small trophies won in the lake fishing derbies, to the navy bedspread that was slightly askew, the room was her son's. She'd been there on more than one occasion, usually when they'd come up from Washington for his birthday, when he'd tugged her upstairs to see his new train, to play with his new Super Nintendo, to hear his new sound system, to try his new laptop.

CJ blinked. She realized she'd been standing in the doorway too long. Too long for memories that were best kept under wraps.

She turned from Jonas's room and continued down the hall toward the master suite, wondering when she'd become such a masochist.

The bedroom was still white, as she remembered.

Inside the room, her footsteps whispered on the thick carpet. Long white drapes were gently pleated across the wide windows. The huge bed, adorned with plump bundles of pillows, faced the tall, white marble fireplace.

CJ moved through the room and peeked into the bath, the steam room, and the Jacuzzi. With a small sigh, she turned toward the sitting room. That's when she noticed that something had changed.

The sitting room had been off to the left in the bedroom. It was a shady nook, the coziest spot in the grandiose house.

But where an archway had been, now there was a door. A closed door.

CJ tiptoed toward it, as if she was being watched. Perhaps Elinor had transformed the space into a closet or a storage room.

With a slow turn of the brass handle, CJ quietly pushed the door open.

It was not a closet. It was not a storage room. It was another bedroom with another door that led back into the hall. The décor was different—not pouffy but plain, with a simple twin bed and a deep leather chair, an overfilled bookcase and a small window garden that held green shoots being rooted in the morning sun.

It was Malcolm's room. The separate bedroom Jonas had told CJ about.

She sat on the bed, then slowly reclined. She turned her face into the pillow and imagined she picked up his scent: musky, woodsy, Malcolm.

Then she rolled over, stared up at the ceiling, and felt the tears slide from her eyes.

Yes, she thought, this bed felt *just right*. In another time, in another life, all of this would have been hers. The house. The husband. The boy.

Twenty-four

For the third day in a row, they were in the city. Alice had no idea if this was a smart thing to do, but she'd grown to enjoy the rush of adventure, the thrill of stepping out of her life into the unexpected.

Besides, today would be foreplay for Bud in Orlando and the real excitement to come.

With a tiny smile, she let the heat fill her body without waving it off.

Of course, they hadn't told Elinor about Manny's warning. She'd seemed annoyed enough by the concept that Poppy's Duane really might be behind this. When Poppy had pressed her again when they'd been curbside at Kennedy, the last thing Elinor said was, "No offense, Poppy, but blackmail is very complex. I don't think your husband is smart enough."

Hopefully, her words also negated Poppy's notion that Duane had been Elinor's lover.

Two blocks south of the Lord Winslow now, Alice pulled over. "Okay," she said to Poppy, "I'll get out here. Take over the wheel and drive around until you see me again." She opened her door and looked out for traffic. But before Alice got out, Poppy said, "No."

Alice turned toward her. "What?"

"I can't drive this thing, Alice. I drive a sports car. This is a truck."

"It's not a truck, Poppy. It's a Cadillac."

Poppy shook her head. "I can't. It's too big."

Alice sighed and closed her door. She set her clenched fists on the steering wheel. "Now's a fine time to tell me."

"I'm sorry. I didn't think about it until now. I guess I forgot Yolanda wouldn't be with us."

"Poppy," Alice said, "you said you'd drive the getaway car. We agreed this is our last attempt to help Elinor."

Poppy nodded, but her face was scrunched up like a scared little girl's. She looked like she'd cry at any second.

"Okay," Alice quickly said. "You don't have to drive. Just sit behind the wheel and stay right here."

"We can't park here! I'll get arrested!"

Alice wondered if anyone would tolerate Poppy if her best friends no longer did. "If a cop comes along, say something's wrong. Say your battery's dead. That you're waiting for the tow truck."

Poppy considered the option. "Well . . ."

"Well nothing," Alice said. "Just do it, Poppy. I won't be long." She slammed the door when she got out.

* * *

She'd worn sneakers, not ladylike heels, which helped make walking the two blocks to the hotel kind of fun. How long had it been since Alice walked anywhere that didn't involve shopping? Shopping wasn't even a pastime she enjoyed. But it was something she was expected to do because she was a woman and her husband was rich.

Breathing in the summer morning, she wondered if it would be tacky to buy a pretzel from the man on the corner. Surely it wouldn't be as bad for her figure as one of her father's tasty guglhuph cakes made with heaps of butter and eggs and raisins and almonds and sweet cherry juice.

Yum.

Good Lord, she thought as she stepped off the curb when the signal changed, when was the last time she'd thought about that? When was the last time she'd thought of her mother, who'd died, and her father, who'd closed up his shop and returned to his homeland and had been so brokenhearted he'd died the next year? Was that kind of devotion a thing of the past?

If Neal died tomorrow, she'd be sad for a while, but she'd carry on. Wouldn't she?

If she died, there would probably be a quick string of ladies willing to jump to his side, eager, even, to do things like go to the big dinner tomorrow that she couldn't, wouldn't make.

A tingle of guilt was swept away by a hot flash. She bypassed the pretzel man and kept walking.

When she reached the hotel, Alice realized she couldn't very well march through the brass-trimmed revolving doors in the tan polyester and sneakers. She turned onto the cross street and studied the building. She spotted a loading dock and an open door. Quickly, she darted inside.

"Wella beetcha moloro," a man suddenly shouted, or at least that's what his words sounded like to her.

She turned, flashed a smile, pointed to her watch. "I'm late," she responded. "I don't want to get fired."

He shrugged, waved her off, and turned away.

Alice walked quickly to another door at the rear of the dock. She turned the handle. It opened easily. So much for security.

Breathing again, she looked around. She was inside a long, gray corridor that looked like the basement Poppy had described. All she needed was to find a service elevator. If she could get to the fourth floor, maybe she could find the housekeeper who took care of room 402.

Then, maybe later, she'd drive to the Lower East Side and buy a guglhuph or two. Neal might enjoy one while she was away.

Elinor was in coach because she did not want to call attention to herself. It had seemed like a good idea when she'd made the reservations. She'd forgotten, however, about the infamous middle seats, and wouldn't you know, that's what she'd been given, between a heavyset man who smelled like a turnip and a girl who looked ten or eleven.

She reminded herself it would only be for four hours and it would be worth it to seem ordinary. One of the crowd. Not Elinor Harding Young, Washington socialite turned slut-on-the-run.

She shivered. Thankfully, she'd brought her noise-canceling headphones. She put them on now and wished it was as easy to do away with what Carly Simon had once called the noise going on in her mind.

* * *

Yolanda had finished her third color of the day when her cell phone danced to "Chilito Lindo." The peppy tune had been a favorite of hers when she was growing up, and now it made her think of her daughter, Belita, whom she hoped would be spicy and confident, with a great zest for life.

It was Manny.

"What are you doing?"

"It's Wednesday. I'm working."

"Oh."

"What about you? Did you win the lottery and now you're retired?"

"Very funny. I need to talk to you about your friends."

"You talked enough yesterday. You scared them sufficiently."

"Are you sure?"

Yolanda glanced up as Rhonda Gagne sashayed into the shop carrying Lady, her Chinese crested dog, who was hairless except for a few tufts of white fur. "Manuel, what do you really want? I am busy."

He sighed. She hated when her brother sighed; it made her feel like such a little sister. "The ransom note," he said. "I want to see it."

Turning from Mrs. Gagne and the pooch, Yolanda replied, "I can't."

"Of course you can. Get it from Elinor."

"I can't," she repeated. "I'm busy."

"Yo, please. If the letters are as colorful as you say, they were probably cut out of magazines. If I can take a look, I might be able to figure out which magazines."

"And that will prove what?"

"I won't know until I see it." He sighed again.

"Manuel," she said, glancing back at her customer. "I have

clients in the shop. Can we discuss this later?" She had a lengthy break before her next customer once the Gagnes were groomed.

"I have to work later."

"And I'm working *now*." Mrs. Gagne had made herself at home on the leather spa chair. She'd slid off her sandals and placed her feet in the whirlpool as if Yolanda had already turned on the sudsy warm water, which she had not. Lady was perched on Mrs. Gagne's lap, probably aware that after her mistress's pedicure, Yolanda would give her one, too. Sometimes, Yolanda thought, she should have stayed in the Bronx.

"If you can get it today, I'll make sure Junior takes you to dinner."

Junior again. Manny was trying to be funny, but Yolanda didn't laugh. She'd heard her brother's plea since before Vincent had come and gone: Junior Diaz had served with Manny in the army and now taught high school history. But Yolanda did not want a Spanish man. She'd come too far from the neighborhood for that.

She leveled her voice. "Manuel, I am going to hang up now." And so she did.

"Yolanda, dear," Mrs. Gagne cooed from the spa chair. "Is there a new man in your life?"

Wouldn't Rhonda love to be the first to spread the news that Vincent DeLano's widow had found a new man—this time, one of her own kind.

Yolanda quickly reminded herself that Rhonda Gagne—and her friends, and their friends—paid big New York dollars for their nails and their hair, dollars that went directly into Belita's education fund and Yolanda's 401(k).

She smiled. "Oh, no, Mrs. Gagne, that man on the phone is my brother. I don't bother with the rest of them."

The woman nodded and fluffed Lady's tufts. "A wise decision, my dear. It's amazing the world has lasted this long with men still walking around."

Yolanda turned on the warm water and poured in the suds. She didn't say that what was truly amazing was that Mrs. Gagne's CEO husband headed an insurance firm on the Fortune 100, and she seemed to enjoy that side of him.

She snapped on the water jets and handed the woman the latest *Town & Country*. Glancing down at the elegant cover that pictured a home of museum proportions covered by teasers for articles within, she wondered if Manny could really learn something from the cut-out letters on the note and if Elinor would still be home after the woman and Lady were groomed.

Twenty-five

Alice made it to the fourth floor of the Lord Winslow without being detected. She stopped by a mirror on the wall near the elevator, primped her hair, checked her lipstick, straightened the tan polyester. Aside from the delayed sex with Leonard, in her younger years Alice never would have dreamed of doing anything sneaky, immoral, or certainly illegal.

Good Lord, she thought with a grim little smile, *I'm glad those days are over.*

She pranced down the hall in search of room 402 and the housekeeping cart. In addition to tracking Elinor's belongings, she'd already decided to do a bit more investigating. How she'd love to learn the name of Elinor's lover!

She'd start with the woman who'd cleaned the room after

Elinor's tryst. Housekeepers noticed things, didn't they? The way the cleaning ladies in Mount Kasteel knew the families they worked for, the way the Yolandas of the world knew intimacies reserved for the moments when their clientele bared their souls along with their roots.

If Yolanda's brother was right—and Alice feared he might be—Alice, Poppy, CJ, and even Yolanda might be in danger simply for butting in. But weren't they entitled to know the whole story if their very lives were at risk?

Elinor must have dumped her lover.

Why else wasn't he involved with the search?

Was he married?

Maybe he was the one doing the blackmailing, a gigolo only after her money.

Had she met him on the Internet?

Was it someone the rest of them knew, not counting Duane?

"Hey, you!"

Uh-oh.

Alice made an attempt at a game face. She turned. "Me?" She faced a young Asian woman who wore a dress that matched the one she had on.

"You late."

Again, Alice tapped her watch. She hoped the woman didn't notice it was a Chopard with seven floating diamonds and a white diamond face. It had been a gift from Neal on their twenty-fifth anniversary before Kiley Kate had started singing and Alice had started doing the rest. "I am not late. You early."

The young woman crinkled her forehead. "You start?"

"No! Where is cart? Where are sheets? Where are towels?" It was all Alice could think of to say.

"Towels," the woman said. "Yes. I have key."

Alice had no idea what she'd do if another housekeeper showed up and staked a claim. "We start in room four-o-two," Alice said as she followed the woman to a closet marked Housekeeping.

"Four-o-six."

"Four-o-two."

The woman shook her head rapidly as she unlocked the door and pulled out a cart heaped with linens and buckets of tiny soaps and shampoos. "Four-o-two occupied. Do not disturb."

"But it's almost noon. Who doesn't 'disturb' by noon?"

The small shoulders shrugged. She pointed to the doorway across the hall. A red and white Do Not Disturb sign dangled from the handle on the door marked 402. The room where Elinor had done what she'd done with whomever she'd done it with.

The woman wheeled the cart from the closet with a swift, practiced move, then started quickly down the hall.

"Wait!" Alice called after her. "I must ask you something."

"You late," the woman muttered again. "We start in four-o-six."

Alice caught up to her fashion companion. "Please. Tell me one thing. Do you always clean room four-o-two? Did you clean it last Friday?"

The cart came to a stop. "What?"

"Last Friday. Did you clean room four-o-two?"

"I no work Friday. I work Sunday, Monday, Tuesday, and Wednesday. No Friday."

"Who worked this floor Friday?"

The scowl returned. "Old lady like you. She here Thurs-

day, Friday, Saturday, when big people come. Not me. I work
Sunday, Monday . . ."

Alice grunted at the "old lady" comment. "Big people?
What big people?" Did she mean big in size?

"Important people. Movie stars."

Movie stars? Alice doubted that Elinor would appeal to
Clooney or Pitt.

"Like who?"

"I don't know names. I work. You work now. You late."

"Right," Alice said. She sensed this was hopeless. The conversation, the dress, the espionage. Maybe the real reason
Elinor wouldn't reveal the name of her lover was that he was
someone she was ashamed of. A Donald in Dallas. A Parker
in San Jose. Someone not worth Alice's time or attention. She
retreated down the hall toward the staircase.

"Hey, you! Where you go?"

"Home," Alice said, without looking back. "Have a nice day."

Finally the damn plane was off the ground. Elinor pulled in her
arms, closed her eyes, and tried to focus on other tedious events
that had lasted four hours and she'd managed to survive.

The implants she'd had done on her molars.

The colonoscopy her doctor had insisted on because she'd
had one of *those* issues.

Father's funeral, of course. They'd lumped the calling hours
and the funeral into one painful morning in order to be done
with the ritual once and for all.

There had been so many people. Faculty, administrators,
students who'd been helped by his public grandiosity over
so many years. There had been parents, mostly mothers, as
the fathers were either working or off playing golf. There

were mountains of flowers, many fresh-cut from the cottage gardens around Lake Kasteel. There were tedious speeches. There was crying. There was the announcement of the Franklin Harding Memorial Library on the grounds of the school he'd lorded over.

Four hours at least. Then it had been done.

With Remy, she never had enough time. An hour and a half was the longest "date" she'd been allowed. She knew, because she'd kept track. She'd kept track of everything: dates, times, locations. She'd even taken a few souvenirs: a fork from the vice president's residence that she might give Poppy one day; a monogrammed hand towel from his private bath; a Cuban cigar from the humidor in his office.

Even at the Lord Winslow she'd only been given an hour of his time in room 402, always 402.

She'd never been trashy enough to keep his DNA in any La Perlas. She wondered if that made her a fool.

The large man beside her slouched toward her now. She angled her spine toward the child and checked her watch. Twelve minutes had passed. Three hours and forty-eight until they would land.

Poppy sat with the four-way flashers flashing. She'd moved to the driver's side, bound her fingers around the steering wheel until her knuckles had paled, and stared into the rearview mirror until she saw little flecks of light. Both the engine and the air-conditioning were running in preparation for the get-away if it needed to be quick.

Ha! As if she could step on it if the situation arose. As if she could maneuver this big boat through Manhattan traffic.

Sheesh.

"Come on, Alice," she whimpered to the rearview. "Make it snappy."

She would have thought Alice might have known she was frightened of the police. It was, after all, part of why she'd continued with this charade. Elinor had sounded believable enough about barely knowing Duane, but, still, he could be behind the blackmail, he was so good at conniving. And if he was, Poppy wanted to know before the police were involved. She wanted to confront him, throw him out, *something!* before the police knocked on their door.

With questions.

And scrutiny.

And reading all those rights.

Yolanda's brother was a police officer, but somehow, he was different. For one thing, he didn't wear a uniform. For another, he really was cute.

Poppy smiled.

Then she blinked. She reminded herself that every time she'd thought a man was kind of cute she'd wound up marrying the louse.

Rap, rap, rap.

She nearly jumped out of her freckles. Without turning her head, she rolled her eyes to the window. Naturally, it was a police officer. He wore a uniform and was not cute like Manny. Her heart started racing.

His knuckles *rap, rapped* again.

She sucked in her breath, said a small, "Oh, Momma, help me, please," and located the button that put the window down.

"Is everything all right, ma'am?"

He had funny-looking teeth, and she couldn't see his eyes through his dark sunglasses.

"Yes," she answered. "I'm just waiting for the tow truck."

"You need a tow?"

She nodded. "Yes, the battery went dead." As soon as she said it, she knew she was in trouble.

He leaned closer to the window. "Sounds fine to me. Looks like you're up and running, air conditioner, included."

"I am?" she asked. "Oh! So I am! Well, thank you, Officer."

She tried to close the window, but he reached in and stopped her. "I need to see your license and registration."

Her license? Did she have her driver's license? And the registration? Where on earth would Alice keep the registration? Poppy fumbled with the Miu Miu—why had she changed back to her big bag at Momma's? And, oh, no! She hadn't left any trinkets in there, had she?

She started to cry.

"Ma'am," the police officer said, "have you been drinking this morning?"

"Drinking? What? Good heavens. It's not even noon!" She fumbled some more.

"I need to ask you to get out of the car."

Poppy froze.

"Now, please, ma'am."

She felt the blood drain from her face the way it always did just before she fainted. Then she heard a familiar voice.

"Excuse me, Officer. Is something wrong?" It was Alice. Dear God, it was Alice. Poppy unbuckled the seat belt and scrambled over the console to the passenger's side.

"I told her to keep driving around the block while I ran an errand. Poppy?" she asked as she leaned past the policeman and poked her head into the car, "didn't I tell you to keep driving?"

"I'm sorry," was all Poppy could manage to say. "I was frightened I'd get lost."

"She doesn't come into the city very often," Alice calmly explained.

"Is this your vehicle?"

"Yes. Would you like to see my registration?"

"No, that's fine. But please get in and move along. Parking is illegal here."

"Thank you, Officer." Alice got in, buckled up, and turned off the four-ways. She cast a side look at Poppy, then pulled into traffic without saying a word.

Twenty-six

When CJ awoke on Malcolm's bed, the odd thing was that she hadn't dreamed about him but about her ex-husband, Cooper. The truth was, she did that often. Throughout the day, the man in her thoughts was usually Malcolm. But during the night, her world belonged to Cooper.

That time they'd been on the ice rink in Central Park, skating to "Lara's Theme," as if they'd been atop a music box, the lights of the Manhattan skyline shimmering against the slate-colored sky.

"What do you want for Christmas?" Cooper had asked as they glided together, hand in hand, like teenagers on a first date. They'd been that-kind-of-comfortable since the beginning: every day sweet and nice, every day a first date.

"I want a rose-colored silk dress to paint for the premiere of your play."

He laughed. "I'll buy you whatever color you'd like. Now ask what I want."

"What do you want?"

"A baby."

"A baby?"

"A son. Or a daughter." His leather gloves squeezed tightly against her thick mittens. The pace grew faster, the music louder, chiming, chiming . . .

CJ woke up.

In a strange room.

On a bed.

Malcolm's bed.

She checked the clock; it was just past noon.

Chimes sounded again. One, two, soft and muted, tuneful and . . .

Oh, my God, she thought, leaping from the bed. *The doorbell is ringing!* The doorbell was ringing and there she was on Malcolm's bed.

She raced from his cozy room, through the master bedroom and out into the hall, pushing her thoughts from Cooper, back to Malcolm, back to Elinor. She prayed it wasn't Janice or even a housekeeper who'd forgotten a key. She'd be mortified if anyone found out she'd been sleeping where she'd been sleeping.

Oh, God, she thought again as she swung around the corner and spiraled down the stairs. *I didn't smooth the comforter or close the door behind me.*

She assured herself that it wouldn't matter if the blackmailer was the one at the door.

It was not the blackmailer; it was Yolanda. Her little girl was perched on her hip.

"Surprise," Yolanda said, which was, of course, an understatement. "Is Elinor here?"

"No," CJ replied as she drooped against the door and tried to catch her breath. "You missed her. She's gone to gather the ransom."

"Did she hear anything?"

"He called. She said she was getting the money."

"Rats."

"Rats," the little girl repeated.

CJ smiled. She wished she could remember the child's name. Then she noticed a look of concern on Yolanda's face. "What's wrong?"

"Well, nothing. I guess it can wait."

"Why don't you come in? I could make tea. Or find something for lunch?"

"I've only come for the note. The ransom note. Do you know where it is?"

Elinor hadn't shown CJ the note or told her where it was. For all CJ knew, Elinor had burned it after Jonas had found it. It was what CJ would have done.

They went into the morning room. Yolanda explained what her brother had said—that if he had the note, he might be able to figure out where the letters had come from.

"And then what?" CJ asked.

"And then, I don't know. He said it would be a good place to start."

"I thought he wasn't going to get involved."

"He thinks Poppy's cute."

"Oh, dear."

"I told him she's married. But my brother is a romantic. For years he's been trying to set me up with a friend of his from the army."

"And?"

"And nothing. I don't need a man."

CJ was about to say she understood when the doorbell rang again. "Good grief," she said. "Excuse me."

This time it was Poppy. And Alice, dressed up like the housekeeper.

"How did it go?" CJ asked. Alice said she'd explain everything if she could first have a glass of iced tea. With piles of ice.

They repaired to the morning room, where Yolanda waited. Her daughter greeted them with a happy squeal.

"Did either of you see the note?" CJ asked as she poured glasses of tea and sat down at the table with them.

"No," they said in unison. "Did you?"

CJ shook her head. "Manny thinks it might provide a clue."

"Manny?" Poppy asked, looking at Yolanda. "Your brother? He's cute."

CJ looked at Yolanda, who looked back at CJ, and CJ thought, *Oh, dear*, again but kept it to herself.

"She probably got rid of it. Or took it with her," Alice said.

"Or she left it here," Yolanda commented.

"In a safe," Alice added.

"Or in her nightstand," Poppy said. "That's where I put important things. Duane would never think to look there for anything."

No one questioned why Poppy felt a need to hide things from her husband.

"Well," Alice said, "we can't very well start going through her belongings. We'll have to wait until she gets back."

CJ thought about the master bedroom, where Elinor's nightstand was. She thought about the open door to Malcolm's room, and the rumpled comforter she'd left. "I can look around a little." It was better to offer than have one of them jump up and go scouting.

"She wouldn't mind if you did."

"You're her twin sister, after all."

"And it might be helpful," Yolanda said, "if you can find it."

"Fine," CJ said. "I'll look."

They sat another moment in curious silence, spritzing lemon, stirring in sugar. Then Poppy said, "When?"

"When, what?" CJ said.

"When are you going to look?"

"Oh, well. I don't know. Later." She didn't add, *"When I'm alone."*

"You could start now," Poppy said. "If you go try on the dress."

"The dress?"

Alice cleared her throat. Then she launched into the story of the housekeeper who didn't work on Thursday, Friday, Saturday, when the movie stars were there.

CJ couldn't follow everything, though Alice was quite clear when she said, "You need to dress up like the housekeeper and go back to the hotel tomorrow. You need to find the maid who cleaned the room and ask her what she knows."

"Me?"

"I'll be in Orlando."

"But I have to stay at the house."

"Poppy can house-sit in case the blackmailer calls. This is important."

"I'll have to go by myself?"

"Yes. And you'll need to find a garage a few blocks from the hotel. No sense letting anyone see that you have your own transportation." Apparently they did not think it made a difference that CJ drove an old Saab, not a Mercedes.

"But we agreed it would be risky because I look like Elinor," she said.

Alice shook her head. "Yolanda can get you a wig like she got Poppy." Yolanda nodded. "Yolanda, can you take a tuck or two in the dress right now? CJ can go to Elinor's bedroom and try it on. Maybe Elinor keeps a sewing kit in a nightstand next to her bed."

CJ knew very well what Alice was getting at, but she agreed anyway. "Wait here," she said. "I'll get you something to wear, and I'll try on the dress." As long as the rest of them stayed downstairs, CJ would agree to almost anything.

By the time Alice drove Poppy home, Poppy was too tired to care that the white Lexus still sat in the driveway. CJ hadn't found the note in the nightstand or anywhere else, so there would be no clues or fingerprints—like Duane's, for instance.

Which was good, because right now, all Poppy wanted was to get out of yesterday's clothes, whether her husband was being a jackass or not.

"Do you want me to go in with you?" Alice asked.

"No," Poppy said. "I'm sick of being scared." She gave quick air kisses to Alice and wished her good luck in Orlando, wondering if Alice knew that Poppy envied her, with her nice, normal family, and play dates with her granddaughter filled with glitter and sequins.

She marched through the garage and into the house. She said hello to Nola, who was scrubbing the kitchen, then asked if she knew where the *mister* was.

"I brought lunch into the study. For him and that other man."

Man?

"Duane has a guest?" Poppy asked, trying to feign surprise. "Who?"

Nola shrugged her shoulders and returned to her mop and pail. "Mr. Duane said the man is his brother. I didn't know that he had one."

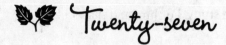 *Twenty-seven*

On her way to the study, Poppy stopped in the powder room and tried to look better than she felt.

Duane's brother?

The one who'd bankrupted the family silver mine?

Her light blue eyes reflected perplexity. Had Duane ever mentioned his brother's name?

At least it isn't a woman, she reminded herself. At least it wasn't a harlot that Duane had brought home to mock their marriage and force Poppy into making a decision she would rather put off because divorce was so unpleasant and who had time for that?

At least it wasn't a conspirator in blackmail.

It was his *brother,* for crying out loud.

Rearranging her hair as best she could, she wondered if

she'd been too hard on Duane. She dabbed on lipstick and pinched her cheeks. She wished she could take a shower and change her clothes before meeting her brother-in-law.

She wondered if he'd be as nice as Yolanda's brother.

She smiled again and put both hands in her pockets. Then she touched something with her right hand. She pulled out the card. Manny's card.

Detective Manuel Valdes.

Twelfth precinct.

Brooklyn, New York.

A shiver shivered through her. She shoved the card back in her pocket, hoping she'd remember to remove it before sending the jeans to the laundry. Not that she'd ever use it. Not that she needed a cop in her life.

"Duane?" Poppy called from the doorway into the study. "Darling, I'm home. I didn't know we had company." She slowly crossed the rosewood floor to where the two men sat facing one another, on opposite sides of the big desk. A pile of papers was strewn over the top.

Politely, the men stood in unison.

"Poppy," Duane said, "my lovely bride. We missed you last night."

She slow-blinked her lashes, a reaction to being called lovely. "Momma had a spell. I fell asleep, and then it was too late to call."

"Oh, poor Momma. How is she today?"

He had always acted as if he liked her mother, though Momma said he knew she could see right through him. "She's better. Now please, introduce me to our guest."

The visitor stepped forward and offered his hand. "Fred

Manley. Duane's brother." He was older than Duane and had weathered, too-much-sun skin. The resemblance, however, was striking, though instead of a polo shirt, he had on denim, and instead of Ralph Lauren pants, he wore washed-out jeans. Oh, yes, and he had on a belt with a big silver buckle. And leather-tooled cowboy boots on his feet.

"Well, well," Poppy said as he took her hand and kissed it with dry lips. "I guess it's time that we met."

"If I'd have known how pretty you are, I wouldn't have wasted all these years."

He apparently had the gift of sweet talk, like Duane. She wondered what Momma would have to say about that. "So," Poppy asked, retrieving her hand, "to what do we finally owe the pleasure?"

Duane folded his arms and puffed out his cheeks. "Fred has a plan to reopen the mine."

"The silver mine?"

"Yes," Fred said. "And I've brought you a small gift."

He picked up a square of black velvet that sat on the desk. He folded back the corners and offered it to Poppy. Nested atop the velvet were several pieces of gleaming silver. Uncut, unstamped, glorious silver.

If Momma had been there, she'd have just died.

"Do you like it?" Duane asked. "I told Fred how much you love silver."

If he was being sarcastic about what he called the family's "eccentricity," she decided to ignore it. "Well," Poppy said, "it is lovely, isn't it?"

"And there's plenty more where that came from," he said. "I've had my men out there looking. They found a huge vein.

All I need is to convince my little brother here to come home and give me a hand."

Home? Was he asking them to move to Nevada?

"Whoa," Duane said. "We have a few other matters to discuss first. Like logistics, brother Fred. I mean, Poppy and I live here in New York. I have no intention of pulling up stakes and going away from poor Momma. Especially now that the spells are back."

Had he moved from sarcasm to being condescending? She'd never been good at deciphering Duane. "Duane's right," she said with caution. "I couldn't leave Momma now." Her gaze fell back to the pretty pieces of silver.

"No problem. After things are up and running, we'll have enough cash flow for you to rent a jet. You can come back and forth on weekends. Once we have a strong workforce, once a month ought to do it."

In spite of the buckle and the boots, Fred seemed rather sensible. And if Duane was out of town more than he was in, Poppy would have a chance to think. After all, womanizing was one thing, but the fact that she'd considered her husband capable of blackmail was quite another. Besides, wouldn't a long-distance marriage be easier to manage than a troublesome, costly divorce? In the interim, maybe Duane would change?

She asked the men to please sit, then she made herself comfortable in the tall wing chair next to her brother-in-law. "Tell me your plans," she said, folding her hands neatly in her lap. "Maybe we could work out the travel arrangements."

"There are other arrangements we need to talk about, too," Fred said.

"He's talking about capital expenses," Duane said. "Start-up funds. You know."

She supposed she'd asked for that. She supposed he would have expected her to be naïve, to never imagine that the whole plan was contingent upon her money. The comfort she'd felt took a decided turn, as Momma would say.

"Really?" she asked, aware of the chill that had crept into her tone. "How much do you need?"

"Only five hundred thousand," Duane's brother replied. "Half a million ought to do it."

Twenty-eight

Alice stopped at the deli on her way home and picked up Neal's favorite for dinner. Since the kids had been out of the house and Neal was often late getting home, she'd seen little point in retaining a cook. For the nights they didn't dine out, she kept the refrigerator stocked with pre-pared things from Whole Foods. But when she was taking Kiley Kate out of town, she made sure to prepare a special meal. Tonight her guilt was called lamb chops.

She rinsed off fresh mint leaves and patted them dry. After three calls from Kiley Kate—should she wear the pink rib-bons to match the pink sequins, would there be time for Sea World, should she bring the mousse to give her more curls, or the gel to straighten them out?—Alice went upstairs to shower and pack. By the time Neal came home, she'd be calm and collected, perhaps even cool. Maybe they'd even make love tonight. She was pretty sure it had been a long time.

Poppy knew she had to go to the police. She retreated to the bedroom after the revelation that Duane's brother was on the hunt for a half million dollars. She locked the door and tried taking a nap, but she couldn't keep her eyes closed. Instead, she soaked in the Jacuzzi for over an hour with only one thought:

Do they think I'm stupid?

She reminded herself that Duane and his brother didn't know that she knew about Elinor and the panties and the ransom for the exact same amount. She reminded herself that the one consolation might be that they'd chosen to blackmail her friend instead of her. Clever Duane wouldn't want to upset his cash cow, whom, he probably figured, he could keep milking until death did they part.

Why had she ever trusted him?

When the water turned cold, Poppy shivered again. She got out of the tub, wrapped a thick robe around her, and went back to the bedroom. She sat on the edge of the bed by her nightstand. Then she opened the drawer and took out the picture of her father and her on the front porch swing. She remembered the creak of the old wooden slats that hung from the long metal chains. She remembered the scent of her father's pipe tobacco, the crinkle of the starch in his shirt, the warmth of his arm that encircled her. She remembered those things, and that she was loved. Her wonderful father, the only man who'd ever looked out for her, who'd ever looked out for Momma.

She held the picture to her chest and stayed very still, too sad to cry, too lonely to even bother with self-pity.

After a while, Poppy was ready.

She dressed in a cream-colored sundress and added a pretty pale orange shawl that CJ had painted and Poppy had insisted on buying when CJ had first been starting out on her own. Though she'd always considered Elinor and CJ just like her, Poppy knew that they hadn't been raised with the same financial perks. As much of a town leader as Mr. Harding had been, he'd still been a schoolmaster, with not much of a financial legacy. Unlike Elinor, CJ had not married smartly, and when that had ended . . .

But why was Poppy thinking about that now, as she stood in the mirror adjusting the shawl?

With a small sigh, she picked up the Miu Miu, which held clean underthings, a skirt and a top, and other essentials she'd need overnight. She double-checked to be sure she'd put Manny's card in the small zippered pocket. She'd call him from the car. Once she'd done that, Poppy knew she couldn't go home again until Duane and his brother were gone.

Elinor did not want to order room service for dinner. She'd been closed in on the plane, stuffed into a taxi, and sitting in her hotel room for two hours. Elinor detested being alone. She blamed CJ for that; she hadn't, after all, even been alone in the womb. For some reason, CJ never minded solitude. Another way that the twins weren't exactly identical.

Elinor marched into the open-air dining room and asked for a table for one.

"In the front," she requested. That way she could gaze at the people strolling on the sidewalk and maybe not feel as alone.

She ordered a dirty martini (not for its taste, but because she'd recently read that olive juice was good for the skin) and a pineapple shrimp dish. She turned her attention to the happy tourists in their plastic sandals and hibiscus-print shirts, with their digital cameras dangling from their necks. Halfway through her martini, Elinor realized she was being watched, too.

CJ decided that reading would be a good distraction from all the nonsense created by her sister. She brought the cordless to the guest room at the top of the back stairs and went into the bedroom that she'd thought was too small. She changed into old sweats and a T-shirt, then sat in the wing chair with her feet on the footstool in order to avoid dozing again. She opened the book and began to read.

An hour or so later she got into bed and napped after all.

She woke up—no dreams this time—and realized the light in the room had changed from late afternoon to pale dusk. As enticing as it might seem, she decided she couldn't very well stay in bed until Elinor came home on Friday.

She could make dinner. Yes, that's what she'd do.

She'd make something elaborate that would take a long time.

She'd pour a small glass of wine and sip while she was cooking.

She'd turn on the news like a civilized American.

She'd call Kevin to check up on Luna.

Maybe she'd call Elinor to see if her cell worked.

Yes, there was plenty to do so she wouldn't be tempted to return to Malcolm's room, to Malcolm's bed.

Running her hand through her knotted hair, CJ grabbed the cordless and trundled downstairs. She scooted into the kitchen and halted abruptly.

There, at the sink, stood Malcolm.

Twenty-nine

"CJ?"

"Mac?" She hated that she'd called him Mac and not Malcolm. She hadn't called him Mac to his face since, well, since *then*.

He laughed a small laugh. "Fancy meeting you here. In my kitchen."

"I . . . I was upstairs. Asleep." She wanted to comb her hair the right way. She wanted to brush her teeth. She wanted to put on the things she'd left behind . . the batik with the matching shrug, the capris, the cropped top. She wanted to thank God that as soon as she'd gone to Elinor's bedroom to try on the housekeeper's dress, she'd ducked into Mac's room, straightened the comforter, closed the door.

"Is Elinor here?" He never referred to E as his wife, not to CJ anyway.

CJ shook her head. "She had a crisis with the dress for the party. Her seamstress is in Philadelphia."

He raised an eyebrow. "Philadelphia?"

"I don't think she expected you here."

There was silence a moment. That's when CJ noticed he had one hand on a wine bottle that sat on the counter.

"Wine?" he asked.

"Sure." She hoped she sounded nonchalant.

He retrieved another glass from the cabinet and filled both halfway. He handed her one.

"Cheers," he said.

She smiled and sipped. Then she realized he hadn't asked why she was there. "My decorators," she suddenly said.

"What?"

"I'm having the house painted. Elinor said I could come here because of the paint smells. You know what that's like."

"Sure," he said, asking no more explanation. "When is she coming back?"

CJ wished she could take out a bowl and some salad greens. It would give her something to do while she stumbled over the lie. But it was his kitchen, not hers, so she stood in one place and drank from her glass. "Tomorrow."

"That must be some crisis."

She nodded. "I guess." She couldn't very well have said Elinor wouldn't be home until Friday. Let her sister deal with her husband on that.

"So," Malcolm said. "We're alone then?"

They'd known each other nearly thirty years. They'd

shared, well, everything once. Almost everything. She still thought about him more than she should. And now she didn't know what to say. "Janice was here earlier."

"I know. She's back in Washington now. She's having a problem with her job. She tried talking to her mother, but you know how well they get along."

Or, rather, don't *get along,* CJ thought. The same way E had often argued with Father, parent and child, too much alike.

"So that's why I came. To talk to Elinor about Janice."

"Well," CJ said, "it's too bad you missed her." She sipped her wine again, trying to avoid Malcolm's eyes. He looked tired. His hair had more gray than the last time she'd seen him; his shoulders were a little slumped.

"We could sit down," he said.

"Or I could make a salad. You could turn on the news." She supposed that sounded odd, but in the moment, it was the best she could do.

"Sure," he replied. "That would be good."

He moved toward the dining area and clicked on the television. CJ opened the refrigerator and pulled out the drawer to the vegetable crisper. And soon they were like an old married couple, saved from conversation by CNN and romaine.

At another time, in another place, Elinor might have been flattered. She might even have been tempted to do God-only-knew-what. After all, the man was not unattractive.

Toying with her martini, Elinor tried to casually study him without being noticed.

He was tall with dark hair. From where she sat to where he sat, she could not tell if his eyes were dark or light. He was young—well, younger than she was. In his mid- to late thirties. A black tank top clung to his rippled abs and curved around well-sculpted arms.

Like Elinor, he was alone.

And he kept looking at her.

She turned her gaze back to the sidewalk, to the colorful paper lanterns that lined the street, to the thatched kiosks with the racks of coconut tchotchkes and bountiful beads and T-shirts in shades of tropical fruits. She had chosen to stay at the Cayman Cabana instead of a downtown or beachfront hotel for the same reason she had flown coach: no one would suspect Elinor Harding Young to mingle with the middle-class, straw-tote-bag set.

Tomorrow morning she'd get a cab. Even then, she wouldn't ask to be driven straight to the bank. She'd already studied the booklet of attractions that was displayed on the rattan table in her room. She'd decided to ask the driver to bring her to the shopping district in George Town. No one would question why a woman was alone if she wanted to shop.

The pineapple shrimp arrived and she said no to a second martini. As much as she would have enjoyed its glow, she could not trust herself while that man sat three tables away.

Picking at the shrimp, she wondered if she'd ever been this damn scared in her life.

Maybe she should call Mac. Tell him what happened. Tell him the truth. Would he be her savior, or would he divorce her? After all these years of marriage, why didn't she know?

Because of CJ, of course. Because of the fire that Father had started between them, then he'd gone and died and left Elinor to deal with the ashes.

Maybe she should call Remy. Ask him what to do. But would he dismiss her as a hysterical woman, no longer worthy of his love?

Love? Ha ha.

"Excuse me."

Elinor pulled her eyes from the sidewalk.

He was standing beside her, the muscle man from three tables over. He held a drink in each hand.

"I hate eating alone. Can I bribe you with a martini?"

She looked at the angle of his jawline, the thickness of his neck. She noticed his eyes were brown, liquid brown. His lips were just full enough to be quite inviting, his black jeans just tight enough to hint at stimulation of the very best kind.

Pushing back her chair, Elinor stood up. She was close enough now to feel his heat. She plucked the glass from his hand, then set it on the table. "You're welcome to sit here, but I'm afraid I can't join you. It's been a long day, and I must meet my husband."

She picked up her bag and exited the restaurant, aware that she'd barely touched the pineapple shrimp and would be hungry by morning.

It might have seemed like a chicken thing to do, but Poppy didn't much care. She went downstairs, slipped past the study, and breezed through the kitchen on her way out the door.

"Tell my husband I've gone to the club and didn't want to interrupt him," she said to Nola, who was emptying the dishwasher.

"Then you'll see him there. He went with his brother. He said you might be sleeping and I shouldn't disturb you."

* * *

When she arrived in Momma's driveway, Poppy called Manny. She supposed she'd reach his voice mail, but she wanted to let him know she'd like to see him in the morning. That way she couldn't back out.

"Detective Valdes."

It wasn't his voice mail but his voice.

"Oh," Poppy said. "Oh, dear, is this Manny?"

"Manuel Valdes, yes it is."

"Oh. Manny. Well, hello."

"Hello. Who is this, please?"

"Well, it's me," she said. "It's Veronica Landry, your sister's friend."

Silence.

"It's Poppy," she said. "The redhead."

He laughed, but it wasn't an unpleasant laugh. "Poppy. Right."

"I need to see you. On law enforcement business." She hadn't known what else to call it. "May I come to your police station tomorrow?"

"Sorry. I'm off duty tomorrow."

"Oh," she said again. "Well."

"How about Friday?"

By Friday she might have changed her mind, retreated into her Poppy, scared-little-girl mode. "No," she said, "Friday might be too late."

For a few seconds, Manny said nothing. Then he asked, "Where are you now?"

"In Mount Kasteel. At my mother's."

"Do you know how to get to Brooklyn?"

Poppy, of course, had no clue. But she did have one of those navigation things that Duane had made sure were installed in both of their cars so they "could always find one another," he'd said. More than once she'd thought it was really so he could find her when he needed an advance on his allowance. "If you give me an address, I can find it." At least she'd paid attention when Duane taught her how to use it.

Manny rattled off an address, then added, "I hope you like kids."

"Kids?"

"It's my house. I have three kids, and they can get pretty loud."

Poppy told herself it didn't matter that Manny had three kids and no doubt a wife. She was not going to do what she was going to do in order to win a man . . . or even to get a date. The truth was, he was the first police officer she'd known whom she felt she could trust. And it was high time she set a few things straight.

For her own sake.

For Elinor's sake.

For Momma's sake, too.

She went into Momma's house and did what she needed to do. Then she entered Manny's address into her car's navigation system and headed for Brooklyn, alone.

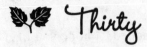 Thirty

A picture of the Virgin Mary hung over the television, which was tuned in to a program where people were dressed like they lived on a deserted island and were playing some sort of game. None of them appeared to have recently showered, and all were shouting.

Two boys (teenagers?) were sprawled in front of the television. One of them wore a sweatshirt with a hood pulled up over his head.

"Gentlemen," Manny said, "we have a visitor. A lady."

The boys hauled themselves to their oversized feet. They were both taller than Manny. They had dark hair and dark eyes and wide, sparkling smiles.

"This is my eldest, Enrico, and my youngest, Alejandro. Boys, this is Veronica."

They took turns shaking her hand and said, "Yo," or a version thereof. Manny said he also had a daughter, Marisa, who was at a friend's.

"They're twelve, thirteen, and fifteen," he said. "And their sole purpose in life is to drive me insane."

"That's right, dude," the eldest jested. "And don't you forget it."

The boys laughed and resumed their positions in front of the TV. Manny rolled his eyes and looked at Poppy. "I am blessed," he said, and she could tell that he meant it.

They returned to the narrow entry hall, where Manny picked up the large satchel she'd brought.

"Follow me," he said, and so she did, through a French door that, like the rest of the house, was framed in dark wood. "It's an old house," Manny said. "It's a little tired, but it's home."

She wondered what it was like for Manny's kids to have a father who lived under the same roof, a father who protected them, loved them, every day. For all the money Poppy's father had left Momma, it hadn't filled up the hole Poppy felt whenever she saw kids with their dad.

The room they went into was too small for the overstuffed sofa and the wide wooden desk and had the aura of a man. In place of end tables, there were stacks of magazines with book bags teetering on top. Manny grabbed a bunch of newspapers off the sofa and gestured for her to sit down. He moved to the other side of the desk and sat. Behind him was a wall-length bookcase that held more magazines, books, and a number of trophies, though Poppy couldn't make out what sport the little gold man on top played.

The trophies, however, reminded her of her satchel.

"So," he said, as if reading her thoughts. "To what do I owe the pleasure?"

She'd sat too far back on the cushiony couch, so she had to struggle to move forward to open her bag. "I think my husband is blackmailing my friend, Elinor, because he knows I'm a thief," she said. "Actually, at first I thought he was sleeping with her, too, but now I think it's just blackmail." She dipped into the satchel, surprised that her hands were not trembling. Then, one after another, extracted the trinkets. "This is from the Lord Winslow," she said, pulling out the call bell. "And this from the Waldorf, and this from the Plaza before it was turned into condos. That was a shame, don't you think?"

In less than a minute she had a dozen of Momma's treasures lined up on Manny's wooden desk.

"There are more back at Momma's," she said when she was finished. "Now you'll have to arrest me."

Manny cleared his throat and inspected the collection assembled before him. "Well," he said. "Before I arrest you, I'd like you to explain what this has to do with your friend and the half million dollars."

She adjusted her shawl and curled a few strands of hair. Then she took a long breath and launched into a full explanation of Duane and his brother and the old silver mine and the money they needed to get it going again.

"It's too much coincidence," she added.

Manny nodded. He was a nice man, she was sure she'd been right about that. She guessed his family was lucky to have him.

Then he said, "But Poppy, help me understand. Does your husband really think he can get away with the blackmail? These trinkets are pretty, but they're hardly worth five hundred thousand."

"Oh, they're just the beginning," Poppy replied. "He overheard me talking to Momma about our big secret one day, about how it was me, not Momma, who killed the gardener."

Manny didn't flinch or squirm or even look aghast. "What gardener?"

"It was a long time ago, but I killed him all right. Momma took the blame. She said he was peeping in the window. At me. Alice. Elinor. CJ."

"But he wasn't?"

"No. We'd been there earlier, but we'd gone down to the lake. He wasn't there then. By the time he arrived, he saw Momma. She was on the couch having sex with Mr. Harding, Elinor and CJ's father."

Poppy paused for a breath. Manny said nothing.

"I forgot my movie star magazine, so I went back to the cottage to get it. I saw Sam Yates peeping through the window. I came up behind him and saw what he saw. He was laughing and muttering something about his ticket 'straight to retirement.' Then he spotted me. He raised his rake and tried to hit me. But it got tangled up in my hair. I grabbed the pruning shears. I stabbed him in the back." Saying it out loud was not as difficult for Poppy as she'd once thought it would be. She'd never told a single, solitary soul, not even her therapist. Momma had made her promise; she'd said it was for Poppy's own good, that Momma would handle confinement much better than Poppy could.

Manny stayed silent.

"Don't you see?" Poppy asked. "Momma let them arrest her. She served five years in jail. Poor Momma!"

"And your husband heard all of this?"

"I told him he misunderstood. But he knows about these

little trinkets. And I think he also knows how to use other people's indiscretions to his advantage." There was no need to reveal that each time he had asked for more money, Poppy had been afraid to say no. "Don't you see?" she went on. "If he doesn't get what he wants now, he'll expose Elinor's secret. If you arrest him for blackmail, she should be safe."

"So it won't matter to you what he says about you?"

Poppy shook her head. "It's time I paid for my crimes. But Elinor doesn't deserve this. It's not like she killed anyone." She didn't add that Duane wouldn't even have known Elinor if Poppy had listened to Momma and not married him.

Alice waited in the kitchen until eleven o'clock, until the lamb chops had dried up and the fresh mint had wilted. It wasn't like Neal to be so late without calling.

Four times she had tried to reach him, but his BlackBerry had only connected to voice mail. She would have sent him a text, but she didn't know how. When Kiley Kate had tried to show her, Alice had pooh-poohed it. Texting was only for kids, wasn't it?

She poured another glass of club soda and wished it was wine. But she'd learned long ago that flying with a hangover was like stuffing one's head in a sock.

At 11:36, she heard the garage door go up. She stiffened her hold on her glass.

"I thought you'd been in an accident," she said coolly when her husband walked in. "I thought you were dead."

He laughed, dropping his briefcase on a tall chair at the breakfast bar. He loosened his tie. She detected the faint scent of bourbon.

"I thought you were gone," he said.

"Gone?"

"Where are you going this time? Phoenix? Orlando?"

"Orlando. But for heaven's sake, Neal, I'm not leaving until tomorrow."

"Oh," he replied and helped himself to her soda without asking.

"Have you had dinner?"

"Sliders at Max's." He took off his jacket and draped it over the chair. He'd pick it up later, Mr. Self-Sufficient.

"Alone?"

He laughed again. "No, Alice, I wasn't alone. I was with five women from the office who've been dying to fuck me. They drew straws tonight. They all won."

Neal was only crude when he'd had too much to drink or had played a good round of golf, which, for some reason, seemed linked to testosterone.

Alice stood up. "I'm going to bed."

"Aren't you going to ask me?"

"Ask you what?"

"If I've found a date for the dinner with Tang?"

"No, Neal, I'm not going to play games tonight. I'm tired and my flight leaves at ten."

He raised his right hand in a mock salute. But as she passed by him, Alice caught another aroma that smelled a lot like Bijon mixed in with the bourbon.

CJ slipped off to bed just before midnight. She'd waited until Mac was in his office, monitoring in real time the Asian pharmaceutical markets as Elinor once said he often did. Or, CJ suspected, he might have simply been waiting for her to retire, to avoid an awkward "Good night, CJ," "Good night, Malcolm" exchange.

She turned off the light and wondered if she could possibly sleep, what with her naps during the day and Mac in the house. She stared at the red digital numbers that read 12:13.

Sleep is the poor man's Prozac, Cooper had written in one of his plays. The line was delivered by a middle-aged woman who reluctantly contended with an elderly uncle who visited each afternoon and napped in the living room chair. After all, the old goat had money. The niece and her husband and their kids shaped their comings and goings—indeed, their lives— around Uncle Sol, turning up the volume on the remote to drown out his snoring, acknowledging to one another that some day it would be worth it. At the end of the third act, the poor man was dead. In his pocket was a diary, an amusing journal of daily observation about his niece and her husband and the kids who'd tolerated him in hopes of inheriting his money, of which, it turned out, he had none.

It was a comic tragedy on the human condition.

The play had been brilliantly written, had won several awards, and had been produced in many major locations around the country.

CJ had been so proud of her husband. They'd celebrated by making love each opening night in every city and town: Phoenix, Des Moines, Wichita.

She'd gotten pregnant in Albuquerque.

She tried not to think of what had followed. It had been so long since she'd felt loved.

The red digital numbers flipped to 1:00. CJ closed her eyes, then a moment later she heard the door handle turn.

She sensed a soft light spill in from the hall.

She tried to breathe normally, then wondered why she felt a need to avoid Mac.

Why . . . when Elinor had been cheating on him?

Why . . . when Elinor's charade involved so many others that she didn't seem to care if she hurt?

Why . . . when CJ deserved happiness, too. Didn't she?

She wanted to push back the covers and let Mac in. Let him into her bed and into her heart once again. But as CJ started to stir, the door gently closed, and he was gone.

 ## Thirty-one

Manny said he wasn't going to drag Poppy to the station in handcuffs. At that hour she'd have to share a cell with the hookers and junkies, and he said there was no need for that. She was a lady, after all.

He also said he couldn't put her under house arrest at his house because the kids would make her nuts. She suggested that his wife might keep them under control, and he countered by saying he didn't have one of those. Not anymore, anyway.

So instead of incarcerating her in Brooklyn, Manny drove Poppy upstate to New Falls, to Yolanda's.

He parked on Main Street. The shop stood in Victorian splendor in the quaint little hamlet where only the very rich once trod—until Yolanda had moved in with her shampoo and mousse. Manny had a key to the front door. They crept in quietly, so as not to awaken Yolanda or Belita, who were no doubt sleeping soundly upstairs. Inside, the only light spilled in from the streetlamps.

Poppy followed Manny past the pedicure spa chairs and the upright hair dryers and the sinks and the stylist booths. It reminded her of a time thirty years ago when she and Alice and Elinor and CJ had crept into the study that had been Poppy's father's but Momma had locked up the day he had died. It had been Elinor's idea.

"Maybe he left you a letter or a special present," Elinor had coaxed. She'd been reading a lot of Nancy Drew then, and she'd thought mysteries loomed everywhere.

So they'd crept in one night when Momma was out. The room had the same feel of trespass that Yolanda's did now, as if the lights would flash on at any moment, as if her father might leap from his leather-backed chair and scold her for breaking in.

But he hadn't leaped or scolded—not that she would have minded. Instead, the room was quiet and dusty and no longer smelled of his pipe tobacco, and Poppy retreated to her bedroom for days.

"Shit," Manny whispered now.

Poppy stopped tiptoeing. "What?"

"I don't have the key to the apartment upstairs."

"We could go up and knock."

"Her bedroom's in the back. Besides, I don't want to wake up Belita."

Poppy studied his silhouette. "Well then," she said, "you'll have to lock me up down here. I could use a manicure after all this commotion."

He laughed softly. "You're something, you know?"

Poppy didn't know how to respond.

"At least let's sit down so I can figure out what to do next."

They sat in twin chairs in front of a long mirror that reflected the streetlamps. Poppy's eyes grew accustomed to the dim light. It was, she thought, rather romantic.

"So," Manny said, "what shall I do with you, Miss Veronica?"

"You could kiss me," she heard herself say.

And so he did.

And she was surprised.

And it felt really nice.

And it felt really safe.

Elinor had shut her eyes hours ago, but she still hadn't fallen asleep. If she'd stayed at a five-star instead of a two-star, she could have ordered brandy from room service and drunk half a fifth and then fallen asleep.

As it was, the refreshments were confined to a small bottle of "spring-like" water that had been shipped in from the States.

When the sun finally rose, she decided to dress and go for a walk on the beach. There had been no word from CJ yesterday, no calls on her cell. No news, in this case, was simply no news. She had no delusions that the blackmailer would suddenly vanish.

Outside, the morning air was dry and already warm. She walked past the boarded-up vendor stalls, past a few tourists jogging; they must have been tourists—would islanders jog? Certainly not in new shorts and matching lycra tops. She wandered past a few delivery vans and a stray dog or two. She counted seven blocks to the beach.

The tide was high, which would make walking uncomfortable in the soft sand. Elinor found a big rock and sat down. She wanted to cry, but she dared not. There was too much to do to lose her cool now.

Pulling her cell phone from her pocket, she stared at the keypad. The blackmailer had called her on her cell. How had he found the number?

Then she had a thought.

The cell phone.

Didn't it record the phone number of the person who'd called?

"Oh, God," she said out loud. She stared at the buttons. Wasn't there one that could show her calls sent, calls received? If she were younger, like Jonas or Janice, surely she would have thought of it sooner.

She began to perspire the way Alice did.

Then she pushed one button.

Another.

Another.

And then there it was.

TUES 4:12PM

212–555–7974

Her hand was shaking. Did she dare make the call? Of course. She had nothing to lose.

Nothing.

But everything.

Which was probably lost anyway.

She clicked back to the main menu. Did she have a signal?

Two bars. It might be enough.

Slowly, she punched in the numbers.

In a moment, the phone began ringing on the other end. 212. Somewhere in Manhattan.

She tried to remember to breathe.

She counted two, three, four rings. Surely voice mail would pick up.

Five, six, seven.

Then she was connected.

"Yeah?" It was a man's voice.

"Who is this?" she demanded, as if he would tell her and that would be that.

"Who you looking for, lady?"

"Where . . . where are you?"

"Hmm, well, let's see, I'm on the corner of Sixty-sixth and West End."

Her trembling eased. "Is this a pay phone?"

"Yes, ma'am. And this is Harry. I live on the park bench outside." The man chuckled loudly. Elinor hung up.

She looked out over the water as the sun rose full in the sky. She bit back her tears and wondered why she was surprised there were any pay phones left in Manhattan.

Manny didn't kiss Poppy again until after the sun had come up, until after she'd told him every detail of her life; until after he'd told her all of his.

She didn't expect he'd want to kiss her again, so as he leaned toward her, she turned her head and his lips landed square in her hair. They laughed.

"I still have to arrest you," he said.

"Because I'm a bad kisser?"

"Because you killed a man."

Oh, that.

"My guess is we can get you off on the petty theft if you're willing to return the things. Do you know where they all came from?"

Poppy nodded with a teeny bit of reluctance. She didn't mention the pieces her mother had helped herself to long ago, mostly throughout Europe. It was how Poppy had learned the craft. But this was about Poppy, not Momma, so she decided to keep Momma's part to herself.

"As for the murder," Manny continued, "you were under-age. It was self-defense. Can you prove it?"

The only way to prove self-defense was if Momma came forward and finally told the truth. Fat chance of that. Momma had been a martyr on behalf of her daughter, and when she'd been released, she'd told Poppy it was over, their sins were atoned. The few times Poppy had tried to talk to her about it (like when Duane had popped into the room, unannounced), Momma had not been receptive to discussion. Besides, even if Poppy could convince her, in her current fragile condition, Momma might pretend not to remember the day, the event, or Mr. Harding, for that matter, who was of course dead, so that let him out.

"I can't prove it," Poppy said. "But it doesn't matter. I did it, not Momma. And if Duane thinks he's going to hold it over my head, he's wrong. I'd rather go to jail." For a minute, it was hard for Poppy to believe she was saying those words. But she knew it was time, had been time for a while. It was too late for her, but maybe not for Elinor, who had hurled her life into a blender.

Manny pushed a red curl off her forehead. He traced the

outline of her face, then moved his finger across her cheeks, as if connecting her freckles. "You are a good daughter," he said quietly, "and a good friend."

"Elinor has always been good to me." She felt guilty for having thought Elinor had been sleeping with Duane. "It might hurt her and CJ to learn the truth about their father, but it's better than having my husband ruin Elinor's life." She looked into his dark eyes. "Do you think I can go to jail without anyone finding out about Momma and Mr. Harding?"

"I will do everything possible."

Then he leaned closer again. This time she let his lips travel toward hers. But just before contact, a light flipped on.

"Coffee, anyone?"

It was Yolanda, at the top of the stairs.

Poppy stayed with Yolanda while Manny grabbed coffee and half a bagel and said he was going to pay a visit to Duane. When the ladies were alone with little Belita, Poppy told Yolanda about Momma and Mr. Harding and Sam Yates, the erstwhile gardener.

"He was going to kill you?" Yolanda asked.

Until then, the fact hadn't really impacted on Poppy's brain. "Well," she said. "Yes."

"And you never told anyone what you did?"

"Momma knew. She made me promise never to tell. She said she would take care of it for me."

Yolanda cuddled Belita. "I understand that. I understand that kind of love a mother has for her child."

Poppy blinked. She hadn't thought of it that way before. She'd only thought about the fact that Momma had been doing something she shouldn't have been doing. . . .

"So she went to jail for five years to protect you," Yolanda continued.

"And Mr. Harding, I guess."

Yolanda shook her head. "Having money doesn't mean one has brains, does it?"

Poppy did not take it personally.

 *Thirty-two*

Alice had driven to the airport because she hadn't felt like speaking to Neal. How dare he become so . . . unpredictable? Other husbands did that sort of thing, not hers.

She sat with Kiley Kate in the VIP lounge, waiting for the pre-boarding announcement. She sipped on a weak Bloody Mary while her granddaughter yakked into a Bluetooth connection. Alice thought nine was too young for a phone, but she supposed some people thought it was also too young to be focused on a singing career.

"I packed my pink sequins and my dress with the pale blue pailettes," Kiley Kate said into the air. "I can do the Hannah in pink and the Christina in the blue." She chattered about rock stars as if they were her friends; her hands darted about as she talked, her little fingernails high-glossed and glittered. "If we end up in Hollywood, maybe you can come, too. That would be so much fun. Gram? Can she, Gram?"

Kiley Kate tugged on Alice's forearm. Alice knew she must have been talking with Shannon O'Neill, her *bff*, as she called her, her Elinor.

"We'll see," Alice said. "First we must get past Orlando."

Kiley Kate giggled and returned to her conversation.

Alice stood up and walked to the window. She nibbled on the celery stalk from her drink, a poor proxy for breakfast. She looked out at the planes lined up at the gates, taking people away, bringing people home, from here, from there, from everywhere. She wondered if Neal was cheating on her.

There, she thought with a crunch of the stalk that was louder than she would have wished, *I've declared the possibility.*

She thought about swallowing the celery but feared it wouldn't go down. Raising the square white napkin with the red and orange FlyUS logo up to her lips, Alice discreetly spit into it.

Was Neal really capable?

Was he really sneaky enough, distrustful enough, desperate enough?

She wondered what kind of a woman he would have selected. Young, probably. They always went for the young ones once they passed forty. Pretty, of course. A new trophy.

And smart. Today, the young women were all smart. They zipped up the ladder right alongside the men, their laptops and their BlackBerries and their short-skirted suits with the lace camisoles poking out from the top. And their stilettos that glammed up their calves in the boardrooms. And their dark-framed eyeglasses that hinted of their brains.

Would Neal ask for a divorce?

She plucked an ice cube from her glass and ran it up and down her throat. Why did they keep the airports so frightfully warm in the summer?

As best as CJ calculated, there were five cordless phones scattered throughout Elinor's house: three downstairs, two up. Hopefully no more.

She waited until she heard Mac in the shower, then she quickly swept the place of the handsets. Though she'd forwarded the calls to her cell, she didn't know if the house phone would still ring. She couldn't risk the blackmailer calling with Mac in the house.

After quickly zipping herself into the polyester, she carted the handsets to her car, started the engine, rolled down the driveway, and escaped to the train station, hoping Mac would simply think she'd gone home, retreated from the temptation of him.

Now, she sat on the rumbling, rattling commuter heading toward Manhattan, gazing out the clouded window at the summer-slow Hudson. Maybe she could find some answers this morning that would finally set Elinor—and the rest of them—free.

"Is this seat taken?"

The voice sounded familiar. It belonged to Ray Williams, and it was just what CJ didn't need.

"Hello, Ray."

He sat beside her. "You going into the city?"

She decided not to point out that his question was moot, that they were both on the train headed south. "Yes."

"Me, too. I'm meeting with the Santoris' attorney."

"The Santoris?"

"The people who cut off their trees."

"I thought they paid a fine."

"The association decided it isn't enough. They want the trees removed and mature ones transplanted there. I found a place that will handle the job and move trees up to fifty feet tall. But we're looking at more than a dozen trees. It will cost some big bucks."

He was talking as if nothing had happened. He was talking as if he'd never told her that he'd slept with her sister and thought it was okay now to be sleeping with her.

Men, she thought. The only one she'd truly ever trusted was Cooper. *Sleep is the poor man's Prozac.* She wished she'd had some of either. Or both.

"So," Ray continued, "you're back? From your family business?"

CJ adjusted her purse on her lap, hoping that because he was a man, he wouldn't notice her suspicious attire. "I'll send Kevin home tonight." She could not, of course, go back to Elinor's. She supposed Mac would stay there until Elinor returned and they went to Washington for the party. As for the party, it was anyone's guess what might happen there. She was too tired of trying to figure it all out.

"CJ?" Ray asked, "is everything all right?"

"Sure," she replied, "everything's fine. There's just so much going on, with Jonas getting married and all."

He seemed to believe her. "Can we hook up for lunch in the city?"

She shook her head. "Sorry. I have an errand to run, then I have to get back."

Ray nodded, and CJ looked back out the window. She wondered if, after Jonas was married, she should go back to Paris once and for all, if she would find happiness in the cafés and galleries, away from the melodrama of Elinor's life, which always seemed to leak into hers.

Yolanda suggested that Poppy take a nap while she went downstairs to open the shop. She was halfway through Kristen Fitzpatrick's highlights when her phone rang.

She figured it was Manny with news about Duane.

"Yolanda?"

"Yes." She didn't know the voice. If he wanted a haircut, he would have called the line for the salon.

"This is Junior Diaz. A friend of your brother's."

She reminded herself that the next time she saw Manny, she should kill him the way Poppy had killed the gardener.

"Manny has told me a lot about you," he said.

"Has he?"

"He thinks we should meet. Have dinner, maybe."

"No offense, Mr. Diaz, but my brother also thinks he should run my life. The truth is, I'm not dating anyone right now. And I don't plan to in the near future."

"But—"

"But thank you for calling." She hung up the phone and returned to the highlights before she admitted he had a nice voice and maybe she was being mean.

Elinor went to the bank. The inside was built of marble and glass, with long counters in stainless steel. How bizarre, she thought, that one could stroll in to such a pristine environment and casually withdraw a half million dollars in cash. Five thousand one-hundred-dollar bills.

Of course, it no longer worked that way.

Instead of the cash (for which she'd have needed a suitcase, because it would have weighed more than a ten-pound sack of potatoes), she received credit cards. One hundred prepaid credit cards, each worth five thousand dollars, that she could use at ATMs back in New York.

All perfectly legal.

No questions asked.

No need to report any interest that would be taxed.

Because she was paranoid that the cards wouldn't work, the bank teller went with her to a downtown ATM, swiped one of the cards, and cashed out the five thousand, two hundred dollars at a time.

"It's either this, or I can wire the transfer," the teller said.

A check would take too long to clear (up to seventeen days), and the wire transfer would alert her bank and maybe Malcolm, too.

"The cards will be fine," Elinor said.

An hour later she stood on the wharf where the tenders came in. She called her home number.

The connection went through, but CJ didn't answer.

She tried calling again, this time to CJ's cell.

Thirty-three

CJ reached in her pocket and flicked off the ringtone. The last thing she needed was to attract attention. She wedged herself into the revolving door between two men in gray suits and slipped through the lobby, which was crowded with more suits and luggage on wheels.

The elevators weren't hard to find. She stepped inside one and quickly pressed 4.

On the way up, she tucked her wispy curls behind her ears. She'd never seen a wig that looked natural; she'd decided the dress and the sneakers would provide sufficient disguise. It felt strange, though, carrying only a small wristlette that held lipstick, a few breath mints, and a twenty-dollar bill. Other than her driver's license, which she'd stuck inside her bra, CJ had left all her IDs in her car at the train station. No sense advertising who she was in case she was stopped by security.

The doors opened on four and she stepped into the hall. So far so good.

She scanned the area for a housekeeping cart but saw none. A brass plate on the wall had an arrow that pointed to the right for suites 401 to 412, so that's where she went. To the right, past the ice machine, around the corner. There it was. A rolling miniature Bed Bath & Beyond.

CJ inhaled a long breath and promised herself this was the last time, the very last time, she was going to enable her sister.

She went to an open door across from the cart, though it was marked Suite 406, not 402. She pushed open the door and looked in.

The living room of the suite was cozy yet plush, in a prewar-building sort of way. Ivory wainscoting belted taupe silk-papered walls that were topped with crown molding, artfully carved. A latte-colored sofa sat beside a mahogany bar; two dark leather wing chairs hugged a wide-manteled fireplace that CJ would bet wasn't faux.

"Hola," she said into the room, though who knew what language anyone spoke in New York anymore.

A short, round figure emerged from another doorway, a squirt bottle in one rubber-gloved hand, a box of disposable something in the other. The woman stared at her but didn't respond.

CJ smiled. "Are you the woman who cleans four-oh-two?"

The woman stared at her blankly. She didn't move.

CJ repeated her request, this time in Spanish.

No recognition.

Great, CJ thought. French was the only other language CJ knew, but she doubted the woman had come to New York by way of Paris.

She smiled again.

The woman screwed up her face.

CJ stepped back to the door, pointed to the numbers, then made a four, a zero, and a two with her fingers.

The woman set down her squirt bottle and reached into her pocket. In an instant she was on a cell phone.

"No!" CJ said, waving her hand. "No, it's okay!" She backed out of the room, her face frozen in its smile. Not wanting to alarm the housekeeper any more than she apparently had, she spun around just in time to come face-to-face with another woman, a larger woman, who had on a dress identical to hers, except that it puckered at the bulge of her breasts.

"You need help?" She had unpleasant breath and a furry dark moustache that Yolanda would no doubt love to wax.

"Oh," CJ said. "Hello. You speak English."

The woman shifted her New York Giants' shoulders.

"I'm trying to find whoever cleans suite four-o-two. A friend of mine stayed there last week and left something behind." Perhaps it was too soon to have mentioned her quest. This woman probably wouldn't believe that a housekeeper had a friend who'd actually stayed at the Lord Winslow in a suite that cost at least a thousand dollars a night.

The big woman laughed. "What did your friend leave? The room service tray with the leftover scones?"

CJ blinked. Elinor always had dry toast and jam unless she was away. Then she ordered scones, a lapse into decadence she thought would go unnoticed, undeniably like the affair.

"I gave them to the birds," the big woman said, revealing a row of surprisingly small teeth. "Why do you want them, Miss Elinor?"

CJ sucked in her cheeks. "I'm sorry," she said. "Apparently you can't help me." She snapped her face away from the woman and walked down the hall at an unreasonable clip.

"But, Miss Elinor, I was just teasing. I'm the one who is sorry. Please don't tell . . ."

CJ waved her hand and called back, "I don't know who you think I am, but my name isn't Elinor."

"I like what you've done with your hair. I think your man-friend will like it, too."

Man-friend, CJ thought as she pushed through the exit door and scrambled down the stairs. She wondered if the large woman had any idea that Elinor's man-friend was who he was.

❧ Thirty-four

Manny didn't get back to Yolanda's until after one o'clock in the afternoon. While Yolanda worked in the shop, Poppy played with Belita in the apartment upstairs, brushing her hair, tying it with ribbons, painting her fingernails and toenails bright pink. Who would have thought Poppy could make a little girl giggle just by being silly, by being herself?

"He's gone," Manny announced.

Poppy looked up from her seat at the tiny child's table, locked eyes with him, and reminded herself she was a married woman before she realized what he'd said. "What?"

"Duane. He left town with a couple of suitcases and his brother. Your houselady saw him go."

There was something sweet about the way he called Nola her "houselady" and not her "housekeeper" or "maid."

"Where did he go?" Poppy asked.

"He didn't tell her. They packed up his brother's car and drove away."

"Bye-bye," Belita said, making her small, manicured fingers open and close in her hand.

"Yes," Poppy said. "Bye-bye is right." She straightened the bottles of polish and creams on the table, then lifted Belita from the soft rug on the floor. "They must have gone back to Nevada. But Elinor's gone. If he's the blackmailer, he needed her money. . . . Oh! Maybe I've been wrong. Maybe my husband isn't involved in any way—"

"Or maybe he is."

"I don't understand."

"Your woman—Nola—said one of the suitcases was very lightweight. As if there was nothing in it."

She gasped a small gasp, then Belita did, too. "Elinor's gone to get the money. Do you think Duane found out and followed her there?" Poppy asked breathlessly.

"Where is she?"

"Grand Cayman. She went yesterday."

"Why didn't anyone tell me?" He seemed more slighted than angry.

Poppy tried to smile. She didn't want to say she hadn't thought that he cared.

"When will she be back?"

"Tomorrow."

"Is she alone?"

The question surprised her. She had no idea if Elinor had gone by herself. Had her lover gone with her? "I . . . I don't really know. I think so."

"Is she traveling under her own name?"

"Of course. I doubt she has a passport with an alias on it just because she is rich."

Manny winced.

"Sorry," Poppy said, standing up, so small beside his tall, hard-bodied self. She went up to her tiptoes and kissed him on the lips. "I'm so scared for Elinor, and I'm so confused. Are you going to go to Grand Cayman?"

He paused. "Someone should. To make sure she's okay. It can't be me, though. She doesn't know me. I'd probably scare her to death."

Poppy didn't say that Elinor didn't scare easily. "But CJ's guarding the house, and Alice is in Orlando, and Momma's too fragile, and I'm under arrest."

He put his hands on her waist. They were so big and she was so small that his fingers and thumbs nearly clasped together, from front to back. "Which leaves my sister."

"Yolanda?"

"I'm sure she won't mind rescheduling appointments. In the meantime, you and I will be at your house."

"At my house?" Poppy asked, trying to drag out the conversation so he wouldn't remove his hands from her waist, so he would hold her and hold her and never let go.

"Yes," he said again. "Your house. I need to search it."

She blinked and she blanched and her throat went quite dry and she wriggled from his grasp because suddenly she couldn't breathe.

They were able to get Yolanda on a 3:40 flight. Poppy paid for her to travel first class. After a quick scramble to gather Yolanda's and Belita's things (Belita would stay with Poppy and Manny tonight), and several frenetic attempts to call CJ at Elinor's (*There was no answer! Why was there no answer?*), they piled into Manny's black SUV and drove to JFK.

Thankfully, Belita fell asleep in her car seat and did not have to say *bye-bye* to her momma.

"Before we go to my house, can we please go to Elinor's?" Poppy asked as Manny pulled away from curbside drop-off. "I need to find out why CJ hasn't answered the phone."

They were pretty quiet on the return trip to Mount Kasteel. Poppy's stomach was all knotted up, like those macramé plant hangers the girls had made in art class at McCready's back in the '70s.

"Prepare to turn right in three hundred yards," the faceless woman inside the navigation system said. Manny had been impressed that Poppy had known how to program the thing, which might have mattered if she weren't so damn nervous. About Elinor. About Duane. And now, about CJ. Not to mention Manny searching her house.

It was, of course, what Poppy *didn't* know that had her cat-nervous. She'd never gone through Duane's things. She might have told herself that his things were none of her business, but the truth was, she hadn't wanted to find what she might find: love notes from ladies; receipts from restaurants and hotels and Victoria's Secret; photos in his darkroom that didn't involve nature, at least, not the flora and fauna kind.

And now, Manny might unearth it all, right there in her presence, where she could no longer deny Duane's out-and-out obsession with women.

Oh, Poppy moaned to herself, what had she ever seen in Duane? Why hadn't she listened to Momma?

The female inside the navigation system said they had

reached their destination. Poppy told Manny to turn left up the drive. As Elinor's house came into view, Manny said, "Well, it's almost as big as yours."

Poppy detected a sad undertone in Manny's words, but she didn't dare ask. She couldn't possibly think of one more problem right now.

There were no cars around, which might mean that CJ had parked in the garage. Duane, too, for that matter.

"I'll go," Poppy said, but Manny said no.

"Stay here with the baby."

She didn't protest. If CJ was hurt . . . if Duane was there . . . well, Poppy knew she was better off in the car.

She watched Manny walk to the front door. She wondered why his wife hadn't loved him, or, according to what he'd told her last night, had stopped loving him, the way Poppy was pretty sure now that she'd stopped loving Duane. It was hard to believe that Manny was a scoundrel or a louse. It was hard to believe he was anything but a really nice guy and a really good kisser. It was hard to believe he wouldn't take good care of anyone that he loved.

He rang the bell and waited. No one came to the door. He rang again. Nothing.

A few seconds later, Manny left the door and followed the Italian stone sidewalk across the front of the house, to the side. Then, he disappeared around back.

Poppy held her breath.

Belita woke up.

"Mommy," she cried, or something that sounded like *"Mommy."*

Poppy turned around in her seat. "It's okay, honey. Poppy is here. Uncle Manny will be right back."

The little girl who, just a few hours ago, had savored her

fun time with Poppy now took another look at her and let out a wail.

"Oh, hell," Poppy muttered and did not know what to do. Then she remembered the bottle of apple juice Yolanda had tossed in the bag. She climbed over the front seat into the back, where Belita still bawled as if she were the one being blackmailed.

In less than a minute, Poppy got the bottle all set, unbuckled Belita, and took the child in her arms. Vaguely aware that something in her lap felt rather damp, she inserted the nipple into Belita's little mouth,

Poppy was pondering how on earth one changed a diaper when Manny finally reappeared. Malcolm was walking alongside him.

"Poppy," Malcolm said. "I was out in the garden."

He was supposed to have been in Washington. He was supposed to have been in Washington and CJ was supposed to be there at the house. Poppy couldn't very well ask what had happened, if the blackmailer had shown up and if it had been Duane.

"But where's your car?" Poppy asked, as if Malcolm was the one who needed interrogating.

"I flew up last night. Took a cab from the airport. Hey—is that a baby you're holding?"

"It's my friend's baby, yes. I see you've met her brother, Manny?"

"I told him we stopped by to see Elinor," Manny jumped in with a quick lie. "I said she wanted to see Yo's little girl."

Poppy forced a smile. "Right," she said. "Well, here she is."

"Very cute," Malcolm said and gave a childlike wave to Belita, who studied him carefully but kept sucking the juice.

"Elinor's in Philadelphia," Malcolm continued. "At the seamstress or something. Having her dress fixed for the big party Saturday."

"Oh, yes, well, you'll have a good time. I know she's excited." Poppy wanted to say she was still upset that they weren't invited, but she supposed the whole thing was irrelevant now.

"Well," Manny said, "we'd better get going. Nice to meet you." He shook Malcolm's hand, got into the car, and they drove off, with Poppy and Belita in the backseat, and Manny acting like the chauffeur in front.

 *Thirty-five*

CJ hadn't wanted to talk to Elinor until she'd returned home, changed out of the polyester, and poured a glass of wine. She'd decided to tell her she was done with the charade.

Sitting on the sofa now, her feet propped on the footstool and Luna stretched out, with her chin on CJ's lap, CJ took a long drink and turned on her phone. There were seven messages, which she chose to ignore. Elinor, no doubt, whining for help.

Slowly, she dialed. If she was lucky, Elinor wouldn't have reception.

"Where the hell have you been?" her twin's voice bellowed before CJ had even heard the other end ring.

"I've been trying to clean up your messes, E."

"Don't start, CJ. You're not attractive when you're mean."

"And you're not attractive when you're a train wreck. Are you still coming home tomorrow?"

"If you mean, did I get the money, the answer is yes. All in untraceable debit cards. Has there been any word from my . . . friend?"

CJ told her that Malcolm had come home, that she'd stolen the handsets, that she was back at the cottage and not at Elinor's.

Her sister paused for a long time, because it was so rare for anything she'd planned to go so awry. "Well, that's great," she finally said.

"Sorry. I did my best."

"What about Alice? Did she learn anything at the hotel yesterday?"

"No." Even as *done* as CJ was, she couldn't bring herself to tell Elinor about the debacle that had ensued, and that she'd gone today and been mistaken for Elinor by the housekeeper. Some things would keep until Elinor was home.

"E," CJ said, "have you given any more thought to telling Malcolm about it?"

"No, and I won't."

"It's just that he's a lobbyist, E. He understands give and take. Maybe he'd have some ideas."

"About how to shake up the current administration?"

"No, Elinor. About how to get out of this with grace and dignity."

"I'm afraid it's too late for that. I've called Remy three times, but now I can't get through. His assistant says he'll let me know when he can schedule a meeting, but I think Remy's angry that I'm being pushy."

In spite of her annoyance, CJ felt a twinge of sorrow. "Oh, E, I'm so sorry—"

"Don't be sorry. You know it's my own fault. What did I expect? I'll tell you what I expected. I expected not to be treated like somebody's whore. I expected not to be tossed out like yesterday's champagne gone flat."

It was a lousy analogy, even for Elinor. Still, it reminded CJ of the glass in her hand, so she took another long drink. After she swallowed, she asked, "What will you do, E?"

"I will fly home tomorrow, and you will pick me up. I will act as if nothing happened, because so far, nothing really has. And I will go to Washington on Saturday for Jonas and Lucinda's big party. And when I see Remy, I will be polite, even reverent, because he is the vice president, and that's what Daddy would expect." Then Elinor started to cry.

CJ teared up as well, because that's the way CJ thought it worked with identical twins, as if both of their hearts were simultaneously pierced. She'd never been sure, though, if Elinor had ached when CJ had. She'd never been sure because she hadn't dared ask.

After a moment, CJ said, "E, there's something else. Something small, really." She closed her eyes, as if that would make what she had to say easier. "You'd better call Malcolm tonight. I was backed into a corner. I said you'd be home today. I thought he'd ask too many questions if I told him you'd be gone until Friday."

Elinor let out a long rush of air. "Well, this keeps getting better and better."

"Sorry, it's what I had to do. And don't forget to call his cell number, because the handsets for your land line are out in my car."

Elinor didn't say thank you. She merely said, "Pick me up tomorrow" and hung up before CJ could say good-bye.

Alice turned on the laptop she'd brought in order to make arrangements to meet Bud, the theme-park magician. She and Kiley Kate had already signed in at the registration desk and picked up their packet of instructions, agendas, and requisite nametags. Now Kiley Kate was having a bubble bath in the pink garden tub of their petite suite.

According to the agenda, preliminaries would be that evening, finals in two sessions tomorrow: one morning, one afternoon.

Alice logged on and went to her mailbox. A little red dot indicated a message.

Her hand hesitated before clicking. She did love Neal, really she did. What would life be like without him? At her age. What would she do?

What would Elinor do if she were Alice?

Alice stared at the little red dot. Elinor, she knew, would take care of herself. She would get a huge alimony and end up with the property and carry on pretty much the same way.

Until she found another man. And started all over again.

But what about Alice? Despite all these years, despite all her attempts, she was not Elinor and never would be. Oh, she'd go for the alimony, all right. But then what? She wasn't manipulative and calculating the way Elinor apparently could be. She didn't know one-tenth of the people Elinor did. She could hardly step into the job market. She'd married Neal before finishing college. A few hours a week in her father's bakery thirty years ago wouldn't translate into marketable skills.

She thought about Neal again. Her eyes stung with betrayal.

Her little game was just that: a game. Somehow she suspected Neal's was much more.

She clicked the red dot. Preliminary auditions started at 6:00, with Kiley Kate scheduled for 7:15. They'd be wrapped up by 9:00, leaving plenty of time for Alice to hook up with Bud around 10:00.

She might as well start her new life now. With the one chance that she had.

"That's where it happened," Poppy said to Manny as she pointed to the garden beneath CJ's cottage window. "That's where I killed him." Manny put his arm around her; she could have died right then and been fine.

"Let's go in," he said quietly. "It looks like she's home."

Poppy took a last look at the rhododendron now planted where the gardener had once been. It seemed like such a long time ago now. Almost as if someone else had done it, not her.

CJ opened the front door. "I saw you pull in. Is everything all right?"

"Have you seen Duane?" Poppy asked.

CJ shook her head. "Why?"

"He's gone. We thought he might have gone after Elinor. But Malcolm is at the house. I think he's alone. We were afraid Duane had found you."

"And done what?"

"I don't know. Oh, CJ, I'm so afraid he's the blackmailer. I'm so afraid he found out about Elinor having an affair and decided to get money to reopen his mine and, oh, Lord, I'm so afraid about everything!"

Manny stepped forward. "She thinks everything is her fault."

"I know," CJ said. "She always has."

"We've sent Yolanda to be with Elinor," Manny continued. "In case he followed her to Cayman."

But CJ didn't look terribly frightened. "I don't think Duane did it," she said.

"But his brother wants a half million dollars! For all we know Duane really is the one E's been sleeping with! And now he wants the money to keep quiet!"

"I don't think it's Duane." CJ sounded insistent.

"You don't know that."

"I'm pretty sure," CJ said.

Poppy stared at her, then looked at Manny, then looked back at CJ.

"Sooner or later," CJ continued, "twins find out everything."

"Do you know who her lover is?"

"I know it's not Duane."

"You're sure?"

"Absolutely."

"Well, he could still be the blackmailer."

"I doubt it. I think this is out of his league."

"Have you seen the note?" Manny asked.

"No."

"Get it from your sister. Please. It's the only real clue we have at the moment."

"She'll be home tomorrow. Would you like to come in? Would you like a drink or something?"

Poppy shook her head. "No, thanks," she said. "We have to go. The baby's in the car, and I'm under arrest."

 Thirty-six

Yolanda stepped off the plane just before dusk and was greeted by a warm rush of tropical air. She was Cuban by blood, 100 percent, but she'd never had a desire to visit the Caribbean, even though Vincent had often asked her to go. She'd wondered if her disinterest had come from a secret fear that if she'd gone, she'd have wanted to stay.

It was her heritage, after all. Palm trees and steel drums and bright-colored clothes.

Dios mio, she thought. *I might as well go out with Junior.*

Slinging her Coach signature duffle—a gift from a happy, white-haired customer—over her shoulder, Yolanda headed straight for the rental-car counter. She had not checked any luggage: she'd been more concerned about what Belita would need overnight.

Using Poppy's credit card, she rented a Ford Escort and picked up a map of the island. Once situated, she turned on her phone and called Elinor. Thankfully, the call went through.

"It's Yolanda," she said when Elinor answered. "Are you all right?"

"No, I'm not all right. I'm stuck here on an island with a half million dollars."

"Tell me where you are. I'm coming to be with you."

"What?"

"Don't ask questions. Just say where you are. My brother and Poppy think you might be in danger."

Instead of going back to Poppy's for the dreaded house search, Poppy convinced Manny they should go to Momma's. She said there was something she had to do.

Momma was resting, so Poppy cooked supper—grilled cheese sandwiches, the only thing she knew how to make. But there was ice cream in the freezer—strawberry swirl, which Manny said was one of his favorites, unless he was lying because he was still hungry.

Never having had grandkids, Momma did not have a crib, but she did have a large cradle that Cain and Abel had shared before they'd been allowed to join Momma in bed.

Under Poppy's directive (Momma was feeling better by evening, but Poppy had suggested she stay under the covers), Lucky, Momma's companion, scrubbed down the cradle and brought it from the storeroom into the silver room, where they could keep an eye on the child while Poppy tended to her task. She lined the cradle with a soft comforter, though Belita didn't seem to care very much; she fell asleep right after her uncle Manny whispered something in Spanish, kissed her goodnight, and safely tucked her in.

"Now," Poppy said, "I'll need paper and a pen." She went to the secretary's desk opposite the grand piano and plucked out a sheath of engraved ivory paper and a ladies' platinum-and-diamond Montblanc.

She was aware that Manny's eyes were upon her as she went to the bookshelves and carefully started her task. The fact that CJ was sure Duane wasn't Elinor's lover did not mean he wasn't her blackmailer. Not that it mattered. Duane and his antics had nothing to do with Poppy's need to finally purge the weight of her own sins.

Sterling humidor, she wrote on one line. *Grand Hotel, Mackinac Island, Michigan, 1992.*

She moved a step to the left. *Sugar shell,* Queen Elizabeth II, *1986.*

"Poppy," Manny said with a grin, "what are you doing?"

"I'm making a list. For when I go to prison. Everything I took should go back to its rightful owners. In the morning I'll tell Momma her trinkets have gone to a museum. That will make her feel good. Her special things on display in a big museum."

Suddenly he was behind her. "You don't have to do this."

"Yes. Yes, I do. I want a clean conscience, Manny. I don't want to give anyone power over my secrets anymore." She gritted her teeth to stop from crying.

Ashtray, Fountainbleau, Miami Beach, 1991.

His hands rested on her shoulders. "I can help if you want."

She shook her head. "You've helped me enough. If it weren't for you, I wouldn't have the courage to be doing this. When

I'm in prison, I'll remember this, Manny. I'll remember how kind you were to me."

He turned her around, took the paper and pen from her hands, tilted her chin, and kissed her. Gently. Long. With warmth like Poppy never had known. This time, she couldn't hold back her tears.

"I'll do everything to help you get through this," Manny said as he pulled from the kiss and held her close.

She shook her head. "I'll get what I deserve, Manny. But maybe it isn't too late to help Elinor."

Kiley Kate sailed through the preliminaries like the star she was becoming. As did Morgan Johnson and Taylor LeDuc.

Grrr.

Unfortunately, Alice was not a good judge of whether or not the others had done well: Her focus had been not on the glitter of the stage but on her ten o'clock date, which had taken on a whole new importance.

She'd bought Kiley Kate a light supper, helped remove her makeup, then tucked her into bed. By now her granddaughter knew the routine: Alice left the girl's cell phone on the nightstand while she went downstairs for a "nightcap." She instructed Kiley Kate to call right away if she was afraid of being alone: to date, Kiley Kate never had.

Still, Alice felt guilty as she stepped into the elevator and pressed L for the lobby. Guilty and reluctant and no longer sure about much of anything.

She stepped into the lounge and scanned the long bar. A few couples, a few men alone, two women together, whom Alice recognized as mothers of contestants.

She didn't, however, see a man who looked like the rather

bland Internet photo, no one who looked as if he wasn't there on business, no one who looked like a theme-park magician.

The clock over the bar read 10:05. Should she sit down as they'd planned? Or would Bud stand her up? Would that be a sign of things to come for a middle-aged woman in search of a man?

Oh God, Alice thought, *will I become one of those?*

Then again, she thought as she stared at a leather-covered barstool that sinfully beckoned, maybe being stood up wouldn't be the worst that could happen. Since she'd started having the hot flashes, decisions were easier when someone else made them.

"Alice?"

He was so soft-spoken that she'd barely heard him.

"It's me. Bud."

He was taller than she was, with silver-gray hair and a gentle smile. He was one of the men dressed like an executive. He did not look like a theme-park magician.

She followed him to a small table, where he pulled out her chair for her. After she sat down, he seated himself, toyed with the candle, and straightened the little tent card that advertised a fruity drink made of three rums.

"So," he said. "You're Alice."

"Yes," she said. "I'm from Topeka."

He smiled and asked her what she'd like to drink. She asked for a glass of Chardonnay, then the waitress appeared and he ordered her wine and one bourbon, neat.

Bourbon, Neal's favorite.

She shifted on the chair and tried to gather her feelings. Had Neal met his lover in a hotel bar?

"So," he said, "what do you do in Topeka?"

"I'm a hairstylist," she said suddenly, knowing Yolanda would get a good laugh out of that. "I have my own salon. I'm here at a hair-care products convention."

He nodded, as if he believed there were such things. "Divorced?"

"Seven years. No kids. You?"

"Three years. A twenty-five-year-old daughter."

Same age as Felicity. She pushed back a wave of shame that her daughters might somehow learn what she was doing. "I've never met a magician before."

"I'm not very good."

Alice laughed. Bud was charming. Maybe life without Neal wouldn't need to be horrific after all. "Have you been doing it long?"

"Years. I started at hospitals. Pediatric wards. When I finally mastered removing a string of two dozen handkerchiefs from my pocket, I moved on up to the theme parks."

"An interesting way to make a living."

Bud laughed. "Hardly a living. I'm a volunteer. In real life I'm an advertising executive. I started on Madison Avenue in New York. I came down here to get out of the cold."

Had he said he was an advertising executive? If so, this must have been a joke. Neal must have learned what she'd been doing. He must have set her up.

How dare he?

A tingle began in her toes and skated up her legs to her stomach.

"Would you rather I was merely a magician?" Bud asked.

"Actually, yes," she said. "My ex-husband was in advertising." It was a line she supposed she'd have to get used to saying.

 Thirty-seven

"So Alice got nowhere and CJ got nowhere and now everyone thinks Poppy's husband is coming to get me?"

"Something like that," Yolanda said after Elinor let her into her hotel room and locked the door securely behind her.

Yolanda sat down on a rattan chair. She was surprised Elinor was in such a mediocre room in such a mediocre hotel.

The paddle fan droned while Elinor paced. "And you've left your child and your business to come and protect me?"

Yolanda shrugged. "Someone had to. I know I'm not really one of your friends, Elinor, but I do care what happens to you." The last thing she expected was for Elinor to cry.

"Oh, Dios mio," Yolanda said, "it isn't so bad. We'll figure this out."

"No," Elinor whispered. "You don't understand. I was approached by a man. But it wasn't Duane."

"Who was it?"

"I have no idea. He came up to me last night. Right here. He wanted to buy me a drink."

"Did you let him?"

"No. I said I had to meet my husband. Then I left."

"That doesn't sound suspicious, Elinor. You're still a good-looking woman."

Elinor let the compliment go. "I saw him again late this afternoon."

"So?"

"So this time he didn't know that I saw him. He was sitting in the lobby, looking in the other direction."

"And?"

"And he had a wire coming out from his ear."

"A wire? To an iPod?"

"Or a microphone. If he's Secret Service."

Yolanda didn't pretend to know what was going on. She only knew Manny expected her to take care of Elinor, so that was her mission, and that's what she would do. For the first time, however, she wondered if her big brother was right—that they were in way over their heads.

"I'll stay here with you in the room," Yolanda said. "We'll keep out of sight until we leave tomorrow."

"Fine," Elinor replied. "But you take the bed, I'll sit in the chair. I won't fall asleep anyway."

What CJ would really love to do was call Cooper.

She walked Luna around the lake—not something she usually did after dark. But the moon was full and bright, the stars big and bountiful, and CJ needed some air. When they'd lived in Manhattan, CJ and Cooper had walked at all hours of the night, in any weather. Snowstorms had been their favorite. The West Village at Christmas, when the white lights twinkled like the stars did tonight, when CJ felt like they were in a storybook setting, Dickens, perhaps. They held hands and were quiet; there was comfort in love.

She wondered how he was doing in Denver, if the theater he managed had lived up to his expectations, if they knew how lucky they were to have a man of his talent. She wondered if he was still writing.

He'd sent a card at Christmas, another on her birthday, the way he'd done for years. Sometimes he sent a small gift: a music box he'd found in an antique shop, a hand-painted silk coin purse, a button that supposedly had come from Annie Oakley's jacket. He'd often told CJ she belonged in the class of independent, adventurous women.

The cards attached had said little of his life: He hadn't mentioned if he was involved with someone else.

For her part, CJ sent things like red maple leaves and a jar of pure maple syrup on his October birthday, a silly keychain that read I ☺ NY. A few years ago she'd found a *Playbill* from the original production of *Death of a Salesman*. She'd been planning on framing it, but she decided it was too intimate a gift, so she wrapped it in brown paper and packed it in the bottom of a drawer.

She folded her lightweight shawl around her shoulders and smiled. It was always nice to think about Cooper. It reminded her that she really did have happy times to remember.

She wondered now what he'd have to say about Elinor.

"You are so different," he used to say, "for identical twins."

He'd considered writing a play about twins, but the end between them had come before the first act.

Luna pranced up beside her now and nudged her hand. "What is it, girl?" CJ asked. "Have you found a possum, or worse, a skunk?"

The dog ambled ahead, stopped, turned to look at CJ, then ambled some more.

And then CJ saw a figure in the night shadows. A tall figure—a man, it appeared from the clip of his gait. He approached on the dirt road with a purpose. It was Malcolm, of course, she'd know his walk anywhere, anytime, day or night.

"Walking after dark?" he called out. "Isn't that dangerous?"

CJ felt a crimp at the base of her neck. "I have my guard dog along."

In a few more yards, he was next to her. He looked tired and unhappy.

"Mac?" she asked. "What is it? What's wrong? Is it Elinor?"

He shook his head. "I have no idea. I thought you said she'd be home today. I tried calling her cell, but I only get voice mail."

CJ couldn't very well tell him the reception to Grand Cayman might meander in and out with the Gulf breezes.

"I thought you might have the number of the seamstress in Phillie. You didn't answer your phone, either, so I drove over. Your car is here. Your house lights are on. I figured you and Luna had gone for a walk."

She suspected they knew each other's habits more than they realized.

"I'm not sure if I have the number. Let's go back to the house, and I'll take a look."

"Thanks. Elinor has been acting so strangely lately. It's a little upsetting."

She couldn't imagine why Elinor hadn't called Mac. "Well," she said lamely, "it's not every day Jonas has an engagement party." But her heart started pumping a little bit harder at the fear that Yolanda might not have reached her sister in time.

Thirty-eight

"The decorators are finished?" Mac asked when they stepped inside the cottage, because, God knew, he never forgot anything. It was a quality that made him essential as a lobbyist but a tough guy to lie to.

"It turned out the paint they ordered didn't come in." CJ busied herself in her junk drawer, where, only days before, she had pulled out her camera and sworn herself off ever helping her sister again.

Mac stood waiting, watching.

She looked up. "Maybe she forgot to charge the battery. Let me give her a try." Before he could protest, she grabbed her phone and speed-dialed Elinor's cell.

Thank God, she answered.

"E?" CJ said with her brightest possible smile. "Where on earth are you? Malcolm has been so worried!"

She paused, tipped back her head, and faked a laugh. "Well, no, he's not in Washington, he's right here at the cottage. Here, I'll put him on and you can tell him yourself." Okay, so it was a lousy thing to do, knowing her sister would be unprepared to sling a quick excuse at Malcolm. CJ supposed that when E had seen that the caller had been Mac, she'd avoided his calls, leaving any dirty work up to others—namely CJ.

She moved to the jar that held Luna's cookies and extracted two for her good, patient dog. Luna's crunching helped mute Malcolm's words.

She filled the dog's water bowl, then turned to the refrigerator, took out a pitcher of iced tea, and poured a glass. She left the pitcher on the counter in case Mac wanted some, though she preferred that he leave, that he went to the house or to Washington or to the moon, she didn't much care where, as long as he stopped showing up in her presence when she was alone.

"Elinor will be back tomorrow," he announced as he hung up the phone. "She thought I was in Washington."

CJ smiled. At least her sister was okay. Maybe. "Is her dress ready?"

"I didn't ask. Some woman named Yolanda is with her. Isn't that her hairdresser?"

"And manicurist. And pedicurist."

Mac nodded. He stood in one place, with no visible intention of leaving. "I'll talk to her about Janice tomorrow. God, I wish she'd make time for our daughter."

They both knew, however, the odds of that happening. Jonas, after all, had always come first.

She gestured toward the pitcher. "Tea?"

Mac shook his head. "I'd better go."

Yes, she thought. *You'd better.*

He started for the door and CJ followed him, then he stopped, turned, and they nearly collided. "Oh," he said. "Sorry."

She took a step back. She looked at the floor.

"So you're okay then?" he asked. "You don't need anything?"

She could have said she hadn't been okay for years, but what would that accomplish? So instead, she lifted her eyes and said, "I'm fine. I'll see you in Washington. At the party."

He hesitated a second, then nodded a short nod and finally let himself out the door.

Bud was a gentleman, wouldn't you know.

He bought her two drinks, then said he had to call it a night, that he was on duty in the morning, that he had to make a rabbit come out of a hat, and that being a magician was sometimes more stressful than advertising.

If Neal had sent him, he was a really good actor.

He did not ask to walk her to her room. But when he stood up and she was still seated, he said, "How about dinner tomorrow night?" and she said, "Yes," because she was a moron and menopause clearly had made her more insane than she already had been.

After she said yes, she smiled. "My commitments are over at eight o'clock. Why don't you give me a call then?"

That's when Alice did possibly the most stupid thing she ever had done: *She gave him her cell number.* It was as if that one whiff of Bijon had made Alice fair game, that if Neal could become an infidel, then so could she.

Besides, who would have thought she'd meet someone online who turned out to not be a loser? Neal probably hadn't sent him. Her husband would not have supplied her a man with such class. Unless he was trying to make the landing softer when he dumped her.

After Bud left, she stayed at the table and ordered another drink.

What she really wanted was to be with her friends—Elinor, Poppy, CJ.

What she really missed was their conversation, their glasses of wine, their being there for each other, their problem solving.

Like when her mother had died and her father closed the bakery and left the country, leaving Alice alone.

Like when CJ left Cooper and came back to Mount Kasteel and said she didn't need their support even though they knew that she did.

Like when Poppy killed the gardener and she and her Momma wanted everyone to think her momma had done it, and they pretended to go along with it because Poppy was so upset, comatose, nearly, sitting in a trance all afternoon in the bed of impatiens.

Like the fact that they'd never spoken about it since, out of respect for all parties involved.

They'd stuck by one another through prom gowns and weddings and babies and now this so-called adult part of their lives, the part that sucked most.

She took another drink and wondered what advice her friends would offer about Bud the magician:

"Go for it," Poppy might say.

"Whatever works for you," CJ would say, then Elinor would add, *"Whatever you do, keep your panties on, or at least keep them in your sight."*

 *Thirty-nine*

The morning sun was orange and pink and some melonlike colors Yolanda had never seen. And there was quiet. Peaceful, blissful quiet, interrupted only by soft sounds of gulls and rhythmic strokes of waves upon sand.

It was not the Bronx. It was not New Falls or Mount Kasteel.

She'd slept better than she'd slept in years, lulled by the *whoosh-whoosh* of the paddle fan. When she'd awakened in the morning, the first thing she noticed was Elinor, sitting in the same position she'd sat in last night, staring out at the dawn from a small slit in the drapes. Yolanda didn't ask if she'd been able to sleep.

After a quick shower, Yolanda's search for a coffee shop had brought her here, to a boardwalk overlooking the beach.

"On a clear day," the car-rental clerk had told her, "you can see Cuba."

She didn't know if it was true. She didn't even know if it was possible to see more than three hundred kilometers on a clear—or any kind of—day.

Maybe.

Maybe not.

She wondered how many relatives were still there. Her father had two brothers, three sisters. Only one brother had gone to the mainland with him on the raft. Yolanda had aunts, Belita had cousins . . . would they ever see them? Would they ever be free?

She closed her eyes and listened to the gentle surf until she was aware that someone stood beside her.

"Good morning," a voice with a thick accent said.

Yolanda didn't want to open her eyes. If this was the man who'd been following Elinor . . . the Secret Service . . . ?

She didn't respond, but the man didn't leave.

Oh, God. What would Manny want her to do?

"Stay out of it," his words echoed, yet now he had sent her smack into the chaos.

She steeled her body, ready to run. Then she snapped her head quickly and flashed open her eyes. "What?" she snarled. "What do you want?"

But the man was barely a man at all, just a slim teenage boy in baggy shorts with dirty blonde hair that needed a good comb.

"Spare change?"

His accent wasn't Spanish but northern European, from Denmark, Sweden, one of those places. One of Yolanda's customers hailed from that region; she'd been a runner-up in the Miss World contest and had married one of the rich men from New Falls.

She dug into her pocketbook. "Here," she said, dropping a twenty into his palm. "Get yourself cleaned up. Get a job. Do *something* with your life. You're luckier than you'll ever know."

"Thank you," Elinor said a little while later when Yolanda returned and took paper cups filled with coffee and rolls with jam from a small bag.

"No problem."

"No." Elinor said. "Not just for the breakfast. Thank you for everything. For leaving your daughter and your business to come down here to be with me. For dragging your brother into my mess. For helping me when I don't deserve it. I've never even tipped you that well."

Yolanda laughed. "Life is about more than tips, Elinor. When I was married to Vincent, I wanted everyone to tolerate me. I learned than in order for that to happen, I had to tolerate them. We live different lives, but we're just women." She shrugged and uncapped her coffee.

"Yes," Elinor said, "we're just women. Thank God for that."

CJ spent the morning wondering how she was going to explain to Elinor that she'd left the house because Malcolm had been there. Before leaving for the airport, she steamed the gray silk that she'd wear to the party, then folded it between tissue to cut down on the wrinkles. She brushed her matching high heels and packed her evening purse with tissue, a lipstick, breath mints. Domestic chores, CJ had found, were often a great distraction.

Still, she left early for JFK, because she ran out of things to do. Naturally, the traffic moved swiftly, because it always seemed to unless one was late.

Thankfully, the Cell Phone Lot wasn't full. She could wait there until Elinor's flight arrived. When she turned off the engine, CJ realized she was exhausted. She almost wished the blackmailer was Duane and they could be done with this. But somehow that would have been too easy. . . .

Her phone rang.

"Where are you? Our plane was early. And the Secret Service is in hot pursuit."

If it had been anyone but Elinor, CJ might have said she'd watched too many movies about Eliot Ness or ones starring Tommy Lee Jones. But Elinor wasn't given to histrionics like Poppy, and she certainly had good reason to fear that the feds might be watching.

A chill shuddered through CJ as she pulled out of the lot and headed toward passenger arrivals. If Elinor was being followed, it probably meant that politics were involved, that politics were playing a role in the blackmail. And where politics were concerned, the one thing CJ knew was that chances were it would not end up good.

Traffic crawled toward the terminal; CJ drummed her fingers on the steering wheel. The women should get together tonight and discuss a next step. But with Alice in Orlando and Malcolm in Mount Kasteel, things weren't going to work as they should. Besides, Poppy had phoned CJ that morning to say she was busy with Yolanda's baby, that she and Manny and Belita had stayed with Momma last night. CJ hadn't asked if Poppy was really under arrest and, if so, for what. She had no room left in her head for additional subplots, though she wondered if something was brewing between Poppy and Manny, and what Duane might do if he found out.

Suddenly, she remembered the note. Manny had said he wanted to see it. He was a police detective. He knew what he was doing, unlike the five women.

She must remember to get the note from Elinor, if it wasn't in ashes already.

Finally, up ahead, she spotted Elinor and Yolanda. CJ looked quickly but didn't see any men in black on their pulp fiction tails.

"The note," CJ said once Elinor had climbed into the front seat and Yolanda was settled in the back and they were headed north on the Hutchinson Parkway. "Do you still have it?"

"It's home."

"In the safe?"

"Hardly. After Jonas found it in my purse, I stashed it in an old evening bag. A Judith Leiber frog. In my closet."

Yolanda supposed this was not a good time to suggest selling the bag on eBay. She'd done a lot of that lately, selling various baubles, mostly things Vincent had bought her. It was expensive to be a woman alone, trying to eke out a living in Westchester County.

She looked out the window and reminded herself that one day it would be worth it. Belita would grow up in a town filled with opportunities. She would not know the struggles of her mother or her mother's parents before her. She would never know life on an island.

For some silly reason, small tears rose in her eyes.

"Manny wants to see the note," CJ continued. "We'll take

E home first, and she can give it to us. Then we can take it to Manny. He called out sick today. He's with Belita and Poppy at Poppy's mother's. They stayed there last night."

Yolanda did not have to ask what Manny had been doing with Poppy all night. After all, she had seen that kiss.

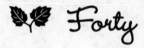 *Forty*

CJ and Yolanda followed Elinor into the house. They waited in the foyer while Elinor went upstairs.

"Have they lived here long?" Yolanda asked as her gaze skirted the lovely paintings, the marble tiles, the movie-set staircase.

"A while," CJ replied. She'd forgotten that Yolanda was usually at Elinor's in the role of hired help and didn't ask questions that might be construed to be personal.

"Except when we're stuck down in Washington," Malcolm said as he walked in from the doorway that led to the kitchen.

CJ felt her blood pressure rise a point, maybe ten. "Malcolm," she said. "We brought Elinor home from the station." She stammered a bit, couldn't very well add that E was upstairs retrieving the blackmailer's note. "Do you know our friend,

Yolanda?" Good grief, she couldn't remember Yolanda's last name. She had only known her by one name, like Cher or Madonna or the artist formerly known as Prince, who, she thought she'd heard, was called that again.

Malcolm and Yolanda shook hands as Elinor appeared at the top of the stairs.

"Well, there's my long-lost wife now."

"Hello, Malcolm." She descended the stairs, carrying the Judith Leiber as if it were a rose. "Sorry I was delayed. I thought as long I was in Phillie, I'd have the girl start my gown for the wedding." The words slid off her tongue like Baileys Irish Cream. At the bottom of the stairs, she handed CJ the purse. "This will match your dress perfectly," she said without missing a lying beat. Then she turned back to Mac. "Do I have time for a bath before we leave for Washington?"

"That all depends," Mac replied as he reached into his back pocket and withdrew a phone handset. "You see, the oddest thing happened while you were away. All the phones were missing from their chargers. Except for the one I keep under my bed. Which is a good thing, because if I hadn't finally figured that out and retrieved this, I never would have received the call from a man who asked if I had the money."

The interesting thing about CJ's sister was that she could manage to rise to an occasion such as this without turning pale or breaking into a sweat, both of which CJ was sure she was doing.

"What money?" Elinor asked.

Malcolm shrugged. "I have no idea. But before he hung up, he said my wife would know what he meant."

Elinor laughed. "So. Was it the paperboy or someone like that?"

"I can't imagine. Any more than I can imagine why the other phones are missing."

"Because I'm having the phone system replaced! We're going digital—didn't I tell you?"

His reply was a cool, curious stare. Then Malcolm went back through the foyer the way he had come.

CJ looked at Elinor, and Yolanda looked at Elinor, and Elinor looked at them both and whispered, "I'm dead."

 Forty-one

Poppy would have been happy if they'd slept together, had sex. But Manny had said that as much as he'd like to, he respected her too much.

She hoped he wasn't afraid she'd nail him with pruning shears, too.

She'd slept until noon, then resumed making lists, while Manny perused Momma's greenhouse and gardens with Belita.

By afternoon, Momma felt up to taking high tea in the solarium, where she could see her orchids in bloom. Besides, she'd heard gleeful delights from Belita and wanted to see the little girl.

"Let's all be like children," Momma said, and so there they sat, Poppy and Manny and Momma and Belita on Manny's knee, and they ate tea party sandwiches with the crusts neatly trimmed and sipped lemonade out of dainty porcelain cups. It didn't matter to Momma that Belita wasn't even two and didn't know, or probably care, what was going on.

Poppy quietly thanked Manny for his patience and promised him that Fiona would make him a big sandwich later. "Roast beef and Brie," she whispered, "grilled on thick slices of focaccia." He smiled.

Over dainty scoops of pink peppermint ice cream, Manny gently asked Momma if she remembered the night the gardener died.

Momma set her spoon into her small tulip dish, looked at Manny, and asked, "What gardener?"

Poppy sighed. "You know, Momma. Sam Yates. I told Manny I'm the one who really killed him, not you. I told him it's high time I cleansed myself of my sins before the good Lord takes us both." If Momma wondered where or why Poppy had so suddenly got religion, she didn't say.

"Momma," Poppy repeated. "This is serious. Manny knows the truth. Tell him."

"Poppy is only trying to set the record straight, Mrs. Landry. From what she says, it was self-defense. And she was only fifteen. Chances are, she won't go to jail. But we'll need your testimony because there's no evidence."

Poppy figured he'd added in the part about her not going to jail because he thought that would be the only way to get Momma's corroboration—if that was the right *Law & Order* word.

Momma picked up the tiny silver hand bell Poppy had bought—actually bought—from a *vendedor* on a street in the south of Spain. "I have no idea what you're talking about. I killed that man and I paid for my crime." She shook the bell and Fiona appeared and Momma said she needed help to get to her bedroom, that she felt another spell coming on.

After Momma was gone, Poppy cried, "What about me? I need to purge my soul! And what about Elinor? If Duane thinks he's still hanging this over my head, he'll get away with blackmailing her."

Belita cried, too.

Then the doorbell chimed.

A few seconds later, Bern escorted CJ and Yolanda into the solarium, and Yolanda picked up Belita, who instantly stopped crying, and CJ sat down in the chair where Momma had been. For some reason, she carried a Judith Leiber frog handbag, a stretch even for CJ, with her artistic leaning.

"I have the note," CJ said. She unsnapped the frog and took out a paper that had been folded into four large squares. Manny and Poppy got up and stood behind CJ with Yolanda and Belita, and they all scrunched forward to examine the goods.

CJ unfolded the paper and carefully smoothed it.

The letters were big and colorful, some bold, some swishy, but most were mismatched.

"These words came from women's magazines," Poppy suddenly said.

All eyes turned to her.

"Do either of you think a woman did this?" Manny asked.

The funny feeling that always found its way to Poppy's stomach whenever she was anxious or scared found its way there now. "I didn't say that. But look. The word *panties* is all one word, not cut out from letters."

"It could have been printed from something online. A

Web site that would give the blackmailer the exact things he needed."

Poppy shook her head. "No," she said quietly. "The words are from magazines."

"It doesn't look like the letters have printing on the back," Manny said. "The lab can determine that, though. We don't want to mess with it ourselves."

Poppy was still shaking her head. "You don't understand. I know these are from women's magazines. Maybe the blackmailer copied them on one of those fancy printers so there's no printing on the back. But I know what I'm talking about. I read these magazines all the time. Momma taught me it helps pass the time and keeps my mind off my troubles." She sighed. "Anyway, I keep a stack of them in my bedroom, right next to my chaise."

They all seemed to know that the next thing they'd do was travel to Poppy's house en masse, head up to her bedroom, and see if Duane had dismembered any of her prized magazines.

Poppy supposed that after that, Manny would search the rest of her house. And she'd be humiliated, once and for all.

Alice sat in the theater watching thirty-six boys and girls sing a rock version of "God Bless America," the theme song for *USA Sings.* The performance opened the show because the producers knew that that was when the contestants would be in top form—which was another way of saying they didn't want the long faces of losers to taint the program.

And there would be losers. Twelve would be cut in Orlando, another dozen in Philadelphia. The *final-final twelve,* as they were called, would win the trip to Hollywood and national television.

Kiley Kate looked stunning in the requisite outfit—red-and-white-striped glittering pants and cropped blue jacket—for which Alice had had to pay an additional four hundred dollars. But the outfit could be used again in Philadelphia and then in Hollywood if Kiley Kate made it that far.

As for Alice's attire, that morning she'd picked up a soft beige sheath in the Grand Cypress Gift Shop. The dress was too short for Mount Kasteel, but what the hell, her legs were still good. And Bud might enjoy looking at them during dinner.

Bud.

She guessed she should smile. But the truth was, she felt a little bit seedy, and she missed Neal.

"They're wonderful, aren't they?"

She did not know the voice, but she recognized the face of the mother of Taylor LeDuc, one of Kiley Kate's rivals. Like her daughter, the woman had mousey brown hair and lips that were too large to be natural. She wore a gaudy print top that made her look pregnant.

"Yes," Alice replied. She had no interest in conversation.

"Kiley Kate is your daughter? She looks like you."

In spite of the nuisance, Alice replied, "Granddaughter." She smoothed the hemline of the beige dress.

"I'm Lorna LeDuc. My daughter is Taylor. She says Kiley Kate's really nice."

Alice didn't reply.

"I always have a little party for the girls after the show. So they can become friends, you know? We invite Kiley Kate, but she's never come; how about tonight?"

Kiley Kate had never mentioned a party. "I'd have to leave that up to her."

"She told my daughter you're usually busy after the show, that it's a tradition for just the two of you to go out. But I think it's nice for the girls to be friends. They're so young, you know?"

Alice hadn't known that Kiley Kate lied. She was a kid, and most kids probably did, but why had she lied about that? Because she hadn't wanted to mention her grandmother's "nightcaps"? And what about mixing competition with friendship? Didn't that matter to kids?

"So we'll be going tonight," Lorna continued. "After the show. If you and Kiley Kate want to come."

On stage, the group launched into the last chorus, and Lorna LeDuc moved away.

Alice watched the kids, wondering what to do, just as her cell phone vibrated.

Bud?

She sprinted for the vestibule. Without her glasses, she couldn't read the caller ID. But surely it was him. . . .

"Hello?" she breathed as the door thumped behind her. "Hello?"

"Oh, God, Alice. Thank God you're there."

It was Elinor.

"Mac knows something's up," Elinor spewed. "And the Secret Service is following me. Poppy still thinks it's Duane, but I'm scared to death, Alice. I wish you were home."

It was the first time Elinor had hinted that Alice might be important to her, someone she needed for something more than childlike pranks or silly escapades.

"Elinor, slow down. What's going on now?"

Elinor told her about the call Mac had received. "I can't blame CJ. She thought she'd done the right thing. When she walked off with the handsets."

Elinor was oddly beginning to sound as scattered as Poppy. "But what does the Secret Service have to do with you?"

From inside the auditorium, a few final notes resounded, followed by applause.

"My lover is Remy," Alice thought she heard Elinor say. "You know. The vice president."

"What?"

"You heard me. And what's worse, he'll be at Jonas's party tomorrow. How on earth am I going to pull this one off? In front of my husband? In front of my kids? With half of Washington looking on?"

God Bless America, Alice thought.

 *Forty-two*

Jordan was the first finalist scheduled to sing. Kiley Kate would go on after her.

Alice stood close to the door, one ear tuned to the show, one to her cell as she called CJ again and again but only got voice mail.

She wondered if Elinor had lost her mind or if she really was sleeping with Joe Remillard. Holy cow. A theme-park magician, executive or not, certainly paled next to a vice president. No, make that *the* vice president.

"Manny's been using my phone," CJ said when she finally answered. "His battery died."

"What the hell's going on? Has your sister gone crazy?"

"She told you."

"Yes. Do the others know? Poppy? Yolanda?"

"I don't think Poppy knows."

"Maybe we should keep it that way. You know how she gets."

"Right. As for Yolanda, well, she knows Elinor was being followed in Cayman by the Secret Service."

"Good Lord, CJ, what's going to happen?"

"I have no idea. I'm at Poppy's right now. She and Manny are upstairs looking through her magazines, to see if Duane cut out the letters for the ransom note."

"And?"

"And nothing so far. Poppy says her magazines haven't been touched by Duane or by anyone."

Alice sighed. "I'll be home tomorrow."

"Well, we won't be. We'll be off to Washington. By the way, how's Orlando?"

"Fine. Interesting. I'll tell you later." But as she clicked off, a sad, lonely feeling crept into her heart and smothered any hope for Bud and the rest. Elinor's predicament was a stiff shot of reality, a wake-up call for Alice to reassess her priorities— priorities like allowing Kiley Kate to make friends, like paying attention to what really mattered, like husbands and families and not self-centered fun.

The party was held at Planet Hollywood, where the dozen or so girls were mesmerized from the moment they walked in. They spotted celebs Monique Coleman and Ashanti, whom Alice had never heard of.

They ordered smoothies and chicken crunch and zucchini chips. And they giggled, as only nine-year-old girls do.

The fact that Kiley Kate had actually won did not seem to affect anyone, most of all Kiley Kate. She seemed to be happiest that she was there with the others.

"This is lovely," Alice said to Lorna LeDuc, who hadn't commented that Alice was a bit overdressed. Then the double chocolate brownies were served and the girls' eyes widened and they giggled some more.

"Girls," Lorna said. "I wish I'd had ten of them. But Henry and I only had Taylor, then Henry got leukemia, and died the next year."

Alice took a drink of her mango-peach smoothie. "I'm so sorry," she said. "You've raised Taylor alone?"

"Oh, we have lots of friends. We're lucky like that."

No one, of course, had to tell Alice the importance of having friends. She reached into her purse to make sure Elinor or none of the others had called. When she'd finally decided to bring Kiley Kate here rather than meeting Bud, she'd turned off her cell altogether. She'd decided that yes, her priorities were what they were. If Neal wanted a divorce, she'd deal with that, too. But she had her friends who would help. She, too, was lucky like that.

After two hours of giggles, they grabbed taxicabs back. As if she still was little, Kiley Kate snuggled up close to her grand-mother. Alice kept one arm around her and one arm on the trophy. *Next stop: Philadelphia,* she thought with a grin.

But when they arrived at the hotel, Alice's heart turned inside out: Bud, the theme-park magician, stood on one side of a palm tree; at the registration desk, stood Neal.

It was, of course, like a scene from a very bad movie that spi-raled quickly downhill as Kiley Kate spotted her grandfather in the same instant Bud approached Alice.

"Hello," Bud said.

"Hello," Alice replied as Kiley Kate scampered toward Neal. Please God, she prayed, please don't let this explode right here in the center court of the Grand Cypress. "Wasn't it a great performance? Good night now," she said to Bud with a halfhearted smile, then turned from him and walked toward Neal, who was walking toward her.

"This is a surprise!" She tried to sound excited, which, of course, she was, not to mention that she was sweating to death. From the corner of her eye she saw Bud remain motionless, watching her watching Neal.

Neal kissed her cheek. "I flew down to see how my favorite girls were doing. I'm sorry I missed the show."

"I won, Grampy! I won!"

Alice held up the trophy with the American flag and the tiny stars all around. "She won, all right. Our Kiley Kate is the best."

Neal gave Kiley Kate a big hug, then said, "You must be tired. Let's go to bed."

"We have a petite suite, Grampy. Everything's pink!"

"Pink!" Neal replied. "Well, that's just what I've always wanted!"

"How was the dinner last night?" Alice asked, because she wanted to sound nonchalant.

"They canceled it until next week when they found out my wife couldn't make it."

If he was teasing, he was doing a great job.

"Let's go," he said. "I want to see our pink suite. By the way, I've extended our reservation until Sunday night. As long as we're in Florida, we might as well have some fun, right?" He winked at Alice, then took Kiley Kate's hand on one side and Alice's on the other, and led his girls to the bank of elevators.

Alice noticed that Bud watched a few seconds more, then turned and went out the front door.

❦ Forty-three

Saturday brought a break in the humidity. CJ had taken the train out of Grand Central because the three-hour ride had seemed more endurable than the possibility of running into her sister and Mac at the airport.

She didn't, in truth, even want to go. If it were for anyone other than Jonas, CJ would have made a polite excuse and stayed far from the fray.

At Union Station, she walked along the marble floors through the magnificent domed concourse of the terminal, past the dozens and dozens of specialty shops that made this more of a tourist attraction than a train depot. CJ knew she should stop in one or two or three places and choose an appropriate gift for Jonas and Lucinda, but she had no idea what to give them, no thoughts on what could be special enough, meaningful enough. Besides, she was sidetracked by the life all around her: hustling, bustling, going-places-life. How could she think about gift-giving when right now she only wished she could fall into step behind someone, anyone, and follow them to their destination? Whatever it was, surely it would be less troublesome than hers.

But this is for Jonas! she reminded herself. *A night to put all else aside and celebrate his love for Lucinda and her love for him!*

Still, the gift would have to wait until she was thinking more clearly.

Juggling the garment bag and her suitcase, she stepped out onto Columbus Circle and found the queue for a cab. Elinor had suggested that Mac send a car, but CJ had declined. The less interaction she had with them now, the better. She suspected there would be drama soon enough, and until then, she had to stay focused.

Jonas. Lucinda.

At the desk of the Fairmont Washington D.C., she was told to go to reception on the Gold Floor, that her room was up there, that the cost had been taken care of. A bellman whisked away her bags, and CJ was told to "have a nice stay."

She made her way up to the coveted floor and had barely given her name when she was led to her room. Her bags were already there; her escort quickly left her alone.

CJ tried to stay in the moment.

Overlooking the lush garden courtyard, the room was spacious and opulent, no doubt hand-selected by her sister. The large king-size bed was layered with white down; the period furnishings were tasteful and authentic. A vase filled with two dozen yellow roses stood on the polished wood desk. No matter the venue, no matter the subtext, Elinor remained the impeccable hostess.

With a small sigh, CJ slipped out of her shoes. She meandered across the thick carpet to the roses and breathed in their sweet scent. She picked up the envelope propped against the vase.

An obligatory sentiment from her sister, no doubt. Or maybe from Mac?

She laughed at her misplaced naïveté, unsealed the envelope, and withdrew the card.

The handwriting was unmistakable. Her hand went slowly to her mouth, then her fingers slid to the base of her throat.

The florist said it was too late for tulips, the card read, *but that roses are always in bloom. Thank you for being in my life. Thank you for being you. Much love, Jonas.*

CJ sat on the bed, still holding the card. Then, one after another, tears slowly spilled from her eyes. And CJ suddenly knew the best gift she could give.

The room phone rang at six fifteen.

"Are you here? Are you ready? Why aren't you downstairs?"

It was Elinor, of course. CJ sat on the edge of the bed and tried donning her Elinor armor. "I thought the party started at seven."

"I need you now! You're my family! The Perrys have dozens of relatives who've flown in from all over creation. For God's sake, I'm all alone!"

CJ didn't mention that perhaps Elinor should have insisted that Alice and Poppy be invited after all. They might not have been blood, but they were like family, which sometimes—like now—could be even better. She also didn't mention that she'd been ready for an hour and only had to slip into her gray silk. "Have you seen anything or anyone unusual?"

"Not yet. But how will I know if anyone is unusual? Half of Washington qualifies for that."

Hopefully, not the half that would be at the party. "Shall I come down in ten minutes?"

"Make it five. Please. I'm not sure I'll survive for ten."

CJ hung up. She straightened the room, smoothed the bed-covers, took a last sniff of roses, then stepped out of her robe and into her party attire.

The band offered just the right balance of strings and brass, romance and zest. The Colonnade was a blend of Washington dignity and New York chic. If this had been Elinor's affair and not Betts Perry's, there might have been an appetizer of lemon confit chicken to accompany the champagne instead of the damn goat cheese mousse on crostini. Chicken was so much more universal than overblown goat cheese, and lemon complemented the wine.

But what did a few menu changes matter when one consid-ered all that might have gone wrong? Still, Elinor smiled that she'd been able to keep herself together well enough to have noticed details like that.

Jonas seemed to be having a good time, as was everyone, except perhaps Janice, who noted her surprise that Elinor's nails had been polished in ivory and not in a shade to match the peach-colored Versace. Elinor had laughed and told her daughter that was the latest in fashion, didn't she know that? She could hardly have said Yolanda hadn't brought her polish to Grand Cayman, so Elinor had done her own nails that morning.

Thankfully, Janice hadn't pressed that issue—or others—but had trotted off to the dinner bar to find the man Jonas said she'd been introducing as her boyfriend, though Elinor had not had the pleasure of meeting him. She was simply grateful that Janice had shown up at all. Just as she was grateful when Betts informed her that the vice president's wife had phoned their regrets. "Remy's down with the flu," Betts bemoaned, and Elinor said, "What a pity," then dug her heels into the travertine floor.

Across the room, Mac was occupied with a group of men and women Elinor had met, but she couldn't recall if they were family or colleagues. It was so hard these days to tell anyone apart. When they'd first come to Washington, the politicians had mostly all been men. Now, it was all too confusing, and it meant she had to be on best behavior with everyone.

Which was especially difficult to accomplish when all she wanted was to go home and cry.

As her gaze traveled the room, she saw Jonas and Lucinda standing by the pastry table, talking with CJ. Lifting an espresso from a waiter's silver tray, Elinor strolled over to join them.

"Mom," Jonas said, "you won't believe what Aunt CJ has done."

Elinor realized that when her sister was nicely dressed, it was amazing how much they still looked alike. Both had their hair pinned up tonight, both looked soft and attractive. Sometimes Elinor thought she wanted CJ to pay more attention to her appearance because it was such a reflection—literally, physically—of her. Elinor smiled. "I can't imagine what your aunt CJ has done."

"She's given us the cottage," Jonas said. "As a wedding gift."

Elinor blinked.

"Only because they've agreed it comes with a dog," CJ said. "Luna needs more people than solitary old me. She needs a real home. Hopefully, a family."

Elinor was speechless, utterly speechless.

"I know Jonas wants to work in New York," CJ continued, "so it only makes sense. Besides, this way it will stay in the family."

"Yes," Elinor said, "but—"

"But what about me?" CJ asked. "I've decided to go back to Paris. I've decided it's time to pick up where I left off so long ago."

It was all too much for Elinor to digest on top of the goat cheese mousse and the rest. "Well," she said, "what a surprise."

"We're thrilled," sweet Lucinda said.

"I'm sure," Elinor replied.

The three went back to chattering about when CJ would leave, when Jonas would move in. Elinor drifted from the group, trying to decide if this news was acceptable or if it was not, and wondering how on earth life all around her was managing to go on while hers was on breath-stopping hold.

Elinor moved out to the garden, looked at the night sky, and wondered what Father would think of all that had gone on. Chances were he would not be surprised at his daughter's transgressions (she was his after all), but he would be displeased that she'd been caught. He would be *cross*, her mother's favorite word.

He would have, however, continued to be proud of Catherine Janelle, because she'd be leaving town, the heroine again, having done what was best for the family.

"Penny for your thoughts." Elinor turned and saw Congressman Perry navigating the terrace toward her.

"Oh, Congressman. Bill." She smiled. "I've only come out for a breath of air. The party is wonderful; the children are so happy."

"And so, thank God, is my wife."

Elinor laughed. "Well, she's done a marvelous job." She did not mention the lemon confit chicken.

"And now she's dancing with your husband."

"With Malcolm?" Mac hated to dance, said he was born with two left feet and no right.

"Shamed him into it, she did. Said she'd get him in practice for the wedding reception."

Elinor suddenly realized the band was playing a slow dance—something Mac detested the most. "He hates to dance. I should go rescue him."

"Or you could come inside and dance with me." He held out his hand and led her to the French doors. In too short an instant she was back in the party, now being held by the man with big hair and big hands, waltzed to the center of attention, right next to Malcolm and Betts.

It was then that the congressman leaned down and said in her ear, "I believe you and my wife have many things in common. For one thing, lavender is her favorite color."

Elinor's ears became blocked. Her head began swirling as if she'd been drugged. "What?"

"Lavender," the congressman repeated. "It's your special shade, isn't it?"

She broke from his grasp. She was going to throw up. She raced from the dance floor, from the ballroom, out into the hallway. She frantically searched for the ladies' room. She dashed inside, locked a door behind her, and quickly crumpled to the floor.

❧ Forty-four

CJ had had enough of the party and felt it was all right to call it a night. She cheek-kissed Jonas and Lucinda and went in search of Betts Perry just as Malcolm moved toward her with purpose.

"Help," he uttered in a controlled whisper. "I don't want to cause a scene, but I think Elinor's sick."

CJ supposed it had been too much to hope that the party would end up unflawed. "What happened? Where is she?"

"She was dancing with the congressman. Suddenly she broke away and ran from the room. Someone saw her duck into the ladies' room."

Well, that made no sense unless it was just as it seemed: that Elinor had simply become sick.

"I'll check," CJ said, and Mac followed her until she left him out in the hall.

Inside the ladies' room, the stalls were not stalls but small rooms with brass-knobs and long louvred doors designed for the utmost privacy.

"E? Are you here?" CJ called out.

"Go away, CJ. It's over."

"I know it's over. It was a lovely party."

Silence.

"E?"

"Not the party. I mean it's over. You know what I mean."

Was she talking about the blackmail?

"E? Are you all right?"

"Go away. We'll talk later, okay? I really don't feel well right now."

"Will you call me? Later?"

"Yes."

"Promise?"

"Yes. Now go away."

Malcolm was waiting out in the hall.

"She's all right," CJ said. "A little too much excitement, I guess."

He took her by the elbow and guided her around the corner, where it was quiet, where it was dark.

"What's going on, CJ? What's happened to Elinor?" His voice was just above a whisper.

"I told you," she began, but suddenly he stepped forward and placed his finger on CJ's lips.

"No lies," he said. "I want the truth."

They hadn't been that physically close in years, that breath-upon-breath close. Between them she could taste champagne that lingered in the air. Then slowly, slowly, his finger began to trace the fullness of her mouth; her old feelings began to stir. She closed her eyes and they were in the greenhouse, she was heavy with his baby, and she wanted nothing more than to feel him deep inside her, to smell his scent, to touch his sweat. . . .

And then she heard her mother: *"Do you love him?"*

CJ jumped away, the way she had back then. "Mac," she said. "No."

He stepped aside. He shook his head and laughed a little laugh. "It's awful, isn't it?" he asked with a halfhearted grin. "It's awful that even after all these years, I don't know which one of you I love. You or Elinor."

She looked into his eyes and loneliness looked back. "Mac," she said again, and in his gaze the answer emerged, the answer for her, for him, for them. "If I looked like someone else, would you even ask yourself that question? If I looked like Alice or Poppy . . . someone, anyone else?"

"I don't know," he replied, the honest lobbyist, the oxymoron of the nation's capital.

She took his hands in hers. "I know I've always loved you, Mac. But I also know my sister's feelings, sometimes as if they're my own. I feel her happiness and joy. Sometimes if I have a headache, I'm not sure if it's mine or hers. Don't you see, Mac? Maybe the love I feel for you really is *her* love for you."

He closed his eyes. "The twin thing."

Then she held his hands up to her face, and he looked into her eyes again. "Elinor really does love you, Mac."

"But sometimes it's hard because of Jonas."

"And yet . . . ," she said.

"And yet we wouldn't trade him for anything." Mac smiled. CJ smiled.

Then the door banged open and Elinor blew around the corner and barked, "Malcolm, take me home."

🍂 *Forty-five*

CJ went up to her room, the glow of the evening gone, washed away by whatever had happened, or not happened, to Elinor, to CJ and Mac.

She didn't know if she was right about her feelings really being Elinor's. But feeling his touch again, being so close to him again, made her know this needed to stop, this doubt, this angst, this . . . love. For all of them, it was time to move out of the greenhouse and get on with their lives.

After all, he was Elinor's husband.

And Jonas's father.

And Janice's father, too.

And CJ wouldn't.

She couldn't.

She was done pretending she could be otherwise.

Yes, she thought, sliding in the key card and opening her door, it was good she'd decided to return to Paris. *A chance to start anew . . .*

She flicked on the light switch . . .

For everyone's sake.

She stopped.

She stared.

Her stomach lurched the way Elinor's surely must have. For there, spread across the neatly plumped pillows, was an unmistakable pair of panties, lavender lace.

CJ shrieked. She slammed the door behind her without thinking that whoever had been there might still be in the room, in the bathroom, the closet.

She shrieked again. No one replied.

She ripped open the doors to the bath and the closet. She dropped to her knees and looked under the bed. No one was hiding. She was alone.

She fumbled through her purse. She found her cell phone. She pushed speed dial.

"You've reached Elinor Harding Young. Thank you for your call. I'm sorry I'm not able—"

Click.

Speed dial. She'd once plugged in the numbers of anyone, everyone, she might have needed to reach in a hurry. There had been few.

"Hello?"

"Who's this?" CJ whispered. "Who's this?"

"It's Alice. CJ?"

CJ spit out the details as best as she knew them. "Please, Alice. Come to Washington."

"I'm in Orlando. With my husband."

"Please, Alice." She told her what had happened. "Hurry," she added.

Click.

Speed dial.

"CJ? What's wrong?"

The voice sounded calm and collected for Poppy. "Poppy? Come quick. We need you in Washington." She repeated what she had told Alice. Poppy told Manny.

"Manny says to get out of that room."

"I've got the bolt on. I'll keep the hotel phone beside me. If I hit zero someone will come running. Besides, it might not be any safer out in the hall."

"Have you called the police?"

"No. I'm afraid."

"Don't worry. I'll bring our own."

Click.

Speed dial again.

"Hello. You've reached Elinor Harding Young—"

Click.

CJ moved to the window, clutching her cell phone. She sat in the plush chair overlooking the garden, but she didn't enjoy the view. Her eyes were focused straight on the panties, and her heart was pounding like the bass in the band that still wafted up from the party.

There was only one person CJ wanted to call. One person who could be levelheaded, and it wasn't Mac.

She speed dialed again. She held her breath, hoping he'd answer, hoping he'd welcome her call.

"Cooper?"

"CJ?" His voice was the same, in spite of the years. She closed her eyes and started to cry.

"CJ? Are you all right? What's happened?"

"Cooper," she repeated, because it was nice to hear herself say his name. Then she said she was fine and he said he was, too, and she launched into the tale about Elinor and the blackmail and their attempts to locate the culprit and the panties now perched on the bed. She did not mention Remy in deference to E. But CJ was as comfortable speaking to her ex as if they'd talked yesterday, as if she'd never left SoHo or him.

"Can you hold on a minute?" he asked once she'd stopped for a breath. "I need to take this in the other room."

Oh God, she realized with a thud to her heart, *he isn't alone. Of course he isn't alone!* Why on earth would he have been without a woman all this time, just because she'd been without a man except for Ray Williams, and he didn't count?

Her bruised ego was about to hang up when he clicked on again.

"Sorry," he said. "I needed to let the dog in before she woke up the neighbors."

A dog. Not a woman. Still, CJ felt foolish. "Cooper, I'm sorry. It was bold of me to think I could call you on a Saturday night and not interrupt your evening. I'm sorry. I'll call back another time."

"Stop it," he said abruptly. "I'm not glad there's a problem, but I am glad you called."

"So I'm not interrupting?"

"If you're asking me if I'm with a woman, the answer is no. The only woman in my life right now is Molly."

Molly?

"My golden retriever."

She smiled.

"CJ," he continued, "you need to call the police. You need to call the police, then call me back if you want."

"I can't," she said. "I can't call the police."

Cooper laughed. "Because it's Elinor?"

"No. Because it's the vice president." Then she told him the rest. "After this is over," she said when she was done, "I'm going back to Paris. I'm going to stop protecting my sister and finally start my life over."

"Ah," he said. "Act two. Maybe this time you can rewrite a few scenes."

She did not ask what he meant.

"You need to divorce me, Malcolm."

Elinor and Mac sat in the back of the black Lincoln Town Car that Mac only used on special occasions. He'd always said it embarrassed him to be chauffeured around, as if he thought he was too important to tackle the Beltway himself.

He sighed. "What going on, Elinor?"

She gazed out the window at the indestructible stone buildings, the historic streetlamps, the sleek limousines that snaked through the grid streets, their dark, tinted windows harboring power within. Elinor had once found Washington exciting. She'd never expected to have to pay for her crimes. Perhaps that was a by-product of Father's example, or maybe she'd simply lived too long in this city.

Beside her, Malcolm breathed. A small hollow grew in her stomach, the same one that had grown the night her mother told her she'd found Malcolm and CJ in the greenhouse. Together. Making hasty, cumbersome love. While CJ was heavy with Jonas. *Their* baby, not hers, not Elinor's, no matter how hard she had tried to believe it, no matter how hard she'd tried to convince the world, because it was what Father had told her to do.

She'd tried to tell Father about the scene in the greenhouse, but he'd said she was overreacting, that they both knew her mother was inclined toward the dramatic.

As with other things—such as the *incident with the gardener*—they'd never mentioned it again.

Still, it didn't seem fair that now, after all these years, Elinor would turn out the villain.

She teared up, and it wasn't an act.

"I've had an affair." Elinor spoke softly, so the driver wouldn't hear through the privacy window, though Mac had once told her that Jimmy was nearly deaf, that, at seventy-six, he needed the job to supplement his Social Security.

Mac didn't answer. He stared straight ahead at the Plexiglas that separated the worlds of employer, employee.

"I'll leave Washington quietly," she continued. "I'll go back to Mount Kasteel. Sell the estate. I'm sure I can move into the cottage with Jonas until I figure out what to do." She stopped herself from adding, "CJ can move in with you, and you both can live happily ever after."

He didn't reply.

Outside, the nation's capital continued to slide past, with its altars to presidents, its homages to the people, its secrets tucked in every corner.

"Congressman Perry knows," she said. "I don't know how he found out."

The seconds, the minutes, gnawed at her pride. She dabbed her tears; he did not seem to notice.

"Malcolm," she said, "I'm being blackmailed. The phone call you received was from the blackmailer. I wasn't in Philadelphia. I was in Grand Cayman. I've kept an account there for years. I started it with my share from Father's estate. I added to it whenever you gave me money for parties or decorating. When we remodeled the town house, I told you the cost was twice what it was. I put the other half in my account. I've let the money grow. I needed to know I'd have money to start over on my own." She stopped for a moment, then added, "I've always been afraid you would leave me, Malcolm."

If Mac was listening, he didn't acknowledge her. It was irritating, painful, humiliating. It reminded her of eighth-grade geography class, when she'd copied the answers off Alice's test paper and Mr. Laufer had guessed.

"I'm not going to give either of you an F," he'd announced to the entire class, "because I'm sure this must be a coincidence. I know that neither of you—certainly not Elinor—would cheat in my classroom." No, certainly not the daughter of the headmaster.

She had been too mortified to admit that instead of studying she'd been helping her mother plan the spring faculty luncheon because it would win praises from Father and did not interest CJ. She'd been too mortified to admit that cheating had seemed preferable to receiving an unacceptable grade.

"Malcolm," Elinor said now because it did not seem the right time to degrade herself further by saying she knew he loved CJ more than he loved her, "the blackmailer found out I've been seeing Joe Remillard."

Mac turned his face in slow motion toward her, as if the planet had stopped revolving and he was quietly catching up. He looked at her briefly, then averted his eyes. "Jesus, Elinor."

That's when she got pissed. She wanted to lash out, call him a bastard, tell him he had no right to judge her after the things he and CJ had done. She wanted to remind him that he was the one who'd chosen to sleep in another bedroom, not her. She wanted to shout to the driver to pull over, then bolt from the car, slam the door behind her, and disappear into the night.

Then Malcolm asked, "Do the children know?"

She fell silent, the eighth grader swallowing guilt. She looked back out the window and wished she had never seen Washington or Remy or even Malcolm, for that matter, wished she had never loved Malcolm, wished she did not love him still.

"There's a train out of Penn Station at three. We'll pull into Washington around seven. If we wait for a flight, we won't get there until later."

"Three in the morning?" Poppy asked, and Manny nodded. "But what about your kids?"

"I've been gone two nights already and they're fine. They know what I'd do if they aren't. I'll tell them I have to escort a prisoner."

"Oh," Poppy said, "right. I almost forgot about that."

It was worse now that they hadn't found any evidence against Duane, that the only clue they'd turned up was when Poppy found some of the words in *Vanity Fair* exactly as they'd been pasted onto the note. But the words in her copies of the magazine were intact, uncut, not used for blackmail. And Duane was still nowhere around.

The three of them—Poppy, Manny, and Yolanda—had

stayed at Poppy's house all night and all day perusing every nook and cranny in search of anything that might link Duane to Elinor and the blackmail. But they hadn't found anything. Not even love letters from ladies that Poppy had feared.

By late afternoon, they'd fallen asleep like Belita, and hadn't woken up until the telephone had rung.

Now Poppy tossed a few things into an overnight bag. Bleary-eyed, the three of them and Belita headed for the Metro bound for New York City, then Washington and whatever awaited.

"I can get into Dulles at eight-fifteen in the morning," Alice said to Neal as she scooped her makeup from the vanity and deposited it in her bag. "I'm so sorry to do this, but Elinor needs me."

"I could say I need you, too, but we've already established that." He had told her the truth, that he'd canceled the dinner with the Tang folks because it would have been too boring without her, that he would have missed the way they talked to each other after those kinds of nights, the way they dissected the people and the power plays and the entrées.

He'd said he missed her.

She'd said she missed him, too. Or maybe it was the *them* that she missed.

She stopped what she was doing now, went back to the bed, leaned down, and kissed him. "You're the best, you know that."

He began to unbutton her shirt. He reached inside, inciting a hot flash between her thighs.

"Neal," she nearly whined and pulled away. "I've got to go."

"Okay," he said. "I'll see you at home."

"After you're finished with the five women?"

He laughed. "There was not even one, O wife of mine."

"You smelled like Bijon."

"I didn't say one didn't try."

Alice laughed, because she deserved that. She brushed off the hot flash. "We are so silly, aren't we? Two people our age acting like jealous kids?"

He narrowed his eyes. "I love you, Alice Bartlett."

She blew him a kiss, rebuttoned her shirt, and said, "Tell Kiley Kate that Grandma's sorry, but I'll see her soon."

"Our granddaughter will be too busy at Sea World."

Alice smiled, zipped up her bag, and reminded herself for the hundredth time since last night that she was glad she was alive, and glad she was his, and he was hers. As she went out the door, she checked her cell phone: there were no messages from Bud. He was a gentleman, as she had suspected.

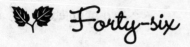 *Forty-six*

Elinor couldn't believe she had slept. She woke up after nine, surprised she was still alive, surprised nothing apparently had happened since she'd taken two sleeping pills and had tried to make the whole night go away.

It hadn't, of course, as the ache in her stomach reminded her now.

She got out of bed and looked around the master bedroom. She supposed Mac was down the hall, asleep in the guest room. How long had it been since they'd slept together? Since he'd started checking the Pacific Rim pharmaceutical markets into the wee hours. Since he'd claimed he had not wanted to disturb her.

Not that it mattered any longer.

They'd had no more conversation after Jimmy dropped

them off at their front door. Once inside, Elinor merely said, "I'll leave in the morning." Malcolm didn't answer, so she went upstairs to bed, numbed by his silence, weighted by her shame.

If she had dreamed, she didn't remember, which no doubt was a good thing.

On her way to the bathroom now she picked up her cell phone and turned it on. Might as well see if the blackmailer had tried to reach her during the night.

The light flashed.

She had three new messages.

CJ.

CJ.

CJ.

The last one sounded frantic.

"Call me as soon as you hear this, E. It's important. I'm in trouble, big time."

Manny warned everyone not to touch anything in CJ's room. Yolanda reminded him this was about panties, not murder. Still, Alice and Poppy and Yolanda sat in the chairs and avoided the bed and the lavender lace. Manny stood by the window, holding Belita. CJ waited by the door for Elinor.

They remained in place like a sculptor's tableau until she finally showed up.

"Well," Elinor said, "I see you've come to Washington after all." Her face was drawn and tinged a bit gray, as if she'd changed her foundation or been swallowing silver. She did not ask why everyone had assembled—if they'd come to rally around her or if they were somehow connected to the "trouble" CJ had claimed to be in.

No one responded. They let Elinor's eyes scope out the room, then alight on the panties the way theirs had done.

Like CJ, she shrieked.

When she'd quieted down, CJ told her what had happened, how the panties had been lying in wait, a lace land mine poised to explode on the pillow, shooting shrapnel of feathers and shards of La Perlas. Her description, she knew, was over the top, but, damn, she was angry—angry at her sister, angry at herself, for getting involved.

Elinor blanched, Elinor blinked. Then she recounted what the congressman had said about his wife's favorite color being lavender.

"And now it's time," Manny said, "to call the police."

"You can't make me," Elinor said. She turned to the others. "He can't make me, can he?"

CJ shrugged along with the others, though she silently hoped that he could.

"I'm an officer of the law," Manny said. "I didn't want to be dragged into this, because I know it's my duty to turn this over to the proper authorities. And the proper authorities are not us."

Elinor shook her head. "Go ahead," she said at last, her skin tone reverting to near normal as she uttered her glum resignation. "It doesn't matter. I told Malcolm last night. And everyone in town will know soon enough, now that the congressman knows."

CJ wondered when—if ever—she'd seen her sister this forlorn, a candidate admitting defeat. She stood up and put her hands on Elinor's shoulder. "E," she said, "I'm so sorry."

Elinor patted her hand. "Before the police get here, can we

order tea? I need caffeine, CJ. You and I know this is going to get worse."

"Sure. Anyone else want anything?"

There were murmurs for coffee and juice and a bagel. "And scones," Elinor added, matter-of-factly. "Have room service bring a basket of scones. I haven't eaten since lunch yesterday, except for that god-awful mousse last night."

It was as if they were going to order tea at the Ritz, with neither a half million dollars nor a nation at stake.

CJ moved toward the phone, then Elinor suddenly cried out, "Oh, my God! I do that every time I'm in a hotel!"

The group raised eyebrows, tilted heads, curled their hair. Well, one curled her hair, anyway.

"Do what?" Manny finally asked.

"I order tea and scones. I did it at the Lord Winslow."

"Anyone who's ever traveled with you knows you do that," CJ added.

Elinor laughed. "You're right. You know. Malcolm does. Jonas. But I would never have dreamed Janice would have remembered. I haven't gone anywhere with her in years."

"Janice?" Yolanda asked.

"My daughter. Three days ago she asked if I'd be staying at the Fairmont. She asked if I'd be ordering scones."

Silence again.

"Don't you see?" Elinor asked, her voice breaking a little. "Janice must have been mocking me. She must have known I had ordered them at the Lord Winslow."

"And that you didn't finish them," CJ added. "That you left them out in the hall, like the housekeeper told me." Her eyes locked with Elinor's in twin perception.

Poppy turned her head. "Does Janice read *Vanity Fair?*"

Elinor tossed Poppy a halfhearted defense. "My daughter and I don't always get along, but I can't believe she's blackmailing me."

"Did she stay here last night?" Alice asked.

"She said she was going to. Jonas said her boyfriend was with her."

"What's his name?"

"I don't know. I didn't meet him. CJ, did you meet him?"

"Yes. I think his name's Jack."

"Could it be Jake?" Poppy asked. "Is it possible he's a security guard at the Lord Winslow?"

"Does he wear black?" Yolanda asked. "Does he have an iPod?"

"I wonder if he was in Grand Cayman," Elinor hissed.

"And," Poppy added, her breath coming out in little bursts, "I wonder if he likes Chinese."

CJ said, "Shit," then Belita said it, too.

 *Forty-seven*

Before calling the Capitol Police, Manny let Elinor call Malcolm. Not that she had a clue what to say.

He didn't answer until the fourth ring, as if he knew it was she, and did not want to bother.

"Malcolm," she said, tying to sound normal, trying not to air any more dirty laundry—ha! such pathetic words!—in front of her friends, "please come to the hotel. I believe Janice is my blackmailer."

"Janice? Our daughter?"

She closed her eyes. If she could die now, everything might work out all right. "Yes," she replied.

"Elinor . . ."

She could not bear explaining the details right then. She could not bear to think she had driven her daughter to hate her so much . . . her own flesh, her own blood, to conjure such betrayal. In that instant, Elinor regretted every moment she had favored Jonas over her daughter, denounced herself for every time she'd clung to Jonas as if he were the sole lifeline she had to her husband. Had she been so insanely jealous of her sister that she'd needed to make certain Jonas would love her, his counterfeit mother?

Along the way, Elinor had been dreadfully unfair to Janice. Why had no one stopped her?

She gripped the phone tightly because she knew the answer: *No one stopped you because you would not have let them.*

Dewdrops leaked from her eyes. "Malcolm," Elinor whispered, "please. We have to confront her, and it will be better if you are here. Janice will need your support. It's obvious she's never felt she had mine." She wanted to ask him to come there for her, too. She wanted to beg him for his support, for his love, though she hardly was worthy of either. "I'm in CJ's room," she added quietly, then gave him the room number.

"I'll be there in twenty minutes," he replied, then quickly disconnected.

Elinor took a deep breath, opened her eyes, and looked at the others, who stood, without motion, like mannequins at Bergdorf's or Saks.

They waited until Mac arrived. He was somber and tense. His khakis were wrinkled, his hair was askew, and his eyes were slightly glazed, as if he hadn't slept. Elinor knew it was her fault. Could it be a sign that he cared?

CJ told him about the panties, because Elinor did not have the strength. Then Elinor asked him to call their daughter.

"Come to CJ's hotel room," Mac said to Janice. "She wants to show you something before she goes back to New York." He told her the room number as Elinor had told him, though everyone now suspected she already knew it.

And so they waited, mostly in silence, except for Belita, who gurgled and giggled and said several words, one of which sounded like "Poppy."

Then, the knock on the door.

Elinor leaned against the wall, her arms folded, her self-respect gone. For the first time since he'd arrived, Mac glanced at her, but she shook her head. She was finished with being in charge.

He opened the door. "Hi, honey," he said to Janice. "Come on in."

Her hair was its usual mess, her clothes tossed together with her usual thoughtlessness. But when Janice saw everyone, she withdrew, like a shy child caught off guard.

Elinor winced.

"What's going on, Daddy?"

Mac cleared his throat. "Honey," he began, "do you know your mother is being blackmailed?"

Her eyes landed on Elinor. Her gaze turned cool. Elinor recognized the chill that always seemed reserved for her, like a Yalumba Cabernet/Shiraz 2001 or a Chateaux Cheval Blanc Grand Cru. "Blackmailed? Why?"

Jonas might be the theater buff in the family, but Janice had always been a competent actor. The chilled look reminded Elinor of that. "If anyone is going to ask why," Elinor suddenly said, "I guess it should be me." She took a step forward but did not raise her voice. "Why, Janice? Why did you do it? Were you trying to scare me to death? Were you hoping your father would divorce me?"

A small furrow creased Janice's forehead. She looked as if she was going to cry.

Malcolm gently placed a hand on Janice's shoulder. "Honey," he said. "Please. Just tell us if you know anything."

"Know anything? About what?" That's when her eyes seemed drawn to the panties, which still lay spread-eagle on top of the bed. *"What is going on?"* She turned to someone in the hallway, whom they couldn't see.

"Is your friend with you?" Mac asked. "Maybe he'd like to come in."

"Unless," Elinor added in spite of her guilt, "he's already been here. Has he?"

The chill turned to ice. "Well. So now it's my mother who's accusing me of something. At least my employer had the balls to say what they thought I had done."

"Janice," Mac said, "don't talk to your mother that way."

Janice let out a sharp laugh. "Why not, Daddy? It's not as if anything I say or do affects her. Nothing ever has."

Elinor stepped forward and raised her index finger. "Now just one minute, young lady . . ."

Mac moved between them. "Stop it!" he shouted. "Both of you. Just stop."

If it was true that energy could be felt in the air, the energy in the room slid from bad to way worse, like Gruyère left out in the sun. Then a short man appeared at Janice's side and boldly marched into the room.

"Jack Dowling," he said, extending his hand to Malcolm. "We met at the party." He wore glasses and had an unfortunate comb-over. "Janice's fiancé."

Janice had a fiancé? Well, it was a fine time to announce it.

Then Poppy twittered. "Well, he certainly isn't Jake from the Lord Winslow."

"And he wasn't your stalker in Cayman," Yolanda chimed in.

"No," Elinor said, with unexpected relief. "It isn't him." She turned to her daughter. "Oh, God, honey, I am so sorry." Then she went to the bed, sank onto the mattress, and cried in front of them all.

"That does it," Manny said. "I'm going downstairs to alert security, so they don't panic when the police show up. Don't anyone leave until I get back."

Yolanda picked up Belita. "We're coming with you."

The coffee and juice, the bagels and scones, arrived as they were leaving.

"What do you think, Manuel?" Yolanda asked as they scooted from the room.

"I think what I said in the beginning. Your friend should have called the police."

He buzzed for the elevator; the doors instantly opened.

"But isn't there some other way?"

They stepped into the elevator; he pushed the button for the first floor. He didn't respond. Sometimes Yolanda forgot that, at the end of the day, her brother was still a man who didn't like talking about people, especially women.

On the first floor, he paced toward the desk, Yolanda and Belita close on his heels.

He ignored the fact that the clerk was registering a guest. "NYPD." He flashed his badge. "Which way to security?"

The clerk pointed to a side door. "But they're busy right now."

"Yeah," the guest added, with a small chuckle. "They caught an old lady stealing the silver."

🍁 *Forty-eight*

"Momma?"

The entourage had moved from CJ's room to security after Manny had called and told them what was going on. They gathered around while Momma held court from the small banquet chair where she sat.

"Hello, Poppy," Momma said, adjusting her navy picture hat. "What are you doing here? I didn't think you'd been invited."

Poppy started to tremble, then she started to cry, and Manny moved quickly to her side. "Momma...," she said, but Momma waved her off.

"Hush," she said. "I knew you were giving my trinkets away. I couldn't resist. Just one little pickle fork. What would it matter?"

"What are you talking about?" Poppy asked. "Why are you in Washington? How did you get here? Where is Lucky?"

It was too many questions, especially for Momma. She closed her eyes and looked as if she'd fallen asleep.

Poppy kneeled down before her. "Momma?" she whispered. "What about your spells?"

That's when Momma laughed and opened her eyes. "Oh, I've been faking my spells. I needed to throw you off track. I didn't want anyone to know I was on to Elinor's shenanigans, and that I was determined to do something about it."

All eyes moved from Momma to Elinor, who stood with her hand to her mouth. "Oh my God," Elinor said. "Oh my good God."

"Oh, don't be so shocked, Elinor dear. Someone had to stop you, before you wrecked your life and everyone else's. I was the only one with the wherewithal."

At least she hadn't said *balls*.

"But how did you know?" Elinor asked.

Momma adjusted the wide brim of her hat. "Well, I knew long before my daughter told me. It was actually pure happenstance! Lucky brought me to town to have my hair done. No offense, Yolanda."

Yolanda nodded and said none was taken.

"We went to the Lord Winslow for tea. I saw you, Elinor. I had Lucky follow you."

"But why did you think anything was, as you say, going on?"

"Because the last time was the seventh time we'd seen you there. After the second time, I realized that even though life is irony, it seemed too much like coincidence. So I paid attention. Did you know you went there the second and fourth Thursdays of every month?"

Momma was no dummy; she never had been.

"So you stole Elinor's panties?" Yolanda asked, and every-one in the room, except Momma, cringed.

"Of course I did. Her daddy would never have wanted her to cause such a scandal." She did not add that she'd known Elinor's daddy quite well, and knew a thing or two about cover-ups.

"But how did you get Elinor's panties?" Yolanda persisted.

Momma laughed. "Well, Lucky and I didn't dress up like housekeepers, if that's what you mean! We slipped a few twen-ties in the right places, and we went into the room after Elinor left. The panties were a bonanza." She turned to Elinor. "You also left a bottle of spray hair gel, my dear, but I didn't think you'd care about that."

Poppy was feeling quite proud in a special place in her heart. Who knew Momma was so clever?

"I . . . ," Elinor stammered, "I was in a hurry. . . ." Her voice drifted off; her eyes drifted to Malcolm, who seemed pretty calm, considering the circumstances.

"Lucky called you for the ransom, Elinor," Momma con-tinued.

"Did he follow me to Cayman?"

"No. That was Jake, the security man from the hotel. He agreed to freelance, and we paid him quite nicely."

The entourage remained silent. Janice's fiancé took a bite of a bagel that he'd brought from the room.

"But why here?" Elinor asked. "Why now?"

"I wanted you to stop before you really were caught. By someone who mattered. I wanted to scare the crap out of you."

Everyone laughed except Elinor. And Malcolm. And poor Janice, who still seemed bewildered.

"But why did you leave my panties in CJ's room?"

"Ooops!" Momma cried, "my mistake! Poppy had a picture of Alice and Elinor in her Miu Miu, which she left at my house one night. I put it in my purse, thinking I'd find a nice silver frame for it one day. Anyway, I brought the picture. I showed it to the housekeeper, and she let me into the room. I said I was your Momma! Imagine that!"

Of course, in reality, she could have been Elinor and CJ's Momma, impregnated by the headmaster.

"It wasn't my room," Elinor said, "it was CJ's. Malcolm and I had gone home."

"Ha ha," Momma laughed, "well the joke was on me. The housekeeper mistook CJ for Elinor! You're still identical twins, after all!"

They stood around, processing Momma's confession, when Poppy said, "But how did you get here?"

"Why, Lucky, of course. He's waiting outside in the limo." She stood up as if ready to go.

"Just a minute." The security man stepped forward and folded his arms. "I'm not going to pretend to know what's going on here, but there's a small matter of larceny we need to address."

The pickle fork, of course.

"Momma," Poppy said, "tell the man you're sorry."

"But it's so lovely," Momma said, her blue eyes twinkling. "It would be such a nice addition to my collection."

Poppy reached into her purse. "Where did you get it, Momma?"

"Some fool left it on a room service tray. I saw it when I went upstairs to deliver the panties." A touch of pride laced her words.

"How much?" Poppy asked the security guard.

He looked at Poppy, then Momma, then the group that had assembled there. He shook his head. "No charge," he said. "Enjoy it in good health."

And just that quickly, the drama was done.

 *Epilogue*

Elinor didn't press blackmail charges against Momma, even when she learned it was Momma who'd planted the dastardly seed in the congressman's mind to tell Elinor that his wife's favorite color was lavender. Momma had cornered him coming out of the men's room in the lobby of the Fairmont and had told him it would be a good way to help warm Elinor up, that she was a good girl but sometimes could be shy.

Even Elinor laughed at that.

CJ declined a ride back to Mount Kasteel in Momma's

stretch limo. She needed time alone, and Amtrak had always provided safe haven. Hopefully, she wouldn't run into Ray Williams.

Once at Union Station, she checked the board: A train left for New York nearly every half hour. One was leaving for Denver in twenty minutes.

Without hesitation, CJ went to the counter and traded in her ticket. The time had finally come to put Elinor and her issues away and pick up the pieces of her own life . . . to rewrite those few scenes that Cooper had mentioned.

When Alice got home, she threw out her computer. She was determined to learn to become herself, not Elinor. Hopefully she and Neal would love each other forever, but she was done tempting fate.

As for *USA Sings*, they were going en masse to the Philadelphia audition: Alice, Neal, Melissa, David, and the two boys. After the show, they'd join Lorna LeDuc and the others to celebrate. Alice had asked Felicity to join them, but she'd said she couldn't make it, no excuses, no explanations, just, "Maybe next time," and Alice had understood.

As it turned out, Momma had made Duane sign a pre-nup way back in Monte Carlo. She'd threatened to have Lucky shoot him if he told Poppy, and Lucky was so devoted, who would doubt his aim?

Still, it was a little insulting that Duane had struck first by sending Poppy a postcard from Reno on which he'd written that his first wife had been waiting and, wouldn't you know, she wanted him back.

Yolanda said the woman must have had *mucho dinero* that she was willing to share with the brothers and their *ridiculo* mine.

Momma said when things were done, they were done. She never told Poppy about Duane's empty suitcase, which she'd loaded with Ben Franklins on his way out of town—her idea, not his. *Insurance*, she considered it. *A small price to keep him away.*

To help pass the time until the divorce, Poppy and Momma went on a world tour, returning the silver trinkets in person. Most places said "Keep them," so Momma was happy. Manny took his vacation in October and met them for a week in Buenos Aires. Alice said that the Lord only knew what would happen with them, but it seemed he might be the man Poppy had always needed.

Because Manny was her brother and she loved him dearly, Yolanda closed up shop that same week and moved with Belita into his house in Brooklyn, because even though his kids would have been okay, a week was a very long parentless time. While she was there, Junior Diaz dropped by.

Holy cow, Yolanda thought. He was really, really nice. Why hadn't Manny told her he was so nice? Or had she just not been paying attention?

The best thing about life, Yolanda decided, was that people really could change, her included.

Elinor had no idea why Malcolm wanted to stay with her. But he said that he did. He said if it hadn't been for her strength, he would not have become the man he'd become; he would have hidden out in a laboratory, making hybrids of trees.

He also said that during the last few years he'd grown distant because she'd grown distant. He wondered if that often happened when people were married such a long time.

But he said they belonged together, that she was the mother of his children, after all, that she'd raised them and loved them, and, like most parents, had done the best that she could.

He told her he loved her.

She did not ask if he loved CJ, too. She just tried to start over again, vowed to try and become a better wife, a better mother to *both* of the children. She hoped it wasn't too late. She also resolved to be rid of the jealousy toward her sister, who, after all, had given her—given *them*—Jonas. Good Lord, what more could Elinor want?

The first thing Elinor did was help Janice prove her innocence about the issue with her job. Elinor still didn't understand what Janice actually did for a living, but she figured that believing in her daughter was the best thing she could contribute. It was all Janice had wanted when she'd appeared in Mount Kasteel in search of her father but had had the misfortune to discover her mother instead.

Thankfully, Janice forgave her mother for suspecting she'd blackmailed her.

"It was reassuring that you knew I was alive," Janice quipped, and Elinor cried, and Janice said she was sorry, that was uncalled for, then Elinor said that she was the one who truly was sorry, that most things she'd said and done to her daughter had been uncalled for.

Then Elinor was touched when she realized that, though years had passed, Janice had remembered that Elinor favored scones when she was in a hotel out of town. It was the kind of detail Elinor would have remembered. How amusing to think that her daughter might be a little like she was! Of course, Janice challenged that once or twice, as Elinor started making preparations for Janice and Jack's wedding.

Remy—or rather, his driver—finally managed to call after the engagement party.

"Your appointment is scheduled for two o'clock tomorrow afternoon," the voice said. "You will be picked up at one forty-five."

Elinor paused. "Please let him know I am sorry, but I will no longer be needing his services."

She did not hear from him again.

She went back to wearing cream-colored silk panties that would hopefully keep her out of any more trouble. But for all of her growth, and all her lessons learned, a small part of Elinor wished she had saved just a bit of his DNA . . . the way that, years ago, she'd saved the rake that she directed Manny to find in the gardener's shed at the lake cottage. It was still where she'd stashed it, still held a few strands of Poppy's red hair, evidence that backed up her story of self-defense. Poppy went to trial, but she did not go to jail, hallaleuigh.

Jonas got the job as theater manager at The Elway even before Cooper made a few phone calls to a few friends back on Broadway. They decided CJ would stay in Denver for the season, then they'd go together to Paris next spring. Cooper's golden retriever, Molly, would be Luna's house guest for the duration of their stay in Europe.

After a while, CJ told Cooper that she was Jonas's biological mother. She wondered about telling Jonas, too, but it would hurt Elinor, and it would confuse Jonas, and it would not change the past.

Besides, CJ reasoned, as she settled into her new studio at the foothills of the Rockies, some secrets—even love—are best left alone.

A+

AUTHOR
INSIGHTS,
EXTRAS, &
MORE...

FROM

**ABBY
DRAKE**

AND

AVON A

Perfect Little Ladies
Reading Group Questions

1. Do you think Elinor should have told Malcolm her problem in the beginning?

2. Two hundred dollars seems like a lot of money for panties, lace or otherwise. What's the most extravagant item you've ever purchased for yourself?

3. Which of the five ladies (Yolanda included) did you feel most connected to? Why?

4. Which of the five ladies had the most solid, enviable relationship, past or present, with whom and why?

5. Which of the five ladies would you most want as a friend you could turn to even in the darkest or the weirdest of times?

6. Was CJ right to have done the things she'd done for Elinor? Would you have done them for your twin?

7. What about Poppy and Momma? Would you cover up things for your parent or child that you might not for your sibling?

8. Describe Alice's life in one word.

9. If a high-profile man was handsome and sexy and all those other good things, would you risk your marriage and your lifestyle for the thrill of the moment(s) you could spend together? Would you expect more?

10. At this stage in their lives, would CJ, Alice, Poppy, or Yolanda risk everything the way Elinor did?

Walt Steinmetz Photography

ABBY DRAKE spent most of her childhood and young adult life trying to be a Perfect Little Lady. Thankfully, she traded it in to become a novelist. Instead of martinis, she drinks Diet Coke; instead of silk she wears denim. She has, however, maintained a penchant for diamonds. She now lives in Amherst, Massachusetts, far from the Washington-New York scene, yet plugged into its pulse via Amtrak . . . and plenty of friends in between.

Abby Drake